A Marriage of His Choosing

Taylor K Scott

1

Warning: The following work of fiction has trigger warnings. See Author's Note for more information.

DEDICATION

When I released 'A Marriage of His Convenience', I feared it wouldn't sell very many books, it being more of a niche market than contemporary romances. However, to this day, it remains to be my biggest seller. And so, I dedicate this book to everyone who took a chance on Tobias and Emily. I hope you enjoy Elsie's book.

MUSICAL INFLUENCES

Big My Secret – Michael Nyman

The Heart Asks Pleasure First – Michael Nyman

Bittersweet Symphony – The Verve

Music by Vitamin String Quartet and Duomo

Einaudi Experience

2Cellos

Vivaldi

ACKNOWLEDGMENTS

Thank you to the community of writers and readers out there who have answered questions, read my work, given me advice, and shared my work. Thank you to all of you!

To my beta readers who all took the time to read this book during the early stages. Just to have someone read my work and offer their opinion is always so empowering for me. I sincerely appreciate you offering me your time, support, and advice.

I must also thank my poor, suffering husband for supporting me through my obsession with writing. Not only has he had to live with my reading habit, which is becoming more and more consuming, but also has the added bonus of losing me to my own works of fiction. Know that I love you dearly, as well as our two beautiful girls, and appreciate all the encouragement you have given me.

Finally, but most importantly, thanks to everyone who has taken a chance on my novel. I hope it hasn't disappointed, and that you might take a chance to read some of my upcoming releases. Thank you so much again.

Author's Note

I like to write about what inspires me and not be confined to specific subgenres, which is why you will find romantic comedies, contemporary romances, dark romances and now, historical romances in my back matter. I will admit that I am no historian and do not pretend to be. I research my books as much as I can, including visits to English Heritage sites and seeking the advice of those who are more knowledgeable that I am. If I have included details that might not be wholly accurate for the time, know that this is an oversight, not a purposeful distortion of the facts. This is a work of fiction, including the characters, the settings, and the plot. It is by no means meant to be used as a non-chronological report of the time. I have also intentionally written in a more contemporary style to make the story accessible to a wider audience. My aim is to share my stories, not to pretend I am a historical expert.

Trigger warnings: This book contains scenes of a sexual nature. It also contains scenes that refer to, and detail injuries involving blood, childbirth, still birth and loss.

Prologue

Edmund

When I was eight years old, I attended a birthday party at the Rothschild house. I was instructed by Mama to be on my best behaviour, and to be extra polite to the daughters of the viscount, for one day, one of them was going to be my wife. Such a concept seemed strange at the time, like make-believe. After all, Elsie had barely ever spoken to me, and Emily, whose birthday it was, had only just turned six years old. I could not take the notion seriously enough to make any real judgement. And so, I attended, bowed my head in reverence, and said all the things I was supposed to, mere moments after I had arrived. I was met with smiles, the odd chuckle, even a few handshakes to make me feel older than the small boy I was. Elsie returned the pleasantries, performing as the perfect little lady she was being brought up to be. Emily, however, Emily was something else entirely.

"Delighted to see you, Miss Emily," I greeted her formally, "thank you for inviting me to celebrate with you today."

"I didn't invite you," she replied with child-like honesty, "but now that you're here, can I show you something?"

"Erm…" I looked up at my mother, silently asking her what I should do, for the youngest Rothschild had gone off script.

"It's ok, Edmund, perhaps Emily wants to show you her birthday presents," she replied at the same time as accepting a glass of punch from one of the serving staff.

"Alright," I uttered to the little girl with curly locks, wide eyes, and a distinctive lisp.

"This way, Edmund Barton," she said as she about turned and began leading me through a crowd of adults who didn't even look twice at the birthday girl.

It took us a good while to finally reach a destination she was yet to share with me. She had led me to the back of their extensive garden, where a small rockery with blooming wildflowers took centre stage. The forget-me-nots matched her pretty blue dress which was now dipping into the fresh soil. Her hands reached down to where an upturned clay pot lay next to a patch of poppies, but before she lifted it, she turned around to check no one else was watching. I did the same, for what reason, I have no idea, but I was already excited over the thought of what she was about to uncover.

"Promise not to tell my mama, or Elsie?" she whispered, even though we were far out of the hearing range of anyone else. I gave her a quick nod, then looked to the flowerpot with greedy anticipation. She began to move it a tiny fraction when she suddenly froze, then turned to face me again. "And best not tell Papa either."

"I won't tell anyone, Emily," I promised, my impatience revealing itself in my unsteady voice. "Now, show me!"

She grinned in such a way, it revealed one of her missing

front teeth. I smiled back at her, then nodded my head towards the pot. When she finally turned the thing over, I could see not one, but two giant warty toads lying on top of one another. The light had hit them so suddenly, they had begun to croak, and were attempting to slip away. I grabbed the biggest one, leaving Emily to catch hold of the second one's back leg. Once secure in our hands, we started studying them more closely, showing keen fascination over these two ugly creatures.

"Do you think they're brother and sister?" she asked me with her lispy, little voice, still staring intently at her captive.

"Unlikely, Emily," I told her truthfully.

"You are right, they could be brothers," she said decidedly, "or sisters."

"I would say this one is the female, and that one you have, is the male," I tell her, having studied toads a little in my free time. Most boys of my age do at one time or another. "The girls are usually bigger than the boys, and your one has a much louder croak."

"Really? How interesting," she said with sincerity in her voice. "I wish I was a toad."

"Some days I think you are," a voice said from behind us, causing us both to jump and drop our captives. They instantly began their escape, hopping away towards the river that ran through the back of the property. "Oh, Em, Mama is going to have a fit when she sees what you've done to your brand-new dress!"

"You won't tell her what I was doing, will you, Elsie? Please don't tell her!" Emily begged her sister, who was now rolling her eyes in utter despair. Luckily, it was obvious she cared for her sister, even if she did find it an exhausting undertaking to constantly have to watch out for her.

"Oh, alright, but go and change," she said, sounding much older than her eight years. "We'll say you fell over or something."

Emily didn't say a word before running back towards the house, readying herself to hide the evidence of our toad studying. I could not help but laugh as she picked up her skirts, and ran like an ungraceful rabbit, jumping over patches of dirt and wet grass. However, I soon ceased my laughter when I noticed Elsie glaring at me with the same judgement my own mother would bestow upon me whenever she caught my brother and I up to no good.

"You should not encourage her," she said with her arms firmly crossed, "it will only lead her into more trouble."

"Oh, lighten up, Elsie," I scoffed, "try to have a little fun like your sister. This is why people are wary of you, you are too uptight. Perhaps if you were more like Emily, your father would love you as much he does her."

By the way she was now looking at me, I could tell I had deeply wounded her with my careless words. She looked as if she was close to tears, or wrath, I could not tell for certain. I immediately regretted saying anything, so looked to the ground to avoid seeing the evidence of my thoughtless cruelty.

"I am the eldest," she said through gritted teeth and a sob caught at the back of her throat, "I cannot run around trying to catch warty toads with any blunderbuss! Mama looks to me to be a role model for Emily, to show her how to be a lady in training."

"I am sorry, Elsie, I did—"

"You are beastly, Edmund Barton, a wicked beast for saying such things!" she cried before about turning to run after her sister. I felt awful, especially as I watched her bring her hands to her face to rub away what were sure to be tears.

When we eventually left the Rothschild household, my mother asked me if I had had a good time. She also asked what I thought of Emily and Elsie. I remained silent for a while, trying to ignore the pang of guilt that hit me hard when she voiced the eldest daughter's name. I had barely seen Elsie after our altercation and had even heard her mother telling the maid to go and check on her. I tried not to acknowledge the fact that it was my fault for her crying; I tried to convince myself that she was taking it all too seriously. In fact, I had even tried to blame her for making me feel so bad, but I knew, deep down, that I had been cruel to her. She was right; being the eldest does mean she bears the weight of more responsibility. It is little wonder she took my words to heart.

"Mother?" I asked her on the way home, to which she smiled, giving me permission to ask her whatever I needed to. "If I am to marry one of the Rothschild girls, can it be Emily?"

"Of course, my darling boy!" She laughed with my father before taking hold of my chin and delivering a kiss to my cheek.

Emily and I simply made sense; we were one and the same. Besides, Elsie would never forgive me after today. She deserved to marry someone much grander than me; someone who would think before he spoke.

Chapter 1

Edmund

"Edmund Barton, as I live and breathe!" Viscount Rothschild greets me with a hearty handshake and a complexion that speaks of one too many shots of brandy. "How were your travels to Europe? I can see it must have been rather hot."

I take in the warm tan of my skin and smile in acknowledgement. Truth be told, I am rather fond of the Mediterranean complexion; it reminds me of sunnier climes. A full year away has given me the opportunity to leave behind my troubles and broaden my horizons.

It had been necessary after having to finally let go of my adoration for Emily. She was blissfully happy with her family, and, after a rocky start, I had to concede that Tobias Hardy was the right man for her. I, on the other hand, was in no fit state to be the right man for any lady.

"Good evening, My Lord," I greet him rather formally, for it has been a long time since we last spoke, and I feel as though I have grown in that time.

"Oh, come now, it's George, you know that, Edmund!" he laughs as we fall into step around the grand hall of Lord and Lady

Bartlett. They have two daughters who are hoping to secure an engagement this season, having already been through one last year, just before I left for France.

"Of course, George, forgive me for being so formal," I reply, ignoring the young ladies who are eyeing me up with curiosity. I must look a little different, or they have simply forgotten who I am. I have not yet much thought about seeking a wife, though it was the first topic of conversation upon my mother's lips when I returned home. Unlike the ladies all around me, I am fortunate enough to not have to rush into such an institution. I can take my time, try to find someone who sets my heart to racing just as Emily once had.

"Your mother must be pleased to have you home safe and sound?" George chortles on, grabbing two glasses of punch for the both of us. "And your father will be keen to have you working alongside him, no?"

"Actually, I shall not be staying in London long," I inform him, "I have been left an estate in my cousin's will. The poor man died of consumption not too long ago. I was the only person listed in his will, so his estate, including 'Maybrook House, and effects have been passed onto me."

"Why, Edmund, that is excellent news!" he beams before shrinking back with a more contrite expression on his face. "My condolences for your cousin, that is not so good to hear. Were you close?"

"Once upon a time," I tell him with genuine sadness in my voice. "A family dispute put an end to our trips to the countryside. He taught me how to swim, to fish, and to fence. He had the outdoor education my father was never interested in and had insisted he pass it onto me. Alas, when I turned nine, there was an argument and I never saw him again."

"Oh, I never knew there was such a fray within the family," he says, looking thoroughly pensive over the matter. My parents are close to the Rothschilds, so I understand why it would be surprising to know such an incident had occurred without his knowledge. "He must have been your mother's cousin, mustn't he? Your father is an only child."

"Indeed, William was an only child to my mother's uncle. He was an earl, though William never much indulged in the title."

"So that means you are a man of property, the lord of the manor as it were?"

"It would seem so," I reply uncomfortably, for I do not wish to advertise the fact with so many mamas trying to secure a husband for their debutante daughters in the near vicinity.

"Well, then, this is cause for celebration!" he beams at the same time as sloshing his drink over the side of his glass. "Colletta, did you know about young Edmund inheriting a—"

"Er, if you don't mind, George, I would rather keep it quiet for the moment," I cut him off before he announces my newly acquired estate to the entire room.

"Oh…alright," he says, looking at me as though I have taken leave of my senses.

"Is Elsie here at all? It feels like such a long time since we last spoke."

"She'll be hiding somewhere, staying out of the way," he says with a sad look on his face. "She's become rather reclusive since her sister moved to Kent."

"She remains unmarried from what my mother tells me," I comment. I was convinced both Rothschild daughters would have been happily married by the time I returned home. It was surprising to hear of Elsie's single status. "Have there been no offers?"

"Oh, plenty, but she has refused all of them," he replies, shaking his head in what looks like exasperation. "If only I could have one easy daughter, ay, Edmund?"

"Now, where would be the fun in that?" I laugh to try and lighten his mood.

"Quite," he replies, raising his brow skyward. "I dare say you will know all about it one day, when you have a family of your own."

"Perhaps," I utter, smiling awkwardly. "But for now, I might try and find your lovely daughter so I can bore her with my travelling stories."

"Excellent, I am sure she will be pleased to hear all about it," he says, looking a little excited over the notion if I am not mistaken.

George was always so reluctant to let go of Emily but appears to be more than willing to marry off his eldest. It has me feeling sad for Elsie, for she more than knows he does not feel the same level affection for her. She has been the perfect daughter, always doing everything that is asked of her, and yet, she still finds herself lacking. And when Tobias Hardy completely bypassed her for Emily, I suspect it took away what little confidence she had once possessed. I do not blame her for wanting to shy away from marriage; she most likely does not feel like she is enough for anyone. I can understand that feeling on some level, after I was seemingly rejected. I think everyone can agree that I went a little wayward after I lost the battle for Emily's affections.

As I make my way through the hall of dancing couples, their chaperones, and elders, I try to avoid making eye contact with any of the debutantes or their mamas. I am in no mood to dance with anyone, and once word gets out about my inheritance, there will be no escaping such attention. I would like to enjoy one last night to myself, to converse with friends without being interrupted.

That is not to say I do not wish to ever form an attachment. I have always wanted a wife and family, but I always believed that life would be with Emily. Now that this dream is an impossibility, I have come to accept it. That being said, I do not wish to rush into another situation whereby my heart is rejected in the most painful and humiliating manner. I shall take my time, protect myself, and find a lady who will choose me for love, not my fortune.

Elsie

The air is cooling this evening, and extremely welcome after being stuck inside of the stuffy dancing hall. I would have preferred to have made my way outside as soon as we had arrived, however Mama has grown increasingly concerned for me over the past year. She worries I will never find a suitor, that I shall become a spinster just like Tobias' Aunt Elizabeth.

As such, it did not please her to find out I was going to stay with the very lady next week. I, on the other hand, am feeling positively over the moon for the reprieve. A whole week to hide away with good books, good company, and my loveable dog, Stanley. He is all I have left now, after Sally passed away at Christmas. I was so heartbroken, Mama had offered to buy me another one. However, Papa put a stop to that notion, explaining that if I was to have any hope of finding a husband, I should not tie myself down with pets. After all, it might make me less attractive to a prospective match.

We rarely talk, him and I, even less so than when Emily was at home. I cannot say I miss our relationship, but I do feel my presence is becoming less and less wanted in the family home. I have tried to stay with others, to keep my distance, but it only makes it all the more uncomfortable when I return home. Emily has been so good to have me to stay, especially with her son crawling about the place and keeping her busy. I do hope she finds me a help rather than a hindrance when I travel to their estate in Kent.

Last week, when Lord French had asked to take me for a turn about the park, Father had been positively giddy over the prospect. Lord French is a portly old gentleman who is frequently drunk and cannot hold a conversation beyond food, drink, and women. I told him I had twisted my ankle and was unable to leave the house for the foreseeable future. This had angered my father to the point of not talking to me until just yesterday. I suspect his decision to break his silence was based on this evening's enforced attendance at this ball. I believe even my mother is beginning to grow tired of me, and I was once her favourite, though, only because I did as I was told. I did not earn her love based on my own merits. I am not like Emily; I have nothing to offer other than subservience.

As I stand here, under the watchful eyes of my mother, who is now gossiping with some of the other mamas, I notice a small group of ladies who I had once considered friends. They now look at me and whisper with one another, no doubt talking about how I was completely overlooked when the duke chose my younger sister over me. The breakdown in our friendship is not entirely their fault, for I chose to shy away from society after Emily was married. I withdrew more and more as the months passed by, to the point whereby I avoided attention as much as Emily once had.

There is no duke to rescue me, however, no one to show me a love I have been so desperately craving, a love that would be all mine.

"Lady Rothschild," a familiar voice says from behind me, and I smile, knowing that this voice is at least a true friend.

"Edmund," I reply before turning to reveal my sincere happiness over seeing him. "It has been almost a year, has it not?"

When I finally turn around to see the boy who had once felt the pain of Emily's marriage as much as I did, I am blown away by how much he has changed. No longer a boy, or a 'calf' as Tobias used to call him, but a man. Edmund Barton is tall, broad, and masculine. A man who is sure to be whipped up by some young debutante in the very near future, for no other gentleman compares. To prove my point, I notice some of the ladies now staring and pointing in our direction. I look around for Mama, to make sure she can see us and prevent any tongues from wagging.

"Just over, actually," he says as he leans in to kiss my hand, safely encased within my silk glove. "Elsie, as always, you look beautiful this evening."

"Oh, come now, Edmund, let us not fall into such flippant pleasantries," I laugh, "I thought we were friends."

"Elsie, I count on you as one of my best friends, but it is only a 'flippant pleasantry' if I do not mean what I say. With you, Elsie, I stand by those words," he says with a charm I do not remember him possessing. "But why are you out here, Elsie, hiding away in the dark?"

I choose not to answer him straight away, instead, I glance at the giggling ladies over his shoulder and make a decision that will risk their gossiping about me. I link my arm through his and begin to pace along the terrace. Mama's eyes are still very much on the both of us, and I will not lead us anywhere beyond her line of sight, but I wish to speak to someone who might offer me friendship rather than unwanted advice. Advice about how I should be finding myself a husband, making my family proud, and fitting back into society.

"Elsie Rothschild, if I didn't know any better, I would think you are using me," Edmund utters with a suggestive smile.

"And do you take offence to such a thing?" I giggle at the same time as noticing every set of eyes turning to watch as we promenade up and down the lavish garden.

"Not at all," he says proudly, "I could never refuse a turnabout with a Rothschild."

"My sister especially," I accuse, thinking how I will always come second to her.

"Perhaps once upon a time," he says with a now serious expression. "But she is now a taken woman, a wife, and a mother, Elsie. I left thoughts of Emily far behind me on my travels."

"If only it were that easy, Edmund," I tell him, "I know how much you loved her. Any woman would give all her beauty away for such affection from a man. Emily was blessed with two men who felt that strongly for her."

"And what makes you think you won't find such a match, Elsie?" he says, stopping us from walking and looking at me in such a way, I feel vulnerable before him; his eyes peeling away at my modesty. "You are just as exquisite as your sister, Elsie."

"If that is true, what made you fall for her over me?" I ask, only to immediately wish I could take it back. "I am sorry, that was much too forward of me. Please, forget I said such a thing."

"Elsie, you will find your match, trust me," he says, but his words only make me feel all the more convinced that I never will. I choose not to reply, so we fall into step again. "Will you let me take you for tea next week? I should very much like to catch up properly with you."

"You would?" I awkwardly laugh, for Edmund has never sought to take me anywhere, especially if it was without my sister before she married.

"Yes, I would," he laughs with the sound of incredulity in his voice. "Why does that sound so amusing to you?"

"No reason," I reply as I trail off my laughter. "Though, I am afraid I am away next week. I am staying with Lady Elizabeth in Oxfordshire for the week."

"Lady Elizabeth? Then I am glad; I think the lady will teach you some lessons in how to think more highly of yourself. It certainly sounds like you could do with a few reminders, Miss Elsie Rothschild."

"Do not tease, Edmund," I smile as I tap him on the arm for being so cheeky.

"I tease not," he smiles along with me. "Then perhaps I shall see you when you return? I will speak to your father about it."

"If you insist, Edmund." He stops me all of a sudden, and looks me straight in the eye, completely catching me off guard with the intensity of his stare.

"I do, Elsie," he says softly, glancing down to my lips for a moment or two.

"Elsie, my dear," Mama cuts in, "your father is asking for

you. He would like you to meet one of his business associates."

"Oh," I gasp before I finally manage to pull back from Edmund. "Until I return, Lord Barton."

"Of course," he says, nodding his head formally, "I look forward to it."

As Mama walks me into the main hall, I notice the sashaying couples, the fluttering of fans and obvious glances between debutantes and their admirers. I find myself sighing, feeling dejected and like I want to run away from the bright lights and floral decorations masking what is essentially a cattle market. All of it feels so pointless and tedious.

My father is standing next to a gentleman who I have seen with him many times before. He is considerably older than me and always appears to have a stern look upon his face. He isn't unhandsome, but I still feel unsettled in his presence. When we are close enough, he looks me up and down, assessing me like a piece of furniture to put on display inside one of his country estates. My father, slightly to the side of him, smiles proudly as I approach, and in such a way I want to run back to where Edmund will soothe me with his friendly familiarity.

"Ah, Elsie, my dear," Father says, reaching out his hand to embrace me, as though we are as close as he and Emily. It has me feeling sad, angry, and a little guilty for possessing such ugly emotions. They tell me that I am more than done with this ball. Indeed, I believe I am done with all of these balls.

"I would like you to meet Lord Boreham. Richard, this is my daughter, Elsie Rothschild."

"Delighted," he says as he takes hold of my gloved hand to deliver a kiss to it. He lingers much too long for my liking, but I do not wish to embarrass my father, so I let him. "George, you are truly blessed to have such a beautiful daughter."

"Indeed, Colletta and I have been blessed with two beautiful daughters," Father replies. "Her sister, Emily, is married to the Duke of Kent."

"I heard," Lord Boreham says, still with his eyes on me, "though, I cannot imagine how he overlooked your beauty, Miss Rothschild. The man is obviously a fool."

"Thank you, Lord Boreham, but you have not seen my sister," I reply politely. "My father will tell you how desirable she is; she is much more dazzling than I."

"You do yourself a disservice," a voice from behind me says, a familiar and friendly one. "Do not believe a word she says, Lord Boreham."

"Lord Barton, I did not realise you had returned from your travels," the older gentleman says, reaching out to shake his hand and nod his head respectfully.

"I returned just this Friday gone," Edmund says with a charming smile as I sit back to watch the two men perform their social niceties. "I am meant to be travelling to Witney in Oxfordshire, but I could not resist coming to see the Rothschilds first."

"Oxfordshire? I did not know you had a residence that way, Edmund?" I question him, his statement having piqued my interest.

"It had belonged to my mother's cousin," he explains, "and was recently bequeathed to me. It is in desperate need of renovating, I am afraid to say, and urgently needs my attention. Perhaps I might call on you when you travel to Lady Elizabeth's house in Faringdon next week?"

I pause for a moment or two, feeling a heat in my cheeks as I contemplate the idea of him wanting to come and see me. Only me. Indeed, I find myself warming to the idea and completely forgetting about our current company. That is until Lord Boreham coughs rather loudly.

"That would be most agreeable, thank you," I reply shyly.

"Wonderful," Edmund announces, "I am due to visit Emily and the Duke before I travel to that part of the country so I can pass on any messages you might have for her. I cannot wait to meet James; he must be over a year by now?"

"Oh, indeed he is," my mother pipes up, looking ever the proud grandmother.

She begins to regale him with tales of my nephew's milestones and how much he looks like his father. Without meaning to, I feel myself sinking in the knowledge that I shall always play second fiddle to my sister, especially when it comes to the man before me. Edmund was so in love with Emily, it is hard to believe he does not still have feelings for her. I glance at the doorway, suddenly wishing I could run from this place and block out the sound of everyone gushing over my younger sibling.

"Oxfordshire? An extremely beautiful part of the country, I hear," Lord Boreham suddenly says from beside me. "I have always wanted to visit the area. Perhaps, George, you might pass on Lady Elizabeth's address so that I too, might come and visit one day?"

He looks at me with an expression that tells me he wishes to become romantic with me, that this visit would be to further pursue things. I meet his gaze, trying to find some attraction to him, alas, I only see him as a parental figure, a man who is much too old for me to think of him as anything more.

"That would be wonderful, would it not, Elsie?"

My father beams with delight over such a prospect. My heart drops even further when I see how excited he is to pass me on so easily, and without even having spoken to me about it first. I know Emily had to endure an arranged marriage, as well as a quick engagement, but it was never my father's intention for her to marry so young. Tobias had practically twisted his arm to agree to such a union, and he was by no means happy about it. This is different; this is my father's way of getting rid of his least favourite daughter.

"Yes, of course," I reply with as much of a smile as I can muster. Lord Boreham smiles as widely as my father, whilst my mother looks on with concern. She holds her tongue, just as she had with Emily's match, but she already knows my heart isn't in it.

"Until next week, Elsie," Edmund, who I momentarily forgot about, says rather stiffly. He looks irritated, as though I have offended him in some unspeakable manner. "I shall send you word of my arrival."

"Lord Barton," I reply with a curtsey, to which he nods his head. He barely looks at me again before stomping off through the crowds of debutantes and their mamas.

"Father," I all but whisper, "I am afraid I am feeling rather faint. Might Mama escort me home? I do not wish to cause a scene."

"Oh, my dear, of course," he says with fatherly concern. "Colletta?"

"Yes, of course," Mama replies dutifully. "Come along, Elsie, let's leave the men to their drinks."

"Goodnight, Lord Boreham," I say politely.

"Goodnight, Miss Rothschild," he replies, picking up my hand once more to deliver a kiss. "I very much look forward to seeing you soon."

His words really do cause me to feel lightheaded, so I lean upon my mother and turn to leave. She whispers soothing placations; however, they do nothing to ease me. Emily might have got her happily ever after with the man she was forced to marry, but I cannot see that ever happening for me.

Chapter 2

Edmund

My carriage remains stationary in the turning circle of Lord and Lady Bartlett's lavish estate. My driver does not question my desire to wait here and watch the grand entrance from the safety of behind my carriage door. He has grown accustomed to my need for solace, to accept my brooding silence whenever my mind becomes crowded with too many thoughts. I cannot voice my concerns for Elsie out loud, nor my distaste for her father trying to marry her off to a man who will not understand her at all. I am not a naïve man, I know marriage between gentry is less about love and more about property, bloodlines, and other such unromantic ideals. However, the thought of Elsie being married off to a pompous old man like Lord Boreham, who will no doubt keep her tied to his bed as well as the confines of his estate, far away from the eyes of other men, has me itching with rage. Lord Boreham is as jealous as they come; he covets his possessions like a priest covets his God. He acts the charming fool for the viscount, but everyone knows what a vile scoundrel he is.

When Elsie finally appears in the entrance to the large house before me, it brings back memories of childhood, of that day when I had hurt her feelings beyond reproach. Such a foolish boy who knew nothing of what it meant to be a gentleman, or to be courteous, charming, or dare I say it, alluring to a girl. Emily kept me so entertained with all the things a boy could want from life – excitement, fun and adventure – that I believed we were the obvious couple.

Elsie was pretty as a child, but she has grown into a truly beautiful woman. Unfortunately, she has repressed her true self by falling prey to what society wants from a debutante, a lady, and what men like Lord Boreham want in a wife. She has never given herself the opportunity to find out who she truly is.

Before I can think any more on Lord Boreham or his odious intentions for Elsie, I notice her rushing out with Colletta, her mother. She looks so dejected and sad, I want to rush over and comfort her, to tell her she is enough, and is just as special as Emily, even if her father is blind to it. I cannot fault him, for it also took me some time to see Elsie for who she is. Indeed, it took Emily marrying somebody else for me to see the sister who shines just as brightly, but only when she chooses to let you see it.

A little over a year ago

Edmund

"Edmund?" Elsie says in a surprised tone of voice; she clearly did not expect to find me here in her father's house so early on a Sunday morning. She's smiling today, for the first time in months. She has taken Emily's marriage just as hard as I have; perhaps even more so. They may have fought as siblings do, but they are the best of friends when all is said and done.

"Good morning, Miss Rothschild," I reply formally, nervously playing with my hat as I do so. I am not sure how much she has been made privy to, especially my questionable behaviour, but I would like to think Emily kept my indecencies to herself.

*However, they **are** sisters. I couldn't very well blame her if she had revealed all to her.*

"Oh, Edmund, don't be all stuffy with me," she giggles as she walks past to take up a seat in the morning sun.

Her little dog, Stanley, comes running through the house, closely followed by her poodle. She's an aged thing now, but happy to see Elsie, nonetheless. I sometimes think they are the only things with which she finds happiness and comfort.

"Won't you come sit with us, Edmund?"

"Are you sure? I wouldn't like to put you out," I reply, feeling much more inadequate than I thought I would. Elsie and I have known each other since infancy, and yet, I feel a little shy around her.

"Do stop being ridiculous, Edmund," she says, shaking her head with a smile that instantly puts me at ease. "Now that Emily has gone, I need all the company I can get. Goodness knows Mother is busy enough, and Father… Well, he and I have never been close. His favourite has always been Emily, even you cannot deny that."

"Then, I would love to join you and your pack of ferocious hounds," I tease. She feigns insult on behalf of her two little dogs, then falls into laughter with me. "I suppose you will be next."

"Next?" she asks, looking truly flummoxed over whatever it is I must be talking about.

"Marriage, Elsie," I laugh, though she looks a little dejected over the word. I had always thought marriage was all that she was ever interested in. Perhaps I was wrong.

"Now that one of us is married to a duke, I am sure my

parents will not be so desperate for me to form a union any time soon. Though, I must confess, it is a little strange being at home without Em."

"You must miss her terribly," I say softly, trying to lessen the blow.

"I do, but I am also very happy for her," she says with a genuine smile. "I have never seen her looking so happy. But what about you, Edmund? How are you now?"

"Did Emily tell you of my deplorable behaviour?" I ask sheepishly, not quite able to meet her eyes.

"Parts, but only enough so that I would look out for you," she says with pity. "I worry about you too, Edmund. I have always cared for you, even if you were horrid to me as a child!"

She laughs at me, and I cannot help but laugh with her.

"What can I say? I was young and foolish and completely lost when it came to girls," I try to explain. "Emily was always different, like a boy. I suppose I found her more relatable. I have done a lot of thinking and I now know that Emily and I would have made an awful couple. We were always destined to be the best of friends, nothing more than that. I am glad for her too."

"Then I am pleased for you, Edmund," she says, briefly putting her hand over mine. The contact feels nice; in fact, it sparks a new lease on life within me. I look at her for a moment or two, seeing her as Elsie, not Emily's sister. Has she always had those dimples when she smiles? She seems to notice her hand is still lying on top of mine and withdraws it quickly, blushing the prettiest of pink upon her cheeks.

"I am going away, Elsie," I blurt out before I can stop myself. I suddenly feel reluctant to leave, but after all that has *happened, I must, if only to clear my head once and for all.*

"Oh," she gasps, sounding surprised, "forever?"

"No, but I shall not be back for a long time, perhaps a year," I tell her. "You understand why I must."

She pauses for a moment, looking deep into my eyes, as if under a spell. I too, lose myself within her gaze. It startles me to think she has eluded me all this time, letting her sister outshine her when all along she was just as dazzling.

"I do," she murmurs, her eyes still looking deep within mine. "Though it pains me to hear yet another person I care about is leaving. I shall miss you, Edmund, but I know why you must go."

"I promise to write, Elsie, and you shall be the first person I come to see when I return," I vow, getting to my feet to leave, for being here with her has suddenly become too much for me to bear. She stands with me, letting her little pug, Stanley, drop to the floor with a small yap.

"Yes, do. I will want to hear about all the wonderful places you will visit," she says, but immediately freezes when I pick up her ungloved hand and bring it to my lips. A scandalous action should anyone catch us, but I cannot help myself. Our eyes are locked upon one another, caught in a moment of yearning. Even when she gasps, she does not try to pull away. In fact, it would be so easy for me to lean in and kiss her plump, pink lips.

"I must go," I tell her on a breath of a voice, "goodbye, Elsie."

"G-goodbye, Edmund."

Present

Edmund

I fear for Elsie; it may already be too late to convince her that she is worth more than living in her sister's shadow. She turns to face her mother, who reaches up to wipe away a few tears from her flushed cheeks. She tries to smile, however, even from this distance, I can see it is pretense. The poor girl looks as though she is literally breaking from the inside. I consider going to her, but when she seemingly composes herself, I think better of it. She does not need another reminder of someone who was once blind to her own merits.

"Drive on," I call out with a knock through to the driver. The sound of the horses' hooves has me leaning back against the seat, giving me a reprieve from witnessing such a heart-breaking scene.

Chapter 3

Elsie

The next morning, as I step up to sit inside of the carriage that has come to take me to Lady Elizabeth's, I hear my father running up behind me, crunching the gravel beneath his feet.

"Elsie!" he calls, sounding jovial, which has me feeling anything but. I can tell he's about to give me some fatherly advice about Lord Boreham. He will no doubt tell me what a fine man he is and how delighted and proud he would be to hear of an engagement. In fact, he has probably already given Lord Boreham his blessing.

"Papa," I reply with a small smile I can only just about muster.

"I just wanted to wish you a safe journey," he says with a wide smile, "and to wish you luck."

"Luck?" I question him, even though I instantly regret it as soon as the word leaves my mouth.

"With Lord Boreham when he comes to visit," he chuckles

as though I should have known what he was referring to. "You could do a lot worse, my dear, he is absolutely besotted with you. I couldn't get him to stop talking about you last night. He wants a big family and I know you have always wanted that too."

"I see," I reply, swallowing back a lump that has suddenly formed inside of my throat. "I also hope to see Edmund."

"Ah, yes, of course," he says, looking a little less enthusiastic. "I hope you are not expecting a proposal from him, Elsie, you know how much he felt for Emily, and probably still does. I would hate for you to be disappointed."

"You do not think he could see anything in me?" I ask through the sting of tears.

"You are desirable all on your own, Elsie, Lord Boreham has proved as much. I do not want you to ever think otherwise, but if I am being truly honest, I believe Edmund will only ever see you as second best to your sister. Do you really want that, Elsie? To be married to a man who is in love with somebody else?"

The tears break the barrier I have been trying so hard to keep up as I shake my head in agreement with him. It feels as though I am being stabbed in the heart with about a thousand knives.

"Oh, Elsie, my darling girl," he says with distinct pity in his voice, bringing me against his chest so I can cry with some degree of privacy. His affection feels strange, unnatural, for I cannot remember the last time he ever showed such care for me. "Lord Boreham will love you like no other, and, in time, I am certain you will come to love him too."

"I am sure you are right," I reply, putting on my usual façade of confidence. It works, for I am gifted with a smile and a kiss to my cheek. "I shall see you in a week. Goodbye, Father."

"Goodbye, Elsie," he says, appearing happy and hopeful once again.

As he embraces me, I look over his shoulder to see my mother watching from the window with a handkerchief held to her mouth as she cries for me. I shake my head a little, so subtly, only a mother would see it. I then offer her a sad smile before climbing inside of the carriage, clutching hold of Stanley tightly on my lap, seeking comfort from something that loves me like no other.

Elsie

I arrive at Lady Elizabeth's house just when the sun is setting low in the sky. It is blissfully quiet here, much like when I go to visit Emily. Had I the choice, I think I would very much like to live in the countryside, nestled amongst the trees, far away from the hustle and bustle of London. Though you could hardly accuse me of being an outdoorsy person, I appreciate its beauty and simplicity. It is but another dream that has been afforded to my sister. Not that I would begrudge her any of her happiness, but I do envy her in such a way it makes me feel sad for myself.

"Elsie, is that you?" Lady Elizabeth calls out to me from her wooden front door, complete with its iron fox knocker. "Henry, do get the tea ready, our guest has finally arrived!"

"Good afternoon, Lady Elizabeth," I smile for her, finally shrugging off my self-indulgent melancholy.

"Oh, tsk, child, we do not bother with such titles here," she says as I lean in so she can kiss my cheek and offer Stanley a pat on his head, to which he indulges her by purring softly against her frail hand.

"Apologies, Elizabeth," I laugh softly, "I have been brought up to respect the social niceties of the ton; addressing one's title being one of them."

"Well, the ton is a million miles away from here. Come, we are going to have an excellent holiday away from all the riff-raff. You and little Stanley."

"Wonderful," I reply with a contented sigh and a huge smile on my face. I may well be visited by Lord Boreham, or even Edmund, who has been troubling my thoughts since I saw him last night, but ultimately, this trip away is for me. And Stanley.

Edmund

"Monty!" I yell as the young hound comes galloping towards me, wagging his tail uncontrollably and crouching down low in submission before he's even reached my feet. "You ridiculous boy!"

I cannot help but bend to embrace him, for I've come to love him as much as Emily does. He offers me many kisses, all the while I try not to imagine where his absurdly long tongue has been. Eventually, he calms himself to a point where he simply falls against my legs and accepts my praise without fuss.

"You are wonderful, aren't you, boy?" I whisper to him, just as Emily comes rushing outside carrying a small child in her arms. She looks incredibly beautiful; it is obvious that motherhood suits her. The child is lucky to have her, for she will encourage him in every possible way, break the usual rules of upper-class child rearing, and give him a life full of love and laughter.

"Edmund!" she beams when she finally reaches me. "You look incredible."

"Emily," I reply, standing up straight and nodding my head in greeting. "And you look wonderful, just as you always have."

"Lord Barton," a familiar deep voice says with a teasing tone, "I do hope you are not ogling my wife."

"I would never," I reply jovially, smiling at Tobias when he comes into full view. Fortunately, he smiles back at me, just before shaking my hand. We are not close friends, but we have a friendship of sorts. Enough of one to be able to tease the other. I consider his forgiveness of my past transgressions extremely gracious, for he could so easily have prevented me from ever seeing Emily again.

"I see you have caught a lot of sun on your travels," Tobias comments as he snaps his fingers towards the hound who is now lying on his back with everything on show. His tongue is lolloping out the side of his mouth without a care in the world. If only one could have the life of a dog like him, content with the simplest of pleasures.

"Indeed, mostly during my time in Greece," I rely, "a most incredible country with one of the most interesting histories I have ever heard. Myths, Gods and Goddesses, quite astonishing!"

"And extremely incestuous, was it not?" Emily adds as she hands James over to his father, who smiles with pride at his young son. It is quite a wonderful sight, having known how serious and unwarming he once was.

"Well, true, but who are we to judge?" I add. "We all have our sordid histories."

"Quite," Tobias says with an arch of his brow, causing my cheeks to glow with leftover humiliation from my time with Polly. She was paid handsomely for my guilt, but it did not deter her from seeking a wealthy lord elsewhere. Again, who am I to judge her for the life she chooses to live.

"Tsk, ignore my husband," Emily says with a wink she aims directly at him when she thinks I am not looking. He smiles with equal measure of pride and lust. They are still very much in honeymoon love, which is hardly surprising after all that happened between them. "Come, let us go and sit outside for tea."

"Still a lover of the wild, I see?" I ask her with a genuine smile; she has not changed.

"But of course. Being a Duchess, wife and mother was never going to stop my need to straddle the boundaries of social acceptance. My son will be brought up just as I was."

"With some exceptions," Tobias smiles, "he will be a duke one day. He will need to think logically and tactfully."

"And I do not?" Emily gasps, feigning insult.

"You are passionate, emotional," he says whilst lifting his hand to stifle the argument that is getting ready to leave her mouth with a little wrath. "And intelligent. More so than many scholars, my dear. However, you do not always think rationally. Running out in the height of a storm in the middle of the night?"

She slams her lips shut at the same time as he offers her a kiss on the cheek, looking haughty over his winning rebuttal.

"I think it best neither of us mention that night, husband," she says, though with a soft smile, "for there was good reason to be running away from you that night."

"I will never forget that night," he whispers, gazing deep inside her eyes. "It made me realise what a fool I was being for fighting my growing feelings for you."

They give in and begin to kiss one another, the sight of which makes me feel dreadfully uncomfortable. Though, funnily enough, not because I am jealous. I only feel like I am imposing on a tender moment, and my upbringing taught me to feel such discomfort when met with open displays of affection.

In the end, she pushes playfully at his chest, motioning her chin towards me, which does nothing to quell my feelings of inadequacy. He simply kisses her again, this time even harder, to the point where she is giggling against him.

"Edmund understands a man's need to kiss his beautiful wife," he says in a playful tone of voice "especially when he is so in love with her."

"I must apologise on my husband's behalf, Edmund," Emily calls out from behind him, grinning from ear to ear.

"You must not!" Tobias playfully chastises her.

"Tobias—"

"No, on this occasion, he is quite right, Em," I laugh over her blushing cheeks. "I can only dream of being married to a woman who makes me feel as giddy as your husband now looks."

"Touché," Tobias grins over my little quip.

"Tea is served, Your Grace," Mrs Keppel announces as she comes marching up with a smile on her face, all before she nods her head in reverence to the three of us.

"Excellent," I reply, feeling glad to be breaking free from the awkwardness of being witness to young love. "Lead the way, Mrs Keppel."

Edmund

Tobias leaves us to catch up on lost time after we have overindulged on cake and tea. Being a married woman means Emily is almost as free to walk around as she was when she was a child. It suits her, being able to live her life without the social constraints of London. She never was built to be a debutante, which is perhaps what made her all the more attractive to men like Tobias. Men who have never put much stock in the pomp and circumstance of the ton. Men like me.

I cannot help smiling over the fact we are able to walk in comfortable silence just as we once had. I finally feel like we are best friends again, the way it was meant to be. Her hair is falling in honey-coloured waves down her back, and she's wearing a dress not nearly as grand as others in her social standing, and with a smile as wide as mine. Monty is leaping about in the long grass where wildflowers are attracting bumble bees that create a natural orchestra for our ears. This is where Emily belongs, this is her natural habitat, and where she thrives.

"You are happy, Em," I cannot help but say out loud, to which she looks at me and giggles with acceptance of the fact.

"Very much so," she replies. "Who would have thought marrying that stuffy man who insulted me beyond reproach would have made my life complete?"

"If I had been a betting man, I would have lost a great deal of money," I admit. "I was so afraid you would never be happy again. I was extremely wrong."

"I think we all were at one point or another," she says, linking her arm through mine with friendly affection. "But I am also happy to have you back here with me, like this, as the best of friends."

"Me too," I say with a smile as goofy as that of the dog.

"You do look a lot better, Edmund, but you are not yet as happy as I am," she thinks out loud, just as she turns her head to watch Monty jumping about in a nearby stream. "What *would* make you as happy, Edmund?"

At first, I give her nothing more than a nervous laugh, which she accepts without comment. She does not push for an answer, just allows me to walk along so that I might find the right words with which to articulate my verbal response.

"Is it not obvious?" I eventually sigh.

"Is there no one on the horizon for you? Perhaps a young lady you met on your travels? A debutante that piqued some sort of interest when you arrived home last week?"

"I met many fine ladies on my travels, all of them with husbands. It is most unusual to find an unmarried lady galivanting across the continent, Em. Though, I could definitely see you undertaking such a challenge if you had the means to."

"Tobias has promised to take me to France one day. But now we are wandering off course; have you, or have you not, met someone?"

"No, well, possibly…it is difficult to know." I pause to laugh over her dropped mouth and her inquisitive stare. "That is to say, there is a young lady, but I am still unsure of many things when it comes to her."

"Such as?" she pushes, nudging at my arm to encourage me to spill all.

"My feelings are cloudy when it comes to this lady, we still have so much to learn about one another. Not to mention, I am still rather cautious when it comes to matters of the heart. Look how badly the last attraction I had for a lady turned out."

"Oh, Edmund—" she begins to argue but I cut her off by raising my hand. She relents quickly, probably not knowing what to say to my joke, which was in poor taste.

"Truthfully, Em, I do not feel like I deserve such a lady," I try to explain. "What if I am not enough? What if my feelings clear and I cannot offer her anything other than what we have?"

"Well, that is quite ridiculous," she tuts. "Tobias and I practically hated each other before we let our feelings grow into love. And look at us now!"

"The lady in question is already in so much doubt over her own worth," I tell her honestly. "If I were to make those feelings of inadequacy grow even deeper, I do not think I would ever forgive myself. She deserves to have love so much more than I do, Em."

"That is sad, Edmund," she says pensively. "Though, have you not considered that you could do the exact opposite by taking a chance on her? You could make her life as fulfilled as mine."

"I am not sure I should take the risk," I voice out loud.

"You are not like most gentleman in London, looking for a wife for reasons of vanity or family honour, you are a man looking for a woman with whom to fall in love. I think you could easily love this lady; I can see it in your eyes and hear it in your voice when you speak of her. It is merely fear that is holding you back, just as it once had with Tobias. If you can love half as fiercely as my husband, then she will be a very lucky lady indeed."

"Perhaps," I reply, sounding only half convinced of her unfailing faith in me.

Emily does not push for anything more and we walk along for a good few minutes before she eventually says something else.

"You're not going to tell me who she is, are you?" she asks with a teasing smile.

"One day, possibly, but not before I have decided what, if anything, I am going to do about her."

"Fair enough. I am sorely disappointed, but fair enough."

Chapter 4

Elsie

Elizabeth and I have been resting in front of the open fire for some time, feeling contented by the sound of crackling flames and Stanley's gentle snoring. I have never felt more at ease than I do right now, away from all the expectations, the disappointment, and the feeling of inadequacy around my father. And yet, I can feel a longing, a desire for something I see between Mama and Father, and what is more than obvious between Emily and Tobias; something I've never experienced before.

Elizabeth has stopped her hands moving against her needlework and is now staring at me with a warm smile upon her face. She is comforting, even when she is silent. It is a gift very few people have; to force someone to open up through eye contact alone. I cuddle Stanley closer to me before I finally begin to speak to her with an openness that I do not easily share with anyone other than my sister.

"You were a million miles away, Elsie," she begins before I can even utter a single word. "Indulge me with your youthful problems."

"*Youthful?*" I laugh sadly. "I am positively ancient for an unmarried lady. Though, in truth, the idea of being a spinster does not fill me with as much dread as one might imagine for a girl in my position."

"It has its pleasures," she says truthfully, "especially when the expectation for you to find a husband finally dissipates. Acceptance of who you are and the choices that have been made, whether your own or through circumstance, becomes a friend you never knew you needed."

"I feel you are holding back, Elizabeth," I tease, "do I sense a *but*?"

"I suppose I sometimes regret not having had a great love affair, as well as the opportunity to have children of my own; it can be frightfully lonely, Elsie."

"I always thought I would have had at least one child by now," I reply sadly, not quite able to meet her eyes. A painful lump has formed within my throat over the prospect of never having a family of my own. "Still, I have my little nephew, and I am sure your own nephew is likely to gift Emily with another child soon."

"Oh, I have no doubt," she scoffs, "I am surprised the poor girl is allowed to see beyond the bed chamber with the way he looks at her."

"I do not understand; the bed chamber?" I ask with a furrowed brow.

"Oh, er, well, never mind," she says, coughing over her slip of the tongue, or whatever it was she was just alluding to. "I am certain you will find out one day. You were meant for love and family, Elsie, just as much as your sister is."

"Then you have more faith than I do in such a thing," I admit glumly before taking a sip of my tea.

"Is there no one on the horizon?" she asks with what sounds like hope in her voice. "No young lord to whisk you off your feet?"

"I do not think so," I reply, though a familiar face presents itself inside of my mind the very instant I say these words. I blush for fear that I have not been entirely truthful with my host. When I look at her, it is more than obvious she feels the same way, for she is smiling with a glint of intrigue behind her eyes. Elizabeth is nothing if not incredibly perceptive. Emily had warned me of such before I had even met the lady myself. Though, she could not deny that such a quality made her as endearing as it did menacing.

"Oh, come now, Elsie, I am old; do not make me go through the effort of having to pull it out from you," she says with a sly smile and a wink.

"Pull what—"

"And do not pretend to not know what it is I am talking about. I thought you far more compassionate than that; to force an old woman to waste breath on such unnecessary rambling," she says in such a way, I have to laugh a little, all the while twiddling with my braid between my anxious fingers.

"Well, I suppose I might have seen something, a hint if you like, of an attraction between Edmund and I," I begin, the words on my tongue feeling strange. I never thought of anything remotely possible happening between us. He's always been so enamoured by my sister, even after she married Tobias. In fact, as soon as they have escaped my mouth, I shake my head in an attempt to pull them back, even though such a thing is entirely impossible. "Please, do not take any note of what I just said; the very idea is folly."

"Of course, Elsie," she says, but I still brace myself, for it does not sound as though she is yet finished. "However, you must know I cannot leave things as they are without asking why?"

"I suppose I would question if it were really you sitting here if you didn't," I laugh, though it sounds more like a cry than a sound of mirth.

She doesn't say another word, just patiently waits against the sound of crackling wood on the fire. The heat begins to get to me, to the point whereby I have to turn away from it, effectively forcing me to face Elizabeth's questioning eyes. Eventually, she gives a nod of encouragement and I find myself taking a deep breath to begin.

"Edmund and I were never compatible; he was attracted to my sister's rebellious and whimsical spirit, much like Papa. I was always too sensible, and much too obedient to attract the attentions of men like him. Just ask your nephew; he barely gave me two seconds attention before he fell for Emily's…*uniqueness*."

"Dear girl, you and Tobias would not have made a love match," she says with nothing but kindness written across her face. "In fact, you would have made each other extremely unhappy; he needed someone to challenge him whilst loving him at the same time. And you, my dear, you need someone who will give you such unconditional love that for once in your life, you will know it is all yours and only yours."

I look at her with a swell of tears on my lower eyelids. Is it that obvious? I have carried around this burden of being in my sister's shadow for so long, I do not even know who I really am. I always believed I had hidden it from others, that I had kept the pain of being second best to every man who met us both to myself. Perhaps Mama has guessed; in fact, I am sure she has, but Elizabeth? A woman I have seen perhaps only a handful of times in my lifetime. Her words bring a feeling of great shame and immense guilt. I love my sister and only wish her happiness, but I cannot deny I also envy her so much, it stabs at my heart to think about all that she has and all that I do not.

"Oh, Elsie," Elizabeth whispers as she comes to wrap her frail arms around my quivering shoulders.

"Please forgive me, I do not mean to cry," I whimper, but those words only cause me to cry all the harder. I have held it all in for so long on my own, that to have someone acknowledge my anguish is all too much to be able hold myself together. Elizabeth does not pay any heed to my apology; she simply holds onto me until I have exhausted myself into a vacant stare.

"What must you think of me?" I utter as we lean against one another in front of the burning flames of the open fire. "I hope you do not misunderstand me; I love Emily with all my heart."

"Of course you do," she says before kissing my head like my mother would have.

"I did not realise it was so obvious for you to see," I admit, "and now I am scared others can see it too."

"Oh, Elsie, you dear silly girl," she laughs, "of course they don't, especially men. Elsie, I can see it as clear as day because I have been in your very position."

"You have?" I ask, pulling away so I can turn to look at her kindly expression.

"Of course I have," she smiles, sounding as if I am foolish to not already know this. "I did not choose to be a spinster."

"I am sorry, I assumed…" I trail off, shaking my head over not having ever wondered why she never married. "How self-absorbed I have been, you must forgive me once more."

"Now, you must stop apologising, Elsie, or I shall have no choice but to force you to come to tea with Lord Wilton, and you know what an insufferable bore he is," she says with such a stern expression, I cannot help but laugh.

"Alright, I promise to stop," I vow with a smile upon my face. "But please tell me what happened to you, Elizabeth."

"I fell in love with a man who professed to love me back," she says with a casual shrug, though from the look in her eye, I can tell it is a hard story for her to tell. "I refused every other man who asked for my hand, much to my parents' frustration. I think the only reason I was not forced down the aisle was because the object of my affection was a duke. Ironic, don't you think?"

"Quite," I murmur, too engrossed as to what happened to this duke.

"Oliver's mother insisted he travel before he settled down," she says with a sad smile and her gaze now getting lost in the glow of the fire. "If he took a year to travel, then his mother would give her blessing. Reluctantly, my parents agreed to let me wait for his return. A lot happened during that year; my sister married her own duke and Tobias was born. Two blessings within the space of nine months. Alas, my blessings never came. My father died just after Tobias was born, and my mother needed someone to care for her. I did not begrudge becoming her nurse for I knew my love was due home any day."

"What happened to him, Elizabeth?" I ask with trepidation.

"He never came home," she says with such sadness, it causes my heart to ache. "My poor Oliver was accosted by two muggers who left him bloody and beaten on the docks in Calais. I was distraught, too heartbroken to consider another. Tobias' mother tried to convince me to reconsider, but I refused, and accepted that I was to be my mother's nursemaid until she died ten years later. After that, I was far too old for marriage; my window for love had well and truly closed."

"Oh, Elizabeth," I cry as I take hold of her frail hand, which even next to the fire, feels cold.

"Do not cry for me, Elsie," she says with a sob caught in her throat, "there have been enough tears."

"But, Elizabeth, your story is so sad," I whimper, pulling her hand to my mouth so I can kiss it with affection.

"And it was only told to make you understand two things - one, the feelings you have are completely natural, given everything, and two, if I could go back and have my love the way I should have, I would not even question it. So, if Edmund is your chance for love, then do not waste time by second guessing it, Elsie; you grab hold with both hands."

"But what if he only sees me as a second prize for Emily?" I ask with shame, after having heard her heart-breaking story.

"Elsie, trust me, when a man is in love with you, when you are the only object of his desire, you will know," she says with a smile that is no longer sad. It is one of a wisdom I do not yet have. "And if you are still unsure, you bring him to me, and I will tell you. You know nothing gets past Auntie Elizabeth."

"No, I suppose it doesn't," I smile back at her, embracing her once more before we finally retire to bed. I think we have both earnt our sleep tonight.

Chapter 5

Elsie

My mind was still flooded with thoughts of Edmund when I retired to bed last night, and I spent what seemed like hours chasing sleep that refused to come. I am so confused over how I truly feel about Edmund that I find it hard to concentrate on anything else. So, imagine my surprise when I am awoken by Elizabeth informing me that a gentleman caller has come to visit. My heart feels like it is thumping at an alarming rate, so much so, my head becomes dizzy.

"Do not look quite so fearful, Elsie," she laughs, placing her hand on my shoulder in an attempt to calm me.

"But I am not dressed, I am not even washed, and my hair looks –"

"Elsie, even after a night of tossing and turning, you still look every part the daughter of a viscount," she says with a warm smile. "But do not worry, dear girl, I told him to return in an hour, so that gives you plenty of time to sort yourself out."

"Oh, thank goodness," I sigh, laughing a little with relief.

"Why don't you wear the mauve gown; you know, the one with the cream trim. You look simply breathtaking when you wear that one," she says, speaking as though she has seen me wear it many times. In truth, she can only have seen it once or twice, but I am thankful for her suggestion. I am so flustered over having a gentleman coming to visit me here, I have no thoughts of my own for what I should wear.

"Yes, thank you, and I shall wear my hair up, I think," I declare whilst jumping out of bed.

"Lovely, though I should warn you, Elsie," she says in such a way I turn to look at her for further explanation, "it is not Edmund Barton."

"It isn't?" I ask, now even more curious as to who this visitor might be, and if I am being honest, a little disappointed too. "Then, who is it?"

"An older gentleman, but still very handsome," she says with a mischievous grin. "He said his name was Lord Boreham."

"Oh," I reply, sounding thoroughly disenchanted by the fact. My discontented tone only makes her all the more intrigued. "One of Papa's associates; I think he is trying to force a match."

"One which you do not wish to explore?" she asks, now turning intrigue into concern.

"I don't know," I murmur, "he does seem very keen, and he is very handsome—"

"And obviously of good standing?" she tries to clarify, to which I unhelpfully shrug.

"Of course, but—"

"But he is not Edmund?" she asks, smiling with understanding. I merely blush over the truth of the matter. "But he could be seen as…*competition*?"

"Elizabeth!" I gasp with shock over such a suggestion. She merely winks with one of her sly smiles and I have to laugh at her.

"The mauve," she eventually says with a tap of her hand against my leg.

Elsie

Lord Richard Boreham arrives promptly on the hour, which Elizabeth comments upon. Apparently, it demonstrates how keen he must be to see me. She takes this as a good sign; however, I only feel nauseated by his desire to see me so urgently. Try as I might, I cannot begin to feel anything remotely close to attraction or even affection towards this man. Even when he walks inside of Lady Elizabeth's morning room, dressed in the finest of fabrics, I can only look on him how I might when my father walks into a room.

"Good morning, Lord Boreham," Elizabeth declares as he walks inside, looking much too big for the cottage's low ceilings. "You remember Miss Rothschild, of course."

"Of course, how could one forget a face such as hers?" he says with as much charm as he had presented to me on the last occasion we met. I offer a shy smile, and a polite nod of my head.

"You have come a long way, I hear," Elizabeth says, as if poking him for some sort of explanation for his presence.

"Indeed," he says with a wide smile, baring his teeth for us both to see. "I was actually hoping I might escort you ladies into town. I hear there is a marvellous tearoom."

"Oh, yes, we would enjoy that wouldn't we, Elsie?" Elizabeth encourages me and I have to stop myself from rolling my eyes over her lack of tact.

"I shall just get my shawl," I say to them, prompting him to get to his feet with me. "Elizabeth, shall I meet you both by the door?"

"Good idea, my dear, I will ask Anthony to gather the dogs," she replies, her twinkling eyes glancing at Lord Boreham before offering a smile of encouragement my way.

Once out of eyesight, I take a moment to breathe more easily, where I can let my facial expression match my inner turmoil. I so desperately want to feign a sickness that would prevent me from going. I rarely feel comfortable in a man's presence, least of all with this man who reminds me of Father. I do not feel as though I can be myself when trying so hard to be the sort of lady a man expects me to be. Emily struggled with it too, though she often felt brave enough to let her true self out. As it turns out, her bravery landed her with the perfect happily-ever-after marriage. If only I could be so honest.

When I finally feel brave enough to meet the others by the front door, I am already wearing a perfect smile for both Lord Boreham and Lady Elizabeth. The strain of it is pinching at my cheeks, but it is the only thing I can think to do to stop myself from showing them my true anxiety.

"Shall I lead the way?" Elizabeth announces with confidence before walking out with the dogs in tow.

"After you, Elsie," Lord Boreham says with a gesture to go out in front. As I pass by, I feel his hand gracing the small of my back, which ignites a tingle through my body. It is not a natural feeling, it is one that tells me I do not want him touching me, not ever. Although I have been schooled from childhood to not let my true feelings betray the façade of a perfect debutante, I cannot help but emit a shiver over the abhorrence of his touch.

The trip had been spent exchanging pleasantries, discussing the weather, upcoming societal events, and such. I sipped delicately at my tea, only eating a third of the cake that was ordered for me. I must have uttered less than ten sentences, ensuring that whatever I said was kept neutral, polite, and not at all challenging to anyone in any way.

"This is indeed a lovely establishment, Lady Elizabeth, do you come here often?" Lord Boreham asks as he ingests a large mouthful of cake. I cannot help but watch as he demolishes the delicacy of his dessert, breaking it apart without care or appreciation. I half-imagine this is how he would treat a woman, taking what he wants without cherishing who she is.

"Well, yes, as much as a lady can," Lady Elizabeth answers before sipping her tea.

"Of course," he replies between mouthfuls of cake. "Too much cake might damage a lady's delicate figure. I, myself, prefer a lady who can show self-restraint."

"Hmm," she mumbles before covering her look of disdain behind her teacup. Meanwhile, I find myself pushing away my plate for fear he might comment upon my own self-indulgence.

"Tell me, Miss Rothschild, your dog?" he says, turning to face Stanley with a distinct sneer upon his face. From the growl Stanley offers him, the feeling is more than mutual.

"Yes?" I eventually ask when he makes no attempt to elaborate.

"Are you and he particularly attached?"

"Yes, Stan—"

"I only ask because my housekeeper, a dear lady who has been in my family's employment for many years, is very allergic," he says in such a way, no other words are necessary to tell me that the matter of Stanley's accompanying me into any marriage would not be up for discussion.

"Stanley and Elsie are extremely close; he goes with her everywhere, much like my dogs do with me," Lady Elizabeth pipes up.

"Sacrifices must be made sometimes," he says without taking his eyes away from mine, smiling haughtily as he does so. *"For the greater good."*

"Tell me, Lord Boreham, have you been married before?" Lady Elizabeth probes further, purposefully trying to rile him up. I suspect she likes Lord Boreham about as much as Stanley does.

"No," he replies curtly. *"It has taken me some time to find a lady who is worthy of bearing the Boreham name. Girls these days tend to forget their place, speaking far too much while listening far too little. Even my father had to deal with my mother with a firm hand at times. But he taught me well; he taught me to wait until the perfect woman would reveal herself to me. I believe she has."*

He smiles at me with crumbs of cake sticking to the whiskers around his mouth. I feel like I should offer some words of acknowledgement or thanks, however, all I can do is dip my head to avoid him seeing the colour draining from my face. Instead of his being frustrated with me, he appears pleased by my silence.

"Shall we depart?" Elizabeth snaps, unable to hide her distaste for this man any longer. *"I have suddenly lost my*

appetite."

I have worn my perfect debutante mask for so long, it has never occurred to me to feel shameful about it. Not until today with Lord Boreham. I felt thoroughly weak by my inability to speak up for myself, as well as embarrassed in front of Lady Elizabeth. But now, walking back to Elizabeth's cottage, getting ever closer to ending this pretense, I begin to feel much more at ease. Reluctantly, Elizabeth hangs back, allowing Lord Boreham and I to walk out in front. One last betrayal of myself before I can relax in the comfort of Elizabeth's home.

"Elsie, I have enjoyed your company today, especially our conversation," he says to me. I will admit, it takes a tremendous effort not to laugh over such a statement. I have shown Lord Boreham perhaps a fraction of who I really am, my real thoughts, dreams, and aspirations. Had I done so, he would not be making any effort to try and charm me now.

"Yes," I reply, for even I cannot bring myself to return the sentiment. There is playing a role, withholding one's inner self, and then there is barefaced lying. I am an expert at playing a part, but I am not when it comes to telling falsehoods.

"I hope you realise how much I am enamoured by you, Elsie," he says rather forwardly, forcing a quiet, but unattractive noise to escape from the back of my throat. He does not take any note of it, simply ignores the sound, and continues. "Perhaps, if we had more time, I would attempt to court you for longer."

"Had time, my Lord?" I ask with curiosity in my voice.

"Let us be honest, Elsie, neither of us are getting any younger," he says bluntly whilst I inwardly gasp over the insult he has just handed me. "I apologise, but a lady of your age, well, your desirability to younger, sillier gentleman, is beginning to wane. And I, although much older than you, can find a wife at any age. However, I would like a family, and an heir to take on my name and heritage. I would like those things now, and, with your father's permission, I would like them with you."

He looks at me as though I should be grateful, positively swooning over his declaration to want me over all the other ladies he can choose from, especially as I am so *old*. He cannot see how deeply wounded I now feel, how he has made me like him even less than I did before. What a pompous old fool he is. I would laugh to myself if it was not for the last thing he just said - *with my father's permission*. For I know, if he does ask, or *when* he asks, Papa will think nothing of convincing me to marry this odious gentleman. He did so with Emily, and she was his favourite, his darling, his shining light. What hope do I have of refusing his will?

"Oh, I see," I reply with a slip of my usual perfect disposition, for I cannot hide the fear in my voice.

"Do not be afraid of giving yourself to a man, Elsie," he says in such a way, it sends shivers up my spine. "I know you have been holding yourself back from marriage, but I will love and care for you. It is your role in life to bear children, to nurture a husband and family. When your father told me of his concerns for you, I had to see this poor girl for myself. At first, I thought it might be because you were unhandsome, but when he pointed you out to me, I knew you had to be mine. It felt as though you had been saving yourself for me; we are meant to be, you and I."

"Lord Boreham, I—"

"Please, you must call me Richard, especially as we are to be married soon."

"Well, I…you see…" I hesitate in my footing when I see Elizabeth's cottage up ahead, a safe haven away from Lord

Boreham and his plans of marriage and family. However, there is something else causing me to pause in my flustering. A figure of a man whom I know very well, the only man with whom I feel remotely free. "Edmund?"

"Elsie?" Lord Boreham questions my erratic behaviour. When I make no reply, he follows my line of sight to see the very same man as I do. I instantly smile over the sight of my childhood friend. Lord Boreham, however, looks positively disgruntled.

"Forgive my interrupting but Elsie, my dear, is that not Lord Barton?" Elizabeth asks as she strolls up to rest beside us.

"It is, indeed, Lady Elizabeth," I reply, unable to hide my beaming smile over the fact. "I believe he told me he would visit."

I practically begin running towards Edmund without any regard for how I might look under Lord Boreham's watchful gaze. I just see him and instantly feel like I should run for his safety. When he notices the commotion of my attempts to rush over, he offers a genuinely wide smile and removes his hat. If I was not restrained by the rules of society, I am sure I would wrap my arms around him and indulge in his embrace.

"Miss Rothschild," he greets me just before I come skidding to a halt, "I was worried I would not see you. I hope you do not mind me dropping by?"

"I do not mind at all, but please do not address me so formerly, not when we have known each other since we were both in lead strings!"

"I am sorry, Elsie, you are quite right. It is ridiculous to use titles when we go so far back. I cannot even remember a time when you were not in my life," he says quietly, looking at me with such intensity, a different kind of tingling begins to travel through me. I like the feeling of this tingle; this tingle speaks of wanting nothing more than for him to touch me. In the end, however, I force myself to turn away from his brown eyes for fear I shall never be free of them again. "You look well, Elsie, so much more at ease in the countryside."

"Thank you, but I owe some of that to my host and dear friend, Lady Elizabeth," I tell him, turning to point at her approaching figure.

He looks up and nods in greeting, though I am certain she is not going to let that be enough to satisfy her. When she is within reach of him, she offers her gloved hand and waits expectantly for him to kiss it, which he does, with an expertly executed charming smile. Even the old lady blushes under his handsome gaze.

"Lady Elizabeth, I do not believe I have had the pleasure," he says politely, "I am—"

"I know who you are," she says, then turns her voice to a whisper, "I can tell by the blush on this young lady's cheeks who you are."

She offers him a wink whilst I gasp with shock and humiliation. I feel his eyes upon me, but I am too afraid to face him after what she has just disclosed. It is the one time I am happy to have Lord Boreham's interference.

"Lord Barton, you are far from London today," he says with a pompous smile, "any particular reason as to why?"

"Lord Boreham, a pleasure to see you," Edmund lies, "I am on my way to my estate in Witney. My cousin left it to me in his will and I am yet to see the extent as to what needs doing to it. I could not come past without stopping in to see my dear friend, Elsie."

"Why don't I arrange for us to sit out on the lawn; it is such a beautiful day, after all," Elizabeth intercepts. I am hoping that Lord Boreham will be satisfied with our outing and leave me be so I can properly catch up with Edmund without his watchful eyes. I can tell by his stiffness that he is not happy with Edmund's presence here; he feels like my father all over again.

"Alas, I have other business to attend to," Lord Boreham replies, "however, I will see you next week, Elsie. Your father has invited me for dinner to discuss…*matters*."

"Oh, I see," I reply, most likely looking pale, for I know full well what he means by '*matters*', cryptic though it was. "I shall see you then."

"A pleasure, Lady Elizabeth," he says politely. "Lord Barton, I hope you enjoy the ladies' company as much as I have."

After the usual nods and curtseys from each of us, Lord Boreham about turns and marches off over the gravel. Elizabeth soon ushers us inside where we take up residence on the lawn behind her cottage. A gentle breeze gives a refreshing coolness in the midday sun, and I close my eyes to appreciate the sensation. Lady Elizabeth has already fallen asleep in one of the garden chairs, whilst the dogs make for little steppingstones in the grass beside her feet.

"You know we should probably wake our chaperone, Edmund," I murmur with my face still pointing up towards the sun. "If my father knew I was out here with a young man, he would probably turn purple with outrage."

"Oh, come on, Elsie, who is here to see us? Besides, Elizabeth would back up any wild and elaborate story we came up with. She is deliciously wicked, I like her."

"I love her too," I tell him with a genuine laugh, only to turn serious again when I remember her sad story from last night. "She was in love once, with a duke, no less. He was going to marry her when he returned home from his travels abroad, only he never made it back to her."

"He abandoned her?" he asks with curiosity in his voice.

"No, he was killed," I explain. "She refused to marry another, so she became her mother's nursemaid. Such a sad story."

He does not say anything, merely looks at me with a melancholy smile. It is genuine and I feel a warmth from his sympathetic gaze when he glances over to the old lady who is now gently snoring. I pour another cup of tea for us both and wait for the steam to hit my nostrils. It always seems to calm me, and after my outing with Lord Boreham, I am in desperate need of its soothing remedy.

"Elsie, I hope you do not think me too forward for asking, but are you and Lord Boreham courting?" Edmund asks, though he must see my body tense up over the idea, for he releases a sigh not long after. "Has something happened? Something untoward?"

"No, but I fear something is about to happen, something I will not be able to decline," I admit. "Father has told him how desperate he is to marry me off. Apparently, Lord Boreham is a suitable candidate for the job. Despite my age, as he so bluntly informed me, he has chosen me to become his wife and to bear his children."

"Oh," he says, looking away with a frown bunching between his brows. I cannot tell what emotions or thoughts are running through his head. However, I can tell he is not enamoured by the idea. "And you do not return his desire to marry?"

"Not at all," I reply, not even bothering to sugar coat my feelings on the matter. We look at one another and laugh a little over my blunt choice of words. "He does not see me, Edmund, he only sees an obedient wife and a mother figure for his offspring. And before you say so, I am more than aware that most gentlemen only see this in a debutante, but the man does not even attempt to engage me in any sort of meaningful conversation. I daresay if I were to speak a fraction of my mind, I would be chastised for it. He is much too like Father; the thought of kissing such a man makes me feel positively sick."

"You sound like Emily," he laughs, though his words only have me slumping with disappointment. I am not an imitation of my sister. I am me; I am Elsie.

"Well, I do not suppose I shall have a lot of choice in the matter," I tell him, changing the subject, even though the direction is no less depressing. "You heard what he said, he is coming to dinner next week. He has already told me he is planning to ask for my father's permission to marry me. It is as good as done, Edmund."

"Then I shall talk to your father," he says determinedly, "I will make sure you do not have to marry him."

"Like you did with Emily?" I reply rather cruelly.

"Emily was different," he says defensively, "your father had no choice with Tobias; this time he does. Your father has always wanted what was best for you and Emily, and I am certain that he will listen if he knows how much you are against the idea."

"Emily," I correct him, and he stops to look at me for further explanation. "He has always wanted what was best for *Emily*. For me, it is what is convenient for him. This marriage would strengthen his ties in business whilst also getting rid of me."

"Elsie, surely you do not believe that?" he says in barely more than a whisper and with sadness in his voice. "Your father loves you."

"Possibly, but not as strongly as he loves my sister," I admit to both him and me. "It is not a belief, Edmund, it is fact. I am destined to become Lady Richard Boreham."

We fall silent while I contemplate my words. The wind picks up and I take a few sips of my tea to try and ward off the chill. Edmund plays with his teaspoon, looking troubled, as though he is battling with indecision, perhaps whether to try and placate me with more lies about my father's affections. He need not bother, for I came to accept what I had just said about him a long time ago.

"Not if I can help it," he eventually mutters, his hand gently covering my own.

"What?"

"I said, not if I can help it, Elsie," he says more determinedly. "You will not marry that man, not whilst I have anything to do with it."

I simply smile, not believing him at all, but what else is there to do other than to put on my usual mask.

Chapter 6

Edmund

When Elizabeth finally wakes, Elsie is looking tired, probably through worry over Lord Boreham's plans to make her his own. That is something I will not allow, not for a second time. Tobias might have turned into the perfect man for Emily, but Richard Boreham will never be that to any woman. There is a reason he has remained unmarried all this time; his brutish behaviour and vile temper is well known. In fact, I am surprised George Rothschild is even considering letting his eldest daughter marry such a man. He needs a reminder of Lord Boreham's unsuitability, and soon.

Elsie yawns, then begins to laugh when I smile over her obvious fatigue.

"Forgive me," she smiles, revealing rosy cheeks and dimples that I suddenly wish to kiss. "Elizabeth and I were up far too late gossiping and such. Sleep evaded me until the birds began to sing outside of my bedroom window this morning."

"Elsie Rothschild gossiping? Surely not!" I tease, though it causes the blush on her cheeks to glow even brighter, a sight I cannot help but indulge in.

"It was hardly noteworthy," she argues as she gets to her feet. "Would you excuse me for a moment?"

"Of course," I reply, getting to my feet when she stands. I watch her back retreat all the way into the cottage, appreciating the curve of her waist, the curl of her hair, and the way her body seems so much more relaxed in the countryside, far away from all the pomp and circumstance of the city.

"I do believe, Mr Barton, the lady just lied to you," Elizabeth says with a small chuckle. I frown before turning to face her, for I cannot think what she is talking about. No one has ever accused Elsie of such a thing, and neither did she say anything that I can think would be a lie. The lady simply laughs harder at me, teasing me with the knowledge I do not have.

"Forgive me, Lady Elizabeth, but you are going to have to elaborate," I tell her with a smile at the same time as I return to my seat. "Though, I think you knew you would need to, which is why you are laughing at me."

"Women of my age have to grab hold of any opportunity they can to have some fun," she replies. "It is not often handsome gentleman come knocking at my door. And to think, I have had two in the same day."

"You and I disagree on what qualifies for a gentleman," I utter, turning the atmosphere less jovial. It was not intentional but the thought of Lord Boreham claiming Elsie like some sort of trinket for him to wear about town, is more than enough to sour my mood.

"Oh? You do not approve of Lord Boreham?" Elizabeth questions me, purposefully poking to garner more information that

I might not have otherwise given to her.

"Let us just say, he is not known for his good temperament or chivalry when it comes to obtaining what he desires," I tell her with bitterness in my voice. "Whoever has the misfortune to marry him will live a very unhappy, and very controlled life. It angers me to hear Elsie's father is pushing so vehemently for a match between them."

"I see," she says, looking away from me for a moment or two for silent reflection. "Though, if there was to be an alternative to Lord Boreham, someone younger, someone who would treat her with the love and affection she deserves, someone like yourself, Mr Barton, perhaps her father would not feel so strongly about the match."

"I am sure I do not know what you mean," I fluster, even though she can see through my refusal to acknowledge that something might be growing between Elsie and me.

"I am sure you do," she argues, still with her teasing smile. "Why do you deny what is so obvious to me?"

I do not answer her for a while, for I am unsure as to how best to articulate my reasons for not courting Elsie for myself. The lady sitting before me remains silent, knowing I will eventually give her what she is asking for.

"I am ashamed," I reply honestly while fiddling with my cuff, a means of distraction so I do not have to face her perplexed expression. "When it comes to Elsie, I fear I neglected to see her for what she is."

"And what is that, pray tell," she coaxes.

"A lady who deserves far better than me," I admit. "A lady who is beautiful, kind, warm, intelligent and funny."

"Better than you? Like Lord Boreham?" she asks, causing me to shoot my gaze her way. She simply stares back at me, unperturbed by my questioning expression. "Because as much as I enjoy the ramblings of a martyr, like yourself, he is who she will end up with if you do not stop wallowing in your own guilt."

"How will I ever convince her that it is her I truly want? After everything with Emily, how can I make her see that she is the object of my desire?"

"Well, now, I do not have all the answers, dear boy," she says with a tut, and in such a way, I have to smile to myself. "And even if I did, I cannot make it *that* easy for you."

"I suppose not," I reply with a sigh, "neither should I be seeking for you to do the work for me."

"Though, you may well have to secure her hand before you secure her heart," she says wisely. "Right now, you do not have the time to court her properly, not if Lord Boreham has anything to do with it. You shall only have your time if and when you marry her. Are you ready to do that, Mr Barton?"

"What are you both talking about so secretively?" Elsie shocks us both with the sudden sound of her voice. Elizabeth even jumps in her seat, causing her little dog to fall from her lap.

"Elsie Rothschild, you made my heart leap inside of my frail old chest," Elizabeth gasps, placing her hand to her bosom and emitting a laugh. "I swear today has been the most fun I've had in a long while!"

Elsie

Edmund was quiet when he bid us farewell, as though he

was deep in thought. I couldn't help but wonder if I had upset him somehow but chose not to ask.

The rest of my stay at the cottage passed by with a pleasant and calm feeling alongside Lady Elizabeth; I half wished I could stay in this cottage with her forever. However, the final night of my stay was soon upon us, and I was feeling anything but calm. I was feeling anxious about seeing my father again, for he is sure to question me on my visit from Lord Boreham. I know it will sadden me to see him so excited over the prospect of marrying me off to a man I do not wish to spend one single day with, let alone the rest of my life. I was also feeling disappointed over Edmund's strange departure the other day; I suppose I was hoping for something…*more*?

Stanley must have been picking up on my nervous disposition, for he could not settle no matter how he positioned himself on Elizabeth's antique rug. Every so often, he would growl and sigh, causing us both to giggle at the poor creature. In the end, Elizabeth picked him up and cuddled him on top of her lap. He resisted for a moment or two before finally relenting into the comfort of her gown. I smiled at him, for in this moment, he reminded me so much of myself – short term resistance before giving in to somebody else's whims. It is a sad thought. Even sadder is the thought of Lord Boreham not allowing me to take Stanley with me, for he did not seem too keen on my furry companion.

"So," Elizabeth begins, snapping me out of my worried thoughts, "you return home to your father, and possibly Lord Boreham's proposal tomorrow, my dear."

"Do not remind me," I reply with a long, despondent sigh, "I am quite dreading it. I feel as though I am going to be ambushed before I have even stepped outside of the carriage."

"You can always refuse, child," she suggests contemplatively.

"I could, but it would only be a matter of time before Father wears me down," I admit. "I have been brought up to be a good girl, to do as her parents tell her, no matter what. I do not have Emily's wild spirit. Besides, even she could not refuse Father's orders to marry your nephew."

"You think he will force you into the match?" she probes further.

"I know he will…eventually," I tell her with conviction. "Perhaps if I was Emily, his favourite, he would have let me turn down the proposal, but we both know I am not. I am just Elsie."

"Well, *'just Elsie'*, I am not convinced that things will be so cut and dry. I believe you will have other options; you just have to be patient."

"If you are talking about Edmund, I think it would be akin to wishing on a star; a childhood desperation, still believing in magic that does not exist."

"We shall see," she says with a knowing smile upon her face. "Your dog agrees with me, he is now purring."

I do not attempt to argue with her. After all, she is practically impossible to argue with. Though she believes she is being comforting, her unfaltering belief only has me feeling even more wretched. It is as though she is waving a dream in front of me, one I cannot reach, one that will never come true. It is best not to hope; it only leaves you feeling all the more disappointed.

Edmund

"This is worse than I thought!" I declare as I walk through my cousin's estate, his faithful butler at my side. He is older than my father but knows all there is to know about the house, the grounds, the staff, and the nearby town. He mumbles a grave word of agreement.

"Alas, your cousin became quite reclusive," he explains, "he was sick with sadness after your family refused to see him again; he especially felt the loss of you, My Lord.

"I had no idea," I tell him honestly, "I was still very young when my parents fell out with him. To be honest, I am not entirely sure what caused them to stop talking. I remember them once being close, and William always treated me like his own."

"Quite," he utters before coughing and moving further forward with the rather depressing tour of the house. "As you can see, the building is no longer watertight. I have had the building assessed and it would seem the roof needs some major repairs, perhaps even replacing."

"Did William know about this?"

"I advised him, yes, but he refused to acknowledge the extent of the damage," Phillip informs me.

"But with the money left, he could more than afford to have the repairs carried out. Why ever did he refuse to have it fixed?"

"I believe, if I may, it was due to the fact that he would have had to move out of the house whilst it was being refurbished. He could not bear the thought so decided to live out his last years in a damp house."

"How sad," I comment with a sigh, "madness, but also utterly sad."

"How would you like to proceed, My Lord?" Phillip asks, skirting around the issue of my cousin's melancholy.

"I will arrange for the repairs to commence as soon as possible," I tell him. "Are the staff quarters damaged?"

"Being on the lower floors, or from the town, the staff are sufficiently housed, as am I," he says to my relief. "However, your quarters are quite uninhabitable."

"Oh, that is not a worry, I can sort myself out, Phillip, thank you. I am here for but a few days and then I must return to London. I have vital business that requires my presence. We can begin sorting through any damaged items, then move on from there. Does that sound like a plan?"

"A good one, My Lord," Phillip replies with a smile and a small bow.

With one more look around a room full of wet patches and spots of black mould, I sigh heavily and make my way out to arrange for a room at a local tavern. After which, I will plan my return to London, hopefully a day or so before Elsie, so I can try and talk some sense into her father.

Chapter 7

Elsie

The journey back to London was awful; I had felt terribly sick. I knew it was in part due to my fear of meeting my father, or worse, Lord Boreham, the very moment I would arrive outside of my childhood home. It does not feel like my home now that I am an adult; it is my father's house, and I am no longer welcome to live in it. I should be married, having babies, and attending to my husband's every whim. I should remain silent, obedient, and not have a single thought other than my family's happiness inside of my head. It is a woman's position in life, but I cannot help feeling utterly miserable over the prospect. I know Emily feared having such a fate too, but she was lucky. She found a man who wanted to keep her spirited, inquisitive, and happy. Lord Boreham is not such a man. Neither is Father, though at least he is kind and loving towards Mama. I cannot fault him in that area.

Fortunately, when I arrived on the street outside of the Rothschild residence, it was not my father awaiting my arrival, it was Mama. With a beaming smile that put me at ease, she embraced me just as she used to when I was little. I can admit, where Emily had been Father's favourite, my mother had ever so slightly favoured me, though only because she found me easier to school. Emily challenged her, whereas I always did as she said, even going beyond her instruction because I wanted her to be pleased with me.

"Elsie, I've missed you," she whispers inside my ear, tickling me with her breath. "Tell me everything; was the weather fine?"

"I suspect the weather was just as it was here, Mama," I giggle at her, for she always begins with the weather when meeting with anyone. She simply cannot enter into a discussion of any kind without first finding out about the weather. "Warm and sunny?"

"Yes," she confirms as we walk inside, linking our arms and feeling at ease in one another's company. "And Lady Elizabeth, was she in good spirits?"

"Of course, and just as nosey as ever," I laugh as we usher Stanley inside behind us. "Wondering when I shall marry, though she only asks out of concern for my happiness, unlike Father."

"Elsie," she says sympathetically, "he loves you, darling."

"I know, he just doesn't understand me." I release a heavy sigh before sitting in my usual seat in the morning room where tea is already being served. "I take it Lord Boreham has already told you of his visit to see me?"

She looks away from me, her face a picture of sorrow, which cannot mean anything good. I place my hand on top of hers, if only to reassure her that I can handle whatever it is she is afraid to say. It works for a moment or two, and she smiles, but when I fail to reciprocate, she emits a long sigh, knowing she is caught between her child and her husband. Not that it really matters which side she chooses, for we all know a man's word is worth a thousand times more than that of a woman.

"He has been here, yes," she finally replies, "several times actually. He is very keen for a match between you and him; he obviously thinks a lot of you. Do you feel nothing?"

"Does it matter?" I ask with a sad smile, to which she squeezes my hand that little bit tighter.

"Perhaps you will grow to love him, as Emily did with Tobias," she says, though from the look on her face, I know she doesn't believe that.

"Perhaps," I reply, sounding syrupy sweet in an attempt to convince her of something neither one of us believes. "When is Father due home?"

"He should be back any time now," she says, looking relieved for the change of subject.

"Did…er…did Lord Boreham mention my other visitor?" I venture, to which she smiles a little deviously.

"If you are talking about Edmund, then he most certainly did," she says, her smile broadening, which only causes me to laugh. It is very rare to see Mama looking so wicked. "He was not impressed at all."

"Poor Edmund, he is always upsetting gentlemen, merely by being friends with the Rothschild girls," I admit. "I wonder if he will ever marry."

"Hmm, me too," she says, giving me a suggestive look. "He deserves love and happiness, but then, so do you, Elsie."

"What are you implying?" I ask with a hint of chastisement in my voice.

"Just that you and he would make an extremely handsome couple," she says as she pours another cup of tea, first for me, then for herself. "A happy one too."

"A fairy tale notion, I'm afraid," I reply with a sad sigh. "Especially when he is in love with my sister; even Father warned me of that fact."

"Your father knows nothing about such things, and what he does know is often wrong. I saw the way you were looking at each other at Lord and Lady Bartlett's ball, and you are second to no one, my dear. You and Emily are both beautiful young ladies, even if I do say so myself. You both have your own charm about you, but in completely different ways. I am extremely proud of both of you."

"Even your unmarried, reclusive daughter?" I tease.

"A hundred times, yes, Elsie Rothschild," she says, tapping my hand and looking a little stern about the fact.

I begin to feel emotional and try to push back the tears I can already tell are on their way. Fortunately, the arrival of my father helps me to hide the few that escape from my mother's view. He bustles in with the smell of the outdoors and with a beaming smile on his face. I stand to welcome him home at the same time as he comes pacing towards me with his hands held out for mine.

"Elsie, how wonderful to see you," he says as he grabs hold and gives them a small squeeze. "The country air must suit you."

"Thank you, Father," I reply, feeling a little suspicious of his sudden affection for me.

"And I am sure Lord Boreham will agree when he comes for dinner tonight," he says, explaining everything without even knowing it. He must see my face drop, for he looks mildly concerned. "I am sorry, Elsie, are you tired from your journey? He was so desperate to see you, I did not have the heart to refuse him.

Elsie," he says, looking overjoyed, "he's asked for your hand!"

"He has?" I ask, trying to sound surprised, but only to hide my inner turmoil and the painful lump in my throat. "W-what did you say?"

"Why, I told him nothing would make me happier," he replies, completely oblivious to how I am now feeling. "Elsie, the man adores you and wishes nothing more than to give you a family; your own children, Elsie!"

"H-how wonderful," I just about manage to push through my lips, knowing that if I were to refuse and make my true feelings known, he would only be disappointed in me. I cannot bear to face that look right now, so simply nod and try to smile.

"Excellent!" he beams as he brings me against his chest, giving me an embrace he so rarely affords his eldest daughter. "Congratulations, my dear. Colletta, what lucky parents we are to have both our daughters married to such fine gentlemen."

"Yes, of course," Mama whispers, though she is looking just as upset as I am. "Come, Elsie, let us get ready for dinner."

"Thank you, Mama," I reply, my vision turning blurry as a sheen of tears covers my eyes. I step back from Father and begin walking at a quick pace to get to the door so I can release my emotions in secret.

"Elsie?" he calls for me before I can escape once and for all. "I am so proud of you; you and Emily."

I can only offer him half a smile, for he has never told me that before. I remember him telling Emily those words on several occasions, when he thought no one was around. And yet, he is only proud of me for the match I am about to make with a man I would be happy to never see again. As soon as Mama has escorted me up to my room, I fall into her outstretched arms and release everything.

Elsie

I remember Emily telling me about the tremble in her hands when she was first married to Tobias; it only went away when she began to trust her heart to him. My hands are already trembling, and Lord Boreham, my future husband, has not even arrived yet. Perhaps it is because my mother has been offering me sad smiles all afternoon, or maybe it is because my father keeps gifting me with an excited wink every now and then. Whatever it is that is causing me to shake with fear, I do not believe I shall ever be rid of it. Not even when I am married, not even when my husband pretends to offer me love, not even when I am living the life of a wife and mother. Lord Boreham is not a love match; he is a man of business and appearances.

Although I never expected anything more than this, being the daughter of a viscount, I have been offered a glimpse of what love can feel like, and I am ashamed to say, I want it too. I want it so much, I want to desperately cry out 'no' when Lord Boreham makes his proposal.

But I won't.

I will plaster on my fake smile, blush, murmur some sort of acknowledgement, and offer my hand. For this is what I have been trained to do, what I have been brought into this world to do.

"You look lovely, Elsie, I am sure Richard will appreciate your efforts this evening," Father says before sipping on his favourite brandy.

"Elsie, dear, will you come and help me with my dress?" Mother says all of a sudden, probably because I am moments away from releasing tears. I nod before following her out into the hallway where I begin to take in deep breaths to hold off my crying.

"Elsie, I cannot tell you to refuse him, but know that if you find yourself unable to say yes to Lord Boreham's proposal, I will not think any less of you. You will always have my love and support."

I smile, being thankful to have her as my mother, then wrap my arms around her, if only to reassure her that I *can* do this. I *will* do this.

"Thank you, Mama, but it is my duty to accept," I tell her with another deep intake of breath. "I will be fine, honestly."

She opens her mouth to say something, or to perhaps begin crying with me, however, before she can make any sound, a knock on the door stops us both dead on the spot.

"That is him," I utter with a tone of disbelief; the time is finally upon us.

"Come, Elsie, let Rupert open the door," she says, nodding towards Father's butler, "we'll meet him in the drawing room."

Mama lets me clutch hold of her arm whilst leading me into the drawing room; she can see my trembling but understands without needing to ask. She also understands why I will accept Lord Boreham's proposal, almost stubbornly so. She educated me well, making sure I knew what would be expected of me when I came of age and when I would one day marry. And yes, I have refused others, but I know the time for procrastination is over. I am not getting any younger, as Lord Boreham has so bluntly informed me, and I am also well aware that my father's patience is running out. There is no choice for me; Lord Boreham is the only choice.

When I hear the sound of a deep, older voice, I brace myself and cling onto Mama more firmly. She places her hand on top of my arm to not only steady me, but to let me know she is here, that she will always be here for me. Father is already making his way to the door to embrace his guest with a familiarity that speaks of years of friendship. I am to be his gift to his friend.

"Richard, welcome, welcome," Father says as he shakes his hand, placing his other hand upon the gentleman's back to encourage him to come further inside. "You know Colletta, my wife," he says as he brings him up to my mother so he can take her hand and deliver a chaste kiss to the back of it. She smiles out of social etiquette more than anything, though I cannot honestly say whether she likes him or not. She has never said anything to suggest either way.

"And, of course, Elsie, my daughter," he says proudly, prompting me to curtsey and offer my hand. Though Father eyes my trembling hand with a little concern, Richard only has his eyes on my own. I can see his intentions to consume me, right in this moment, without words or gesture, just in those dark eyes of his.

"Miss Rothschild, I have been looking forward to seeing you since the moment I heard of your return from Oxford," he says quietly. "Indeed, I have thought of nothing else."

"Thank you," I murmur, blushing over his words that he spoke so bluntly in front of my parents. A deep, shaky intake of breath has my mother stepping forward to suggest we move into the dining room for dinner. I welcome the reprieve and the distraction from his hungry eyes.

Edmund

A steady stream of breath billows from my lips as the cool air hits London. I have been sitting in my carriage for the past hour, trying to build up enough confidence to go inside and face the Rothschilds. I am sure to break about a dozen social niceties with my intentions tonight. I have not been invited; I have not spoken to Viscount Rothschild, and I haven't taken the time to court Elsie in the proper fashion. Alas, I do not have the time to do such things in the proper way.

When I see the shadows of figures walking into the drawing room, signalling the end of dinner, I move towards the door so I can make my way over to their front door. One more deep inhale, and I finally place my hand upon the doorknocker so I can inform them of my presence. The door opens not long afterwards, and I come face to face with Rupert, Lord Rothschild's personal butler. He smiles in recognition of me; he has watched my face morph from child to man as much as any other member of the family. I, too, have seen the wrinkles and other signs of age change his face over the years, and I cannot help but smile back at him.

"Lord Barton," he says with a nod of respect, "I am afraid the Rothschilds have a guest, Lord Boreham."

"Yes, Rupert, I know," I tell him with a hard swallow, removing my hat as I do so. "I would appreciate it if I could see them. All of them."

"Oh, I suppose…" He pauses while flustering on the spot, as if thinking what to do in such an unusual situation.

"I shall say I forced you, Rupert, please do not look so worried," I try to reassure him. His concern melts a little and he nods before shuffling into the hallway, with me following behind.

Chapter 8

Elsie

Dinner had been a silent affair, for Mama and me at least. Father and Lord Boreham had talked about business, politics, and other such affairs that excluded our input. It was a sad realisation that I would be expected to eat my meals forever more like this, in silence. That I would be expected to have an intimate relationship with someone who wanted me to listen but to not talk or dare to question him.

Now that we are in the drawing room, sitting uncomfortably while the two men continue to talk, they begin smoking on cigars and sipping on expensive liquor. And I am waiting, just waiting for the moment when Richard will ask to take me aside so he can officially propose. I feel sick with it.

"So, George," Richard begins as he looks my way, and I feel my heart drop, "we both know why I came tonight."

"Yes, we do," my father agrees with a haughty smile on his face, also looking my way. "Colletta, perhaps you and I should give Elsie and Richard some privacy."

"Er, yes, of course," Mama flusters at the same time as looking at me with concern. I simply nod at her, wanting to scream but knowing not to. She offers a sad smile before walking over to take hold of my father's outstretched arm, just as Richard moves over to sit beside me, taking my hand inside of his and smiling.

"Elsie, whilst you were away, I came over to speak with your father," he begins even before my parents have fully left the room.

"Y-you did?" I just about manage to utter without breaking down into tears.

"There is no need to be nervous, Elsie, you have already won my heart," he says with a kind of arrogance as he reaches inside of his pocket to retrieve a small box. "I asked your father—"

His words are cut short by the sound of Rupert appearing at the very same door that my parents were just trying to shuffle through. They step back before a collision can ensue and Rupert begins to fluster and apologise profusely for the intrusion.

"Good God, Rupert, what on earth is going on?" Father barks at him, causing the poor man to shuffle about even more so. "Lord Boreham was just about to propose to—"

"My apologies, Lord Rothschild, Lady Rothschild," a familiar voice announces as he enters the room, his eyes finding mine almost instantly. But then he glances to the side to see Lord Boreham upon bended knee, and instantly looks to the floor, as if in anguish. "Lord Boreham, Miss Rothschild, please forgive my intrusion, however, this is a matter of urgency."

"Edmund, whatever is the matter? Is it your father? Your mother?" Father gasps with panic in his voice. "Dear God, it isn't

Emily, is it?"

Edmund looks at him with confusion, no doubt wondering the very same thing as I am; why would Edmund know anything about Emily?

"No, George, of course not," he says as he pats him on the arm with familiarity.

"Then, whatever is it?" Father asks as he leads everyone back inside the room. Richard gets to his feet, looking less than impressed by the interruption. As for me, I have no idea what to think, though I cannot deny I am feeling a little relieved.

"Indeed, Mr Barton, Elsie and I were in the middle of something important," Richard sneers.

"Actually, that is precisely why my business cannot wait. Miss Rothschild, please forgive me, but I cannot allow this engagement to go ahead."

"Why ever not?!" Richard practically spits. "You are not the girl's father."

"Edmund, I have to ask what it is you are thinking, coming here and interrupting what should be a happy occasion," Father adds, though he looks more curious than angry.

"Let me explain myself; you see, Elsie has already been promised to me."

I do not think it will come as any surprise when I tell you all four of us drop our mouths open in shock. Even poor Rupert is scratching his head as he makes his apologies and exits the room altogether. No one speaks for a moment; even Edmund takes a while to process his thoughts and how best to get them out into the open.

"I don't think I follow," Father eventually says, voicing what we are all thinking.

"When I was but a boy, my mother told me that I would one day be married to one of the Rothschild girls. I do believe you had all laughed about it at one of your parties, George. It was a long while ago, so I forgive your memory loss, but I remember it as clear as day. You, George, said I should count my blessings for I would not have to go through the torture of trying to court a young lady, for an agreement had already been made between yourself and my father."

"Goodness, Edmund, that was over a decade ago, and it was a joke between your family and mine. While I had believed you and Emily would one day marry, that was more because of your friendship rather than our so-called agreement."

"Unfortunate," Edmund says with a confidence I have never seen on him before. "I never thought you, George, would go against your own words."

"I'm not, I am simply saying... Wait a moment, are you really saying you want to marry Elsie?"

"Lord Rothschild, you promised Elsie to me," Lord Boreham cuts in, sounding beyond angry about the situation.

"*After* she was promised to me, I'm afraid," Edmund says, sounding and looking just as arrogant as Richard. There is certainly no love lost between these two gentlemen.

"George!" Richard snaps, causing my father to lose a little colour from his face.

"Perhaps, if I may," Mama, of all people, interjects, "if both gentlemen have been promised Elsie's hand, perhaps the most sensible thing to do is to leave the ultimate decision to Elsie herself?"

Everyone stares at Mama, then Father, who simply shrugs, before finally settling their eyes on me. I am left without words, fully unprepared to deal with this new situation.

"As always, Colletta, you have thought of the perfect solution," Father announces to the room, to which Lord Boreham turns a shade of angry puce. Edmund, on the other hand, looks completely accepting of their decision and is now waiting for me to speak.

"Elsie?" Mama prompts me. "You must do what your heart tells you to."

"Erm, well, I...my word, this is so unexpected," I begin, rubbing at my temples to try and soothe my nerves. "M-may I speak with Edmund? Perhaps with Rupert to chaperone us?"

"Splendid idea," Father declares as he opens the door to call his poor butler back inside. Meanwhile, I can feel Richard's hard stare upon my face, making me deeply uncomfortable. But he's unrelenting, so in the end, I have no choice but to turn his way.

"Elsie, think of what I can offer you," he says with a stiff upper lip and a look of authority. "Lord Barton might well be familiar to you, but I will give you your every heart's desire."

"Will you give her love, Lord Boreham?" Edmund asks from across the room, sounding extremely irritated.

"Will you?" Richard snaps. "We all know it is her sister whom you have loved for all these years; somewhat of an obsession, was she not?"

"Please!" I cry, stopping this from becoming something I

do not want it to be, a fight for possession that will only end in insults being thrown at me. I do not need anyone to tell me how much less desirable I am compared to me sister.

"Come along," Father says in a jovial manner, as though none of this ugliness is happening, leaving Edmund, Rupert, and I alone inside of the room.

Once the door is firmly closed shut, Rupert chooses to stare directly at the wall in front of him, whereas Edmund and I spend a few moments watching each other before he finally crosses the room to meet me.

"Elsie, you must forgive me for how I have gone about all this. Believe me, this is not how I would have chosen to ask for your hand, however—"

"Why are you doing this, Edmund?" I ask with emotion clogging up my throat.

"Because, Elsie, you are my choice," he says quietly, now getting so close to me, I can feel his breath upon my face. "I want to explore this life with you."

"Do you?" I retort with a mixture of sadness and frustration. "Lord Boreham may not be the love of my life, but at least I would be the *only* woman in his life. I am not sure I could bear being married to someone who pictured my sister whenever he looked upon me. I have suffered with that my whole life."

"I do not ever picture Emily when I look at you, Elsie," he tries to convince me. "I see you, Elsie Rothschild, and you are my future. Emily was my past."

"You loved her so much; how could I *not* think that?"

"Let me try to convince you," he whispers, lifting his hand

as though he wants to brush it across my cheek.

"Do you love me, Edmund? What I mean is, are you *in* love with me?" I ask, terrified of what he is going to say.

"I have always cared for you, Elsie, both you and Emily. And I will admit, those feelings are changing, blurring at the edges. I am not ready to say those words yet, for I do not deserve to. I have made so many mistakes, Elsie, and when I finally say those magical words, I want to be worthy of saying them to you. But I will say this, I am falling, Elsie. And if you marry Lord Boreham, I know that light I was beginning to see in your eyes, the light that makes me want to make you mine, will diminish."

A tear escapes me, because I know he is right, but he still won't tell me what I am dying to hear; that I am loved, like Emily is loved, like she has always been loved. So, when the door bursts open to reveal an angry-looking Richard, as well as my parents, I am still uncertain.

"Apologies, Elsie, but I refuse to wait another minute longer," Richard declares. "I need an answer now."

"Yes," I whisper before moving from out of Edmund's shadow. "Er, yes, you are right, Lord Boreham. You deserve an answer, and I apologise for making you wait."

"You have an answer, Elsie, my dear?" Father ventures and I nod.

"Richard, whilst I appreciate your recent affection and kind offer, Edmund and I have been friends since childhood; we have a bond I am afraid you cannot sever. I thank you for your proposal, but I must decline."

I fear his reaction, however, he surprises me when he walks up to where I am standing, takes hold of my hand, and delivers a soft kiss to it.

"I would have been extremely lucky to have had you as my wife, Elsie, and I hope Lord Barton knows how fortunate he is." He then leans in and lowers his voice so only I can hear his next few words. "You would never have been second choice for me."

I simply nod, smile as much as I am able to, then watch as he leaves. He says nothing to my father, nor my mother, breaking social etiquette by refusing to thank her for a wonderful meal. I fear I might have tainted my father's relationship with him, and for that, I feel immensely guilty. The door slams and I jump, but I am soon comforted by Edmund standing close beside me.

"Does this mean your answer is *yes*?" he asks, and when I look into his eyes, I can see what appears to be hope.

"It does," I tell him quietly, though the happiness I thought I would feel has been overshadowed by his refusal to declare his love for me. I cannot help but feel as though I am nothing more than Emily's stand-in, that I am his second choice, his *pity* choice.

"How wonderful!" Father beams, and when I look in his direction, even my mother is smiling with joy and relief.

Edmund smiles, though it looks like any other smile he has given me in the past; it is not a beaming smile, it gives nothing away.

"Thank you, Elsie," he utters before Father takes hold of his hand to shake it with renewed enthusiasm.

"Father, will you and Lord Boreham be alright? I feel I have tainted your relationship," I tell him with guilt written across my face.

"I am sure my name will be frowned upon for a while, but I

do believe we will be ok in the long run," he says, walking up to kiss me on the cheek. "Besides, your happiness is more important."

I look at him with disbelief, though it is only for a moment. After that, I give him my usual mask of a smile, like the dutiful daughter I have always been.

Chapter 9

Edmund

"I shall call on you tomorrow after I have set things into motion; the sooner the better, don't you think?" I say to my bride-to-be when she shows me to the door. She looks at me with nothing but doubt, though I cannot deny I am feeling just as unsure. Not because of my feelings for her, nor my choice to propose to her this evening, merely my ability to love, protect, and be the husband she truly deserves. Be that as it may, she hardly needs me to voice these concerns when she is already questioning my intentions. So, instead, I plaster on a mask of confidence in the hopes she will take some form of reassurance from it.

"If you say so, Edmund," she replies, an answer I wasn't expecting. I do not know what to take from it. She's shut down on me, much like when I saw her the time after I had insulted her as a child. Looking at her expressionless face, I realise I am entirely inept to deal with a woman in this state. In fact, I can feel my hands becoming clammy and my breath shallow, so much so, I am not sure I am getting enough air to keep me conscious.

"Elsie, talk to me," I plead, "I thought this would make you happy?"

My words appear to do the exact opposite of what I was hoping for; they seem to have angered her.

"Is that why you proposed? To make me happy?" she asks with venom in her voice.

"Is that not at least one reason to ask a lady to marry you?" I ask, sounding and no doubt looking as incompetent as I feel.

"No...well, yes, I suppose, but what about you? I do not want to force anyone into having to marry me," she snaps.

"Elsie, of course I am happy," I try to convince her, now taking her hands inside of mine, but it would seem my words have come too late. Tears are now running down her face and she is beginning to shake, so I take a chance and pull her in close to me so I might look deep inside of her eyes. "I am happy, Elsie, so happy, but I know it is going to take some time to convince you of that fact."

"There is every possibility that I shall never be convinced," she sniffs, looking so unlike her usual graceful self. However, to me, it only makes her all the more endearing in this moment of vulnerability.

"Well, then at least I only have a lifetime to try," I whisper, smiling as she loses the battle to do the same. "We shall live happily ever after, trust me."

"You realise I know nothing of marriage," she says, looking anxious all over again, "or love, or satisfying a husband...Oh, Lord, I'm going to disappoint you, I'm going to—"

"Be perfect, both of us, in our own way and in our own time," I reassure her, and she finally relinquishes her tense shoulders to lean on me. I indulge in her scent, her softness, and the fact that she is mine. "Let us not forget that we are friends, Elsie, the best of friends. Everything else will come in its own good time. I am in no rush, and neither should you be."

"Edmund, I know you like the company of a woman, and though I do not know the full details of what that entails, I do know a man needs that sort of company in order to be happy," she says uncomfortably, the whole time avoiding my gaze. "And I want to make you happy, Edmund; you've given up your life for me."

"Elsie," I whisper, pushing her shoulders so she is forced to step back and look at me, "I have not given up anything. You agreeing to be my wife, my soul, and my other half? Why, that is nothing but a huge gain for me. And as for everything else, why do you think I took myself off for a year? Yes, I enjoy the feel of a woman, but it has always felt somewhat empty. To share that with a woman whom I love, whom I desire above all else, that is sure to be the most wonderful feeling in the world."

"Have you never felt like that with any of your women?" she asks, looking so shocked, I have to laugh a little.

"How many women do you think I've had?"

"I do not know," she replies, now with a bright blush heating up her cheeks. "You realise it is not something a lady thinks about."

"No, neither should we be talking about it," I agree, now feeling ashamed for having brought up such a sensitive subject with my new fiancée. "Though, when we are married, I hope to get to see the real Elsie, not the Elsie who worries far too much about being a 'lady'."

"That too, will take some time," she admits, but at least she is smiling again. "Edmund?"

"Yes, Elsie?"

"I would like to have that feeling with you too…one day,"

she says, to which I pull her against me again.

"And you will," I reassure her, "as well as the feel of a ring on your finger, which I shall obtain when I inform my parents of our impending nuptials. Be prepared to hear my mother's squeals of delight from across town within the next few hours. Now, go, sleep, and be secure in the knowledge that I want this, Elsie, with you."

"Goodnight, Edmund, and thank you."

"No, Elsie, thank you!"

Edmund

After a sleepless night that had me feeling weighed down by responsibility, I decided to cross town to visit my mother and father. I am currently staying in temporary lodgings, for I have no intention of staying in London once my late cousin's house is fit for living in. The thought of which has me feeling even more fretful; will Elsie be happy to move away from her childhood home? She seemed more than happy in Oxfordshire with Elizabeth. Indeed, she looked the most relaxed and free that I've ever seen. It suited her.

By the time I have reached my own childhood home, a place full of bittersweet memories, it is past breakfast time. My brother died in this house before my tenth birthday. Coincidentally, this was around the same time my parents stopped talking to my cousin. Stephen, my brother, was ten years my senior and a loveable rogue who took life for what it was – a momentary experience. He wanted to live life to its fullest. It was as though he knew he would only be here for but a short time. As you can imagine, when he died, my parents were distraught, especially as it had been so unexpected. A freak riding accident had him laid up in bed for two days before we found him unresponsive in his bedroom. The doctors had warned us that he was unlikely to survive; he had been slipping in and out of consciousness and could no longer feel any sensation below his waist. I still miss him; he was as close to me as Mother and Father.

His loss was perhaps the reason for why I took up with Thomas Grayson, a man whom I both admire and despise. He had fought everything and everyone for his affections for Tobias' sister, the love of his life, but in doing so, he had betrayed Emily and me. And yet, despite his shortcomings, he had reminded me of Stephen in so many ways. Indeed, the way he had always managed to make me laugh, even when I had just lost Emily to a duke, was very reminiscent of my late brother. His heartbreaking story had shocked me for many reasons, though mainly because you would never have believed he had been planning to take his own life to be with her again.

But when all is said and done, this old building will always be the place in which I grew up with the best parents in the world. I was never short of love and comfort, even when I had made the gravest of mistakes. Jane and Charles Barton have supported all my endeavors and have wanted nothing but happiness for me. And when my brother was still alive, there was never any sibling rivalry or questioning of their devotion to either one of us. Stephen's very last words to me were to have me promise him that I would always look after our parents; something I hope I have upheld.

"Edmund! This is a lovely surprise…Charles, come quick, Edmund is here!" my mother shouts over her shoulder, not caring one bit about raising her voice for the whole street to hear. She might be a lady of London, but she is certainly not particular when it comes to social niceties. With Jane Barton, family comes first;

appearances, second.

"Edmund?" Father smiles as he comes to pull me inside. "It is early, this must be important. You have never been an early riser, boy, something must be keeping you from sleep."

"It is, though perhaps we might at least sit down before I share it with you," I suggest.

They stare at one another with a curious smile only parents can give one another when they think their children aren't looking. Subtlety has never been their strong suit, but I try not to let on to the fact.

Eventually, we make it past the front door and into the morning room, where we make ourselves more comfortable. Which is to say, my parents sit expectantly on the chaise, gripping hold of one another's hands and smiling with far too many teeth on show. Whereas I am pacing about in front of the stone fireplace that holds my mother's favorite figurines. Many would consider them gauche, but they came from her mother, and her mother before that, so she refuses to part with them. I love how my mother will always choose loyalty over fashion, especially as she refuses to take them down, even when company is visiting.

"Well?" Father eventually says, gesturing with his hand to hurry this along. "Your mother is about to pass out from all the anticipation."

"I am engaged," I blurt out, coming to a standstill with my back ramrod straight. "As of last night."

At first, they appear to hold their breath, moving in closer together for comfort, as if not quite believing what their own ears have just heard.

"*Engaged*, engaged? Marriage, engaged?" Mother finally

asks for clarification, fighting back a beaming smile that is just begging to be set free.

"That is the only engaged I am aware of being, yes," I confirm with a stiff nod of my head.

"And the young lady in question?" Father asks, his hand reaching out towards me.

At first, I emitted a small laugh, knowing how my parents are about to react over the answer to this question. However, when my mother brings her hand to her lips, unable to bear the tension any longer, I straighten up once more and tell them directly.

"Elsie Rothschild."

Not one of us moves, not for at least a minute or so. In fact, the three of us seem to remain as still as statues while we all take the information on board. Harold, our long-standing butler knocks on the door, prompting my parents to jump from their seats and lunge for me. My mother's squealing of delight, along with my father's hearty laughter and prompt handshake, finally allows my heart to beat at a more regular pace again.

"Oh, Edmund, I am so delighted, you were always meant to marry into that family!" Mother beams as she kisses me on the cheek. "And Charles, think of the grandchildren! Lots and lots of grand babies!"

"But of course, Elsie is a very handsome young woman," my father says with a wink that has me feeling extremely self-conscious. "I am sure they will have a house full of them in no time!"

"Oh, Charles, don't be so vulgar!" Mother chastises him before wrapping her tiny frame around my much taller one.

"I am glad you are happy for us, but let us calm down a little –"

"Excuse me, My Lord, but there is a Viscount Rothschild at the door," Harold announces from the hallway.

"Oh, how wonderful," Father laughs. "Well, Harold, show him in, we are going to be family after all!"

"Of course, My Lord," Harold replies in a bored tone of voice.

"Oh, Edmund," Mother says, having calmed down enough to now look me in the eye whilst Father rushes to the door to meet Lord Rothschild. "You are happy, are you not? You know, as much as we are thrilled about your news, the only thing that has ever mattered to us is your happiness, my darling boy."

"I know, Mother," I tell her quietly, looking at her with the affection she deserves to have from her only remaining son. I then take a moment to really think about what she has just asked me, to push aside all the worries and doubts, and consider how I truly feel. "Do you know, I think I am, Mother. I have not been happy since Emily was promised to the duke, but after everything, after coming to terms with the way things needed to be, I am honestly very happy."

"That's my boy," she beams, and I kiss her on the cheek.

I am happy. I only hope I can make Elsie just as happy.

Elsie

I brace myself when I hear the familiar tone of my sister's voice sailing through the house. She sounds happy, excited even, and yet, I am still fearful over our impending meeting. We have not seen each other since James was only a few months old; he's now nearly a year. I had planned on seeing them on his first birthday, however, news of my engagement to Edmund has spread fast. What will she think of me? Will she warn me of his love for her just as Father did? Or will she be cross with me for seemingly being desperate? I wonder if I did not have all of these worries flying around my head, I might actually be happy over my wedding to Edmund. I am happy, aren't I?

"Oh, you have no idea how good it is to see you again, Emily," I hear my father declare as I make my way along the upstairs corridor to meet them all. His words stop me short; his fawning over my sister always does.

"And we are glad to see you too," she replies, accompanied by the sound of my young nephew gurgling. "Though, I hope you don't think me rude if I leave you with your grandson so I can go and congratulate Elsie?"

"No, of course not, but you must make some time for your poor father," he chuckles in a way he never has with me. I only wish I could ignore it, learn to accept that he and I will never have the kind of relationship they share.

"*Poor*?!" she scoffs with laughter following afterwards. "You, Father, are anything but poor. You have not one, but two ladies looking after you. However, you are soon going to lose another one, Father, and for that loss, I will afford you some of my sympathy."

"Ah, yes, but I am happy to lose her if it means she will finally be happy," he says. His words confuse me, for I did not know he realised how sad I had become over the years. Does he know he plays a part in that sadness? I wouldn't have thought so, but then, I thought he never saw me at all. Perhaps I am wrong about this too.

"Of course," Emily says knowingly, so I decide to finally make my presence known. "Elsie!"

Emily positively screeches with a beaming smile on her face. The sight of which at least allows me to relax a little; she does not seem the least bit concerned or cross with me.

"Emily, you are early," I smile back at her, then laugh when she comes galloping up the staircase towards me. Even though she is now a Duchess, she is still my unconventional little sister, and for that, I am grateful. "We thought you would be at least another...oof!"

We laugh when she bowls into me, taking the very breath out of my lungs as she squeezes on tightly to my body. A wife, a mother, a Duchess, but always the baby of the family.

"I've missed you," she whispers against me, and with her eyes shut tightly.

"Well, things must be slow in the Hardy household," I tease, "could the honeymoon period finally be over?"

"Never!" she declares and jumps back with a grin my mother used to reprimand her for wearing in company. "Alas, Tobias has had to rush off into town for business stuff and nonsense. But he will be here this evening with strict instructions to behave himself. But enough about me, tell me everything!"

"Oh, my, here we go," I grumble through self-consciousness, "I have been waiting for this moment."

"Are you suggesting I cannot restrain myself?" she feigns insult, before giggling. "Though, you are right, I cannot. You have to tell me everything, then Edmund will have to tell me everything, before I finally go to Mother and get the full story behind how my best friend came to be engaged to my big sister."

"And will you one day give away all of James' secrets to anyone who asks?"

"Not to anyone, no, but to their sibling whom I know loves him very much? Of course, I shall," she admits as we finally make it into my bedroom where she wanders straight over to the window to look upon her once upon a time playground. She smiles, as always, content in the knowledge that it has not changed at all since her wedding day, the final one she spent in this house before she moved away with Tobias Hardy, the miserable Duke of Kent. And he is miserable, but markedly less so now that he has found love with my sister. And with her, he positively glows with happiness.

"Poor James, someone should warn him," I tease.

"James should be warned of a great many things, and I am sure Tobias will do so before he turns five. But enough of all that, put me out of my misery," she says with the same eyes I am certain she has learnt to use from studying her dog, Monty. "I heard he stormed in and declared you be his before shoving that awful Lord Boreham out the door!"

"That is a greatly embellished version of events," I level with her before laughing over her excitement. She looks so enthralled; I decide to give the story a romantic retelling. "Though, I can tell you, Edmund was very forceful. In fact, I have never seen him act so authoritatively. I am sure I would have been quite excited myself, had I not felt so surprised. He declared he had been promised the hand of one of the Rothschild ladies, and seeing as you are now married, then he simply must have me."

"Oh, my!" she gasps, still with her hands planted beneath her chin whilst she listens with eagerness. "Of course, I do hope you've put him in his place since then. I shall be having my own words about how I expect him to treat my big sister." She grins and I end up laughing with her, for this is Edmund we are talking about, the cheeky little boy who used to encourage my sister with her tearaway antics. "Who would have thought little Edmund Barton could be so…so…*masculine*?"

"Oh, my goodness, please, Emily," I practically beg as I bring my hands to my cheeks to hide my warm blush, which she finds very amusing indeed. "I know nothing about all of this. Truthfully, I had been warming up to the idea of living a life alone. Well, apart from Stanley, that is."

"Oh, Elsie, I had no idea," she says with a sympathetic voice before wrapping her arms around my shoulders. "Why would you think such a thing? I thought you wanted a family, love, and devotion. Honestly, Elsie, I have always believed you were made for marriage, far more than I ever was."

"And yet, here we are, you with a beautiful family, me becoming someone's second choice," I admit sadly.

"Elsie Rothschild," she snaps, pulling back to look as nearly as foreboding as mother when she is about to give a lecture. "You are nobody's second choice! Edmund and I were never meant to be, and if you were to ask him now, he would fully agree with me. We are best friends, something he confused with romantic love. Besides, why ever would he ask you to marry him if he did not feel something for you?"

"Pity?"

"If I wasn't your sister, Elsie, I would take hold of your shoulders and give you a good shake for saying such a thing."

"Emily, you cannot blame me for thinking he would rather be with you," I argue. "Perhaps I should have said yes to Lord Boreham, at least I would have known he wanted me and only me. Oh, this is such a mess!"

"Elsie, this is worse than I thought," she says with a sigh and a smile, "but nothing I cannot fix."

"I thought you would be mad at me, or try to warn me about him loving you more, just as Father did," I whimper as the tears quickly run down my cheeks.

"Firstly, I would never be angry with anyone for following their heart. Secondly, Father is a simple fellow, always has been, and only knows how it feels to fall in love with the one woman who was handed to him on a silver platter. He never needed to romance Mother, their union had been arranged from such an early age. I doubt he was ever taught the art of courting a lady. He couldn't possibly understand where Edmund is coming from; they are completely different people. Thirdly, Father loves you and is simply trying to ensure your happiness."

"Emily, do not be so foolish as to believe Father loves me as much as he loves you," I huff like a small child who has been sent to bed without any dessert. "He has always preferred your company."

"Only because I make it easy for him to talk to me," she says contemplatively. "As I said, he is a simple fellow and I know how to talk to him as a simple fellow."

"And how does one speak like a simple fellow?" I cannot help but giggle over her assessment of Father, the supposed 'man' of the house.

"You pick a subject that is usually reserved for men in a

smoky gentleman's club and allow him to waffle on about it. You do not need to even worry about knowing that much about the subject; simply ask him about it and he'll do most of the talking for you. But you must keep it neutral. When I was pregnant with James, I made the mistake of asking him whether he wished he had been there to witness one of our births."

"Oh, my, what on earth did he say?" I ask with shock.

"He froze mid-sip of his whiskey, placed the tumbler on the table, coughed to clear his throat, opened his mouth, closed it again, then pretended to hear Mother calling for him. I at least waited until he had left the room before giving into my laughter."

We both fall against one another, laughing over my poor father having to respond to such a suggestion. When we've wiped away the last tear from our faces, we rest against one another and enjoy the moment of happiness we just shared.

"Will you tell me everything, Emily? Will you tell me how a wife is supposed to keep her husband happy? After all, Tobias appears to be one of the happiest husbands I know."

"Of course," she says with a contented sigh. "I shall also tell you how to be a happy wife, for I am the happiest wife *I* know."

"Thank you, Emily, you have cheered me up," I tell her truthfully, "just as you always do. James and Tobias are very lucky to have you."

"And Edmund is extremely fortunate to have you."

Chapter 10

Edmund

With a steady sigh billowing from my lips, I watch the lights flickering in the street where my fiancée lives. Truthfully, I have been both looking forward to and dreading this moment ever since I woke up this morning. I would like nothing more than to have some time alone with Elsie, but that is an impossibility before we are officially wed. I feel as though I need to reassure her that I have no expectations of rushing things. Transitioning from friends to lovers might take some time, though I am hopeful it will happen one day, and soon. But I do not wish for her to feel obligated as a wife to offer what she is not yet ready for.

The dread that is sitting inside of my stomach is for the moment when Emily and I finally come to face one another. Will she question my intentions after everything that happened? Will she think me good enough for her sister? To be fair, the latter of those questions is one I frequently ask myself. I do so want to be good enough for her, to give her all that she deserves.

"You realise, Lord Barton, you are supposed to walk *through* the door," a familiar, teasing voice says from behind me.

"It does not work by simply staring at it."

"Well, thank goodness, the mighty Lord Hardy is here to make things clear for me," I joke back, to which he laughs at me. "Does it always feel so terrifying when one is about to embark on a meal with his in-laws?"

"I try to turn the tables on that one," he says, completely straight-faced, "but I have heard that is the case for most."

"The Rothschilds still fear you, Tobias?"

"Only the viscount and his wife," he replies, "neither of their daughters are intimidated by me. Emily because she more than knows she has me wrapped tightly around her little finger; your future wife because she has learnt how thoroughly ridiculous men can be. She merely plays her role of subservience very well. Ever since she gave me a piece of her mind when I had banished Emily to Kent, she knows I am more bark than bite when it comes to the fairer sex. You have to admit, it is of no surprise that Viscount Rothschild's daughters are both infinitely more intelligent than he is."

"He is harmless…" I trail off when I think of how close he came to giving Elsie to Lord Boreham, a man that would have sucked any life from her.

"Ignorance and arrogance can be far more harmful than even the most villainous of people," he says with a knowing smile. "I would have thought you more than anyone would have been aware of that."

"Yes, quite," I utter sadly, knowing how foolish I had been when it came to my dealings with Thomas Greyson, a man who sought to destroy my best friend through his pre-planned villainy.

"Do not act such the martyr, Barton, we have all been

there," he says with a smile that reminds me he also played the fool when it came to Emily. "What makes us better men is what we choose to do after we have made such follies."

"Well, I am trying," I admit.

"Indeed," he says as we fall in to step across the empty street. "Just be sure you are doing what you are for the right reasons. No lady wishes to be chosen through pity."

"I would never do such a thing to Elsie," I snap, irritated by the insinuation.

"Then, I am pleased for you both," he smiles. "Though she was never an option for me, I can more than see how beautiful she is. She is my wife's sister after all."

"She is more than beautiful," I say to myself more than him, "she is my friend."

"Then you must do all you can to hold onto her," he says as he rings the bell to the Rothschild residence. "For they make the best wives."

Elsie

After my sister had squealed with excitement, things became markedly less awkward, so I was able to relax for dinner with my family and Edmund. We sat side by side but barely spoke due to Mama's and Emily's non-stop questioning about our wedding. As you can imagine, Emily is far more enthusiastic about my nuptials than she was about her own. Her marriage to Tobias was not seen as a happy occasion, for it had been entirely taken out of her hands. And yet, she could not be happier than she is now. I hope mine and Edmund's union works out just as well.

As well as the evening had gone, I was so desperate to have five minutes alone with Edmund. We have not had the opportunity to talk properly since the night he proposed; he had had to return to his new estate in Oxford not long after. The work needed to make the property watertight is significantly more than he was first told, so much so, he had suggested we postpone our wedding. However, Emily and Tobias have since offered to house us while we wait for the work to be completed. At first, I protested, not wanting to put anyone out, but I was told not to talk such nonsense, that I was to think of it as a honeymoon.

But now it is late, and it is becoming more and more apparent that I will not be able to have any time alone with Edmund. The frustration of which has led me to wanting to retire to bed.

"I hope nobody minds if I take my leave," I announce to the room, "I am quite exhausted."

"Might I escort you to bed?" Edmund flusters as he gets to his feet, to which Mama and Papa look at each other with shocked concern, all the while my brother-in-law smiles to himself. "Er…that is to say, might I bid you good evening from the entrance hall?"

I glance at Mama and Papa before I finally nod my reply to a now brightly blushing Edmund. I cannot help but smile over his embarrassment. He then offers me his arm and we walk through the door, being careful to leave it slightly ajar to appease Mama. As soon as we are alone, he covers his ashen coloured face and emits a small groan, just as I allow myself to properly laugh at him.

"Did I really just suggest such a thing in front of your mama?" he asks with a laugh of his own.

"I think you just did," I tease. "But I am glad to have this moment with you; it feels like we haven't had any time to talk since that afternoon in Elizabeth's garden."

"Yes, you are quite right," he smiles, and something sparks within me. "And so much has changed since then."

We stare at one another for a moment or two and I begin to feel a little heady. He pushes back a lock of my hair and allows his hand to linger by my ear. My heartbeat begins to pound between my ears, and I am forced to take in an extra gulp of air. His lips move in towards my own and I feel suddenly nervous. Nervous of my inexperience of such things when he knows so much more than I do.

"Elsie…" he whispers as he leans in so close, I can feel the warmth of his breath.

"W-what did you want to say to me?" I rush out, not ready to disappoint him so soon after agreeing to marry him. Though, from the pensive expression on his face, I think I might have anyway. I clear my throat, trying to push the awkwardness of the situation away.

"What?" he says with confusion, now pulling back and straightening up. "Oh!"

As I wait for him to elaborate, I step back and try to shake away my feelings of inadequacy. I should have let him lead, let him follow through with what I am sure was going to be my first kiss with my husband-to-be. Instead, I let my nerves get the better of me, and because it was Edmund, he let me push him away. Would he have done the same with Emily? Or would he have swept her into his arms and kissed her anyway?

Before I can talk myself into a panic, he shocks me by

pulling out a ring box from his jacket pocket and drops to his knee. Oh, Elsie, how could you have doubted this moment?

"Elsie Rothschild," he says with a shy smile that has me feeling silly for my attack of confidence in him just now, "will you do me the honour of becoming my wife?"

I cannot help but emit a burst of giggles, mostly through nervousness, but happiness too. Now that I am here, looking into Edmund's eyes and the same cheeky smile he has always possessed, I cannot imagine doing this with anyone else, least of all Lord Boreham.

"I will," I accept at the same time as he pushes the antique ring upon my finger, just as my sister and brother-in-law walk through the door. Edmund rushes to his feet while I feel a strange need to hide my hand from view, as though they just caught us doing something inexplicably scandalous.

"Have we just interrupted a private moment?" Emily asks with a worrisome expression.

Edmund and I reply with conflicting answers, with me saying 'no' and him saying 'yes', leaving us both looking uncomfortable. Tobias, being the sort that he is, finds it all the more amusing and quirks his lips into one of his teasing smiles. I fear I have upset Edmund, so flush with heat upon my cheeks.

With too many pairs of eyes on me, I emit a small cough and excuse myself to go to bed, nodding my goodbyes to all of them, though lingering a little longer on Edmund's intensely brown eyes. I want to soothe away my unintentional insult but feel much too embarrassed to do so in front of my sister and her husband.

Without any other words, he looks away first, and so, I turn about and leave, cursing myself for being so timid and callous with his feelings.

Edmund

"Oh dear," Emily winces as I turn to face them with disappointment coursing through my veins. Every time we become natural with one another, giving me hope that we might be able to become more than childhood friends, one of us leaps back.

"Perhaps this was a mistake," I admit my fears to them. "Perhaps we are not suited to being more than what we've always been."

"No, you just need time –"

"Edmund?" Tobias says, cutting off his wife's reassurances.

"Yes," I reply, bracing myself for him saying something entirely blunt and no doubt insulting.

"Do remember you are a grown man," he sighs with boredom in his voice. "Calves do not marry ladies like my sister-in-law and live happily ever after. They disappoint and cause resentment."

"Tobias!" Emily gasps over his cutting words.

"No, he's right," I admit, "though it pains me to admit it."

"Of course I am right," he says with a haughty expression that causes Emily to roll her eyes. "I do believe we already agreed this before you had even stepped through the door tonight. Seeing as you need things repeating, I will tell you something that I am sure you already know. Elsie's bedroom is the third on the right. Go and finish off that proposal properly."

"I do recall your proposal being anything but romantic,

husband," Emily says with as equally a haughty expression as he is still sporting.

"And yet, here we are, with you madly in love with me," he counters.

"Ah, yes, but—"

Before she can complete her side of the argument, he leans down and kisses her so passionately, it prompts me to leave. I know I should not be going up onto the first floor of the Rothschild's residence, somewhere I haven't been since I was a small boy, but I fear if I do not go and do as Tobias has suggested, Elsie's and my marriage will continue this downward spiral before it has even started.

Elsie

With a heavy sigh, I pull back the covers of my bed and prepare myself to slip inside where I can attempt to hide from my overwhelming thoughts. I have always believed this to be an affliction, particularly for the female of the species, we have a tendency to think far too deeply about everything. Perhaps it is a matter of survival, but it does not stop the never-ending doubting of oneself or those around her.

Before I can shut my eyes, a soft tapping comes from my bedroom door, causing me to huff in frustration. I love Emily dearly, however, I am in no mood to hash out what just occurred downstairs. Even Stanley lifts his head with a tired growl, so I wander over to where he is curled up on top of his ancient cushion, tickle his head to let him know all is well, then pace towards the door before she can knock again.

The door opens to reveal someone who ought not to be up here, not before we have officially married. Without any words, I quickly look over his shoulder to ensure no one can be witness to this scandalous meeting between Edmund and me, especially when I am only wearing my nightgown and robe. I pull him inside, which earns me a warning bark from Stanley – even he doesn't think Edmund being up here is a good idea. The man himself, however, simply laughs before grabbing hold of my upper arms to try and soothe me.

"Edmund, do you realise –"

Before I can even finish that question in a whispered shout, he leans down to my face and places his lips ever so gently onto mine. My eyes burst open with shock, only to find his closed and looking fully committed to the embrace. When he finally pulls back to look at me, he smiles rather proudly at my dumbfounded expression.

"Have I managed to silence *the* Elsie Rothchild?" he asks quietly before trailing his thumb over my warm cheek.

"Er…I…that is to say –"

He kisses me again and I think my heart stops beating for a moment or two.

"Still nothing?" he teases.

"Edmund, I've never kissed anyone before…I have no idea how to," I finally manage to say with a sort of shame, which is quite ridiculous. If I had kissed anyone before now, I *should* be ashamed, but my lack of experience embarrasses me. I really cannot win it would seem.

"Then," he says, tipping my chin up with his forefinger, "I shall have great fun teaching you."

"Edmund, if Mama or Papa—" I fluster, pointing to the

door, all the while Stanley gets to his feet to come and sniff about Edmund's feet with his tail wagging at high speed. My traitor of a dog has been easily charmed by my fiancé.

"Hush, Elsie, I am not going to teach you now, but I could not let my proposal have such an underwhelming ending," he says with a smile still in place. "After all, what a disappointing story to tell our grandchildren."

"Grandchildren?" I gasp.

"Of course," he says with a knowing smile, "I thought you wanted a family?"

"Yes, more than anything, but…I…you…hmmm."

"Then I shall make it so," he says as he leans in again to kiss me. "This time, when I place my lips on yours, I want you to close your eyes, clear your mind, and just enjoy it, Elsie."

"You know I have never been very good at clearing my mind," I admit, finally smiling at him. "I worry too much."

"Kissing should be no cause to worry, it is something to enjoy."

"Alright," I tell him nervously, "then, for my fiancé, I shall try my best."

When he is but moments away from pressing his lips against mine, I close my eyes and try to think of him, and only him. At first, I am unsuccessful, and begin worrying about someone catching us, but when his hand reaches for my waist and his lips part to run his tongue along my own, I all but lose myself completely inside of his embrace. A natural instinct takes over me and I open my mouth to let him in. I shock even myself; I let someone in!

My compliance, my undeniable submission to his control, has him pulling at me with more desire than I thought possible from one person. Our tongues connect and move against one another, seeking something inexplicable from each other. I cling to his shoulders as though my very life depends on it, all the while his hands pull at my back to arch against his body, one that is entirely firm and masculine.

"Elsie?" my mother's voice calls out from behind the door, terrifying us both into jumping apart. My hand flies to my thumping heart while Edmund looks at me with equal parts surprise and desire.

"My God…" he whispers, "Elsie—"

"Elsie, is someone in there with you?" Her words prompt him to forget whatever was on his mind just now, and instead, open his eyes wide with terror.

"Er…no, just Stanley," I finally reply, pointing at the other side of the bed, silently telling Edmund to hide. He merely looks at me as though I am quite mad, for it is unlikely to hide him at all. "I think he needs to go outside; I was just on my way."

"Oh, then I shall come with you," she says cheerfully, "I am quite full after that dinner. I could use some air."

"Give me two moments," I tell her before rushing up to whisper to Edmund. "I shall take her with Stanley, you wait a moment or two, and then escape. Agreed?"

"Good plan," he says with a firm nod, "but Elsie?"

"Yes?"

He grabs me one more time and kisses me on the lips, just long enough for me to let go of my fear of Mama hearing us and close my eyes. In fact, it is not until a moment or two after he has released me that I just about manage to open them again.

"Goodnight," he says with a self-satisfied expression on his face, which has me giggling. I always knew Edmund had a mischievous side, but I didn't know quite how naughty he could be.

"Goodnight, My Lord."

Chapter 11

Elsie

A few weeks after Edmund had stolen kisses from me in my room, I am back here alone, unable to sleep, for we wed in the morning. After which, we are to travel to Kent where we shall stay with my sister until Edmund's house is at least watertight. We have spoken often about his cousin and what he can remember about him, as well as memories of his brother, Stephen.

Alas, I remember very little of Edmund's older brother, but knew he was a force to be reckoned with. He was very charming and always made an effort to smile at me, especially when Edmund and Emily had abandoned me to go in search of adventure elsewhere. He tried to teach me the piano, but I was far too intimidated by how handsome he was. I could only focus on trying to keep my cheeks from burning up whenever I was in his presence.

As for romance or real emotions, Edmund and I have not broached the subject since our kiss. We had simply returned to friendship, or perhaps, awkward first meetings, but nothing to suggest we felt any more for one another other than what we'd always been before he had proposed to me. I cannot deny it has me feeling worried, or rather, disappointed.

I had hoped he would have said or done something to let me know he wanted the same as I do; love and devotion to one another. Meanwhile, Father has been doing his best to make things right between himself and Lord Boreham, or so Mama tells me. He was met with stony silence after Edmund's sudden proposal, but as time has marched on, it would appear Lord Boreham has found it within himself to forgive Papa, and to instead, blame the whole thing on Edmund. I cannot help but feel guilty for all concerned; it is a woman's lot in life, to take the burden of a man's hurt pride.

Mama told me not to think about it and to let everything run its course. I wish I could act on her advice; however, I cannot stop thinking about all that has come to pass, or more importantly, all that is about to come.

Edmund

"Dear, oh, dear, how long has he been pacing around like that?" Emily asks Tobias when she finally arrives home from her parents' house. Her words are not surprising seeing as though I am completely losing my mind over my impending nuptials tomorrow.

All of my doubts that our kiss had dissipated, have returned tenfold, and the urge to claw out my hair is upon me. Why I thought Tobias would be of any use, I have no idea. For the last hour, he has merely watched me lose myself while nursing a crystal glass of whiskey. Emily's arrival marks the first time he's attempted to move or change expression. And such an action was only to reach for her hand.

"You see, look!" I gasp as I gesture towards their clasped hands and lovestruck faces, to which they frown over my outburst. "This is what I want, this is what Elsie wants, but what if we never get to this point?"

"Ridiculous," Tobias mumbles, earning a tut from his wife.

"Do you not remember how I was before we married? I was a complete mess and wallowing in hatred for my intended."

"Charming," he utters again.

"But true," she says before kissing him on the cheek, "you were thoroughly awful back then."

"T'was all part of my master plan to seduce you," he retorts. "And see here, it worked."

"Liar," she says, to which he nods nonchalantly. "What I'm trying to say, dear Edmund, is the anticipation of marriage is much more terrifying than the act itself. Once this hurdle is over and done with, you can spend as much time as you need trying to woo one another, without chaperones and without pressure. Trust me, you are in a far better position than Tobias and I were. You and Elsie will become the new grand love story."

"And cherubs will fly about in the sky," Tobias teases. "Though it pains me to say, my beautiful wife is right. You cannot possibly hope to form a romantic bond under such circumstances; it is utterly ridiculous to think one can develop feelings of any depth when you are constantly under someone else's watchful eye."

"So, if we ever have a daughter, will you be allowing her the freedom to be courted with some degree of privacy?" Emily asks with a knowing smile on her face.

"Certainly not, men are contemptable," he replies without expression.

"Alright…yes," I nod in agreement, trying to let their wise advice relax my fears, only to begin pacing about again to rid myself of my excess energy.

"Er, Edmund?" Emily asks in a drawn-out fashion, one that evokes a quirk of Tobias's lips, so I brace myself before cautiously looking her way. "This is entirely uncomfortable for me, I hope you know, but it has been decided that I should be the one to have the pre-marital talk with Elsie. Simply put, Mama is a coward and cannot bring herself to discuss the more physical aspects of marriage."

"Your point?" I snap without meaning to, for this is not a conversation I wish to be having with anyone, least of all my childhood best friend who is a Duchess. It is nothing short of humiliating.

"Well, how much would you like me to tell her? As in…" She pauses to scratch her head and releases a sigh of discomfort. "What I mean to say is…"

"What my wife is trying to evade asking you is whether you plan on consummating your marriage, and if so, how soon?" Tobias asks with his usual bluntness, looking me dead in the eye.

"Oh, dear Lord," I whisper to myself, my eyes now bulging from their sockets. "I had not thought of that. I mean, of course I have thought of *that,* but I never considered the fact my fiancée would have to be schooled in such things."

"Another absurd restraint put on courting couples in our society," Tobias says before returning to his paper.

"So, our hypothetical daughter, she would be schooled –" Emily begins before Tobias replies with a firm 'no' without even looking up from his paper. She giggles in my direction before seeing how anxious I am.

"Look, Edmund, I will educate Elsie the best I can, but I think you need to consider how far you wish to go…I mean, if you are planning to… tomorrow night?"

"You know, our local farmer informed me he is trying to mate his pigs. If you were to wait, you could simply *show* her how the act is done," Tobias suggests matter of factly.

"TOBIAS!" Emily cries out, her outraged expression enough to have me finally smiling. "I am not showing her what marital relations are by taking her to the local pig farm. Good gracious!"

"Perhaps not, but at least our groom is no longer looking as though he is about to swoon."

"Very clever, husband," she sighs before leaning in to kiss him, which only gives him invitation to put his hands on her, making me feel like I could bed Elsie now if I had the chance. However, I think we should take this slowly, let her make her peace with the idea before I try to exercise my husbandly rights. If that means waiting for an eternity, I will, for I respect her too much to force myself on her.

"Er…I shall leave you two to…erm…yes," I fluster before marching towards the door.

"Edmund?" Emily calls out, all the while Tobias kisses her neck with a hunger for more. I avert my eyes, for both her modesty and my sanity. "Try hot milk tonight, it will help you sleep."

"Nonsense," Tobias mumbles against her skin, "whiskey, and lots of it!"

"I shall mix the two together," I reply, taking the opportunity to escape through the door.

Elsie

It is sunny at least, warm for the time of year, though cool enough I shouldn't melt inside of my wedding gown. Not because of the weather, at least. My nerves may well cause me to over-perspire, alas, I am powerless to control them. If I were to hazard a guess as to how many hours sleep I managed to have last night, I would say three at best.

"Tomorrow is when you become a woman, Elsie, and your mother and I couldn't be more proud of you!"

If I am only becoming a woman today, then what was I yesterday? A girl? A child?

I do not have long to contemplate such a thought before my sister barges into my room with a smile as wide and toothy as it often was as a child. Usually when she had unearthed something filthy and slimy from the back garden. The memory has me giggling, momentarily breaking me from my nervous disposition.

"The day is finally here!" she beams at the same time as skipping over to take me inside of her arms. "I cannot believe it is you and Edmund; it is like the fairy tale wedding I never had."

"Oh, that sounds a little sad, Em," I reply with a small dose of pity in my voice.

"It matters not, for my marriage is the stuff of fairy tales," she says whilst guiding me over to the dressing table where she begins to brush my hair. She sees my face fall; does a fairy tale wedding mean an unhappy marriage? She immediately tuts and leans down to stare at me through the vanity mirror. "If you are thinking what I think you are thinking about, then stop it this instance, Elsie! I will not have you doubting something that is supposed to be a happy occasion."

"If I remember rightly, your wedding felt more like a funeral, you were that sad about it."

"Yes, but I did not know it was a good thing until much, much later, when my dear Tobias finally decided to stop being such a fool and see me for the catch that I am," she giggles, and I cannot help but laugh along with her.

"Is Mama coming?" I ask, knowing I am yet to receive those wise words a mother gives her daughter on her wedding day.

"I am sure she will come eventually, though I have to tell you, it has been decided that I should be the one to impart my wisdom when it comes to marriage and what is expected to happen between a husband and his wife."

I cannot help but notice her swallow back what looks like a lump in her throat, an action that immediately sets my nerves off again.

"Which is?" I ask, sounding anxious and unsure of everything I thought I knew.

"Before I begin, understand that it is uncomfortable for anyone to be having such a conversation, even me. I did not have this wisdom imparted to me until several weeks into my marriage, and from Lady Elizabeth no less. Monty was used as an example, along with an apple tree, one sunny afternoon, after only having just—"

"Emily?" I ask as I turn around to look at her directly.

"I am rambling, aren't I?" she asks with an apologetic expression on her face.

"Even more so than usual," I reply, causing her to tut and place her hands on her hips. We laugh about it before she takes hold of my hand and leads me over to the edge of the bed.

"Is it that bad?" I nervously ask.

"Goodness, no! Believe me, the explaining of such matters is a lot more awkward than the actual act itself. When Tobias and I do…well, the, er…*act*, it is not bad at all; it is anything but. It helped our love to grow into something deeper. But when you hear what I am about to tell you, it is going to sound strange."

"Alright," I say, making the word sound drawn out. I'm no longer sure I want to hear this, however, I know that I must. "I feel it best you get it out into the open and stop prolonging the inevitable before I work myself up into a frenzy."

"Deep breaths, Els—"

"Emily," I sigh.

"Yes, of course, right," she says, getting to her feet and beginning to pace. *Please, sister, just get on with it.* "So, when a man and a woman come together in matrimony, they are meant to consummate their union by coming together."

"Coming together? Like hugging…or kissing?" I smile, hoping this is all it is, for Edmund and I have already done that.

"Well, yes, but also no…more than that. Do you remember when we used to visit Edmund's family estate in Hampshire? I was four or five, and you and Edmund would have been six or so?"

"Yes, it was one of the last times we saw poor Stephen. He and Edmund had been… Oh!"

"Yes, naked as the day they were born," she says with a wicked smile on her face, "jumping and splashing about in the river, their entire bodies out on show. Mama had snapped at me when I asked what it was that was hanging between their legs."

"Emily, what has this got to do with marriage?"

"Well, that 'thing' hanging between his legs has to go inside of you," she says, now closing her eyes as a deep crimson coats her cheeks. "It will sting at first, but then it will feel natural...good."

"Oh my, I thought as much," I sigh as I place my face inside of my hands.

"You did?" she says, her eyes bursting open with surprise. "How?"

"Stanley used to try and do this with other dogs, bitches mainly, when he was younger. He is much too old to be bothered nowadays, but I could tell it was a natural instinct for him. I was hoping it was an animal thing," I tell her with yet another sigh.

"We *are* animals, sister," she says rather unhelpfully.

"You know what I mean," I groan.

"Really, Elsie, it is much, much better than it sounds," she says as she places a comforting arm around my shoulders. "I rather enjoy it. Besides, it is how James was made."

"I take it Tobias enjoys it too?"

"Oh, he really enjoys it," she says with a menacing smile, "daily, if not more so."

"And Edmund?"

"Well, I cannot say, I have not asked him," she replies. "Even I know that would be highly inappropriate of me to do so. Though, I do believe most men do."

"We kissed...the other night," I admit, cringing over having to admit to such a thing. "It felt nice."

"Well, take that feeling, multiply it by a thousand, and that is what it will feel like when you and Edmund come together," she says, though I only half believe her. "Honestly, I would not lie to you, sister, you mean far too much to me."

"And you mean the world to me," I tell her, feeling strangely emotional. We have never been the sort to be over-affectionate with one another, but the intensity of today has me feeling grateful to have her in my life.

"Now, let's get you ready."

We move back to the dressing table where she begins to brush my hair again, and I start to contemplate the enormity of everything that is about to happen. My life will never be the same again; I hope it will be better; my fairy tale will come true.

"There's no rush, Elsie," Emily whispers through the mirror, snapping me out of my thoughts. "It is finally your turn to be happy. You deserve love, Elsie, real love. And what's more, you are going to *love* it."

I smile, tapping her hand which is now resting on top of my shoulder in support.

"Thank you, Emily," I whisper back, "I hope so."

Edmund

My palms are sweating, and even when I clasp my hands together, they refuse to stop shaking. I have had all the reassuring speeches from my father, my mother, and even Tobias.

"Calves all need to grow up some day, Lord Barton," he utters as he stands beside me at the front of the church, "and I have every confidence in Elsie to make you do so."

"Thank you?" I murmur, purposefully keeping my back to the guests that are now taking their seats.

"Now, stop trembling like one of those insufferable small dogs your bride so enjoys keeping," he says with a quirk of his lips over his own insult. He then turns to face the congregation and appears to nod his head in recognition of someone. I immediately turn to see if it is Emily or Elsie; the thought of which feels me with relief. Alas, it is neither. It is Fredrick Brown and his infant son, Thomas, named after his wife's late brother. I smile, to which he attempts to reciprocate the gesture, but it is difficult; I can tell.

"How long do they think she has?" I ask in a sad tone of voice.

"Weeks, if that," he replies with a sigh. "I had to force him to come today, if only to have some fresh air. However, now that you have seen someone who has real worries on his mind, stand up straight, put on a stiff upper lip, and be thankful that you are about to marry a handsome, intelligent, and healthy young woman. And a Rothschild, no less."

"Yes, you are right," I murmur, thinking about poor Fredrick and his wife, Victoria, who is fast fading away, mere months after having started a family. "I am beyond fortunate, and I should think of the future, not my past transgressions."

"Good, because here she comes," he says, prompting me to swing around and face my bride.

"Oh, my…"

Elsie

When I see Edmund turning to see me for the first time in my wedding gown, I cannot help but smile. In fact, I have a desperate urge to break free of my father's arm and run to him. Above everything else, he is my friend. He is the only man in my life who makes me feel warm, safe, and happy. And now, he is looking upon me as though I am desirable too.

As the ceremony takes place, I can feel his eyes on me the whole time, drinking me in as though he cannot fully quench his thirst. I try to ignore it, try to act the proper lady in front of the priest, but I cannot help but smile his way every few moments, digging a nail into my hand to stop myself from laughing with happiness. He also looks quite the sight, with his tailored suit in a shade of blue that compliments his eyes, his broad chest and his muscular... Well, a lady shouldn't notice such things, so I shall pretend I don't.

"You may kiss your bride," the priest finally announces, and I take in a gulp of air to try and soothe my nerves.

As we turn to face one another, he takes hold of my hands and pulls me towards him, towering over me before he places a chaste kiss upon my lips. I am left feeling somewhat disappointed. Though, I suppose I should be grateful for his modesty. Or was it modesty? Did he not want to kiss me anymore than that? What if it is because Emily is here? The girl he really wishes he was marrying.

"You look...there are no words, Elsie," he says with a soft smile, "not one word that can do what you look like justice. I am a very fortunate man."

"And you look nice too," I reply awkwardly before he leads me down the aisle and towards the door. The guests are still clapping, but my mind is too preoccupied with doubt to take much note of them.

The wedding reception seemed like a blur, an overwhelming meeting of people who I could not distinguish from one person to the next. A lot of my father's portly old gentleman colleagues were there, including Lord Boreham, which I thought extremely inappropriate, but I said nothing. I smiled, I nodded, and I moved on, not being the least bit surprised by my father's thoughtlessness.

A small speech was made by Edmund's father, who gushed about his only surviving child. His words and glazy eyes more than conveyed how much he loves and cherishes his son in every way possible. He wished us a long and happy marriage; a marriage that will be blessed with many children, love, and kindness. I was officially welcomed to the family before each of his parents took Edmund into their arms and whispered words of pride. The scene hit my heart strongly, for my father, when giving his speech, only mentioned how pleased he was to be welcoming such a fine young man into the family; he said nothing specifically about his eldest daughter. Still, at least he managed not to mention the fact that it was Emily who had initially held Edmund's affections. I should be at least thankful for that small mercy.

I also saw Lord Brown, Tobias' best man, and his small son for a moment or two. Emily had already told me about his poor wife's declining health, so I offered him a smile, but chose to leave him to his discussion with Edmund and Tobias. We do not know one another personally, and I can count on one hand the number of words we have exchanged. It seemed insincere to offer my sympathies when we are barely acquainted, especially at my wedding. The one person I have not seen, the one I was hoping to see the most, is noticeably missing.

"Tobias, is your aunt not coming?" I ask when he finally comes back from waving his friend goodbye. "I was most looking forward to seeing Lady Elizabeth."

"Alas, she is suffering with a bout of flu," he informs me. "At her age, she decided it was best not to attend."

"Oh," I reply sadly, unable to hide my disappointment. "I do hope she is alright."

"She will be," he says with what could be a smile, but also a grimace. "She'll outlive us all."

"Don't fret, Elsie, I have arranged for us to visit once the estate is renovated," Edmund says as he places his hand on the small of my back. "Have you spoken to your mother and father yet, Elsie? It is not long before we will have to depart for Kent."

"Oh, yes, of course," I whisper, suddenly having a new bout of nerves; nerves I feel like I only just about managed to lose. "And Emily and Tobias?"

"We will be leaving tomorrow," Tobias informs me. "We thought you should have at least one night alone."

He quirks a brow at Edmund before excusing himself to go and find my sister. I am sure my cheeks are now bright enough to light the room, though I try to pretend otherwise. Edmund shuffles his hands for a moment or two before turning to face me with a serious expression.

"Do not take any note of your brother-in-law," he says with a degree of awkwardness. "Go and say your goodbyes; we can discuss anything else later."

"Of course," I smile nervously, trying to remember this is my dear friend, Edmund. I have nothing to be afraid of when it comes to him. Except, perhaps, rejection. "Thank you, Edmund, I shall be back soon."

I turn to leave before stopping myself so I can face him again. I place my hand to his cheek, catching him off guard and making him silently gasp over my sudden affection.

"Edmund, I am glad it is you I shall be discussing such matters with," I say quietly. "I cannot imagine doing it with anyone else."

"Me neither," he says, smiling as he puts his hand over mine, "Mrs Barton."

Just as Emily had done on her wedding day, I make my way up to my bedroom, which is now empty of my belongings, even Stanley. It barely even looks like my room anymore; it is as though I was never here. Mama is sitting on my bed, waiting for me with her handkerchief already dabbing at her damp eyes. As soon as she looks at me, the sobs come thick and fast, and I have to run and hold onto her warmth, just as I did as a child. I wonder if Emily had felt just like this when we had all said our goodbyes to her on her wedding day.

"I do not know what I am meant to do anymore," she whimpers, "my babes have gone, left the nest, and now I am empty."

"Oh, Mama, we will always be your girls, you know that," I argue, even though I sound just as sad as she does. "Besides, you are a grandmother now. And who knows? Maybe one day I will be able to give you another grandchild."

"That would be wonderful," she says, pulling back so we can wipe away each other's tears. She then turns serious all of a sudden, and I find myself bracing for what it is she is about to say. "Your sister spoke to you? About how such things occur?"

"She did," I reply, averting my eyes so we do not have to face one another during this awkward conversation. "And we do not need to mention it ever again."

"Yes, quite right, Elsie," she says as she taps my hands with her own. "I knew I made the right decision in asking her to explain things."

We remain sitting in silence for a moment or two before looking into each other's eyes and allowing ourselves to fall into a fit of laughter. It is the perfect way to say goodbye.

"I found him!" Emily announces as she bursts inside the room with her usual lack of grace. She pulls my father inside and I notice his red cheeks and swirling eyes. He is drunk. Completely drunk!

"Elsie, my darling girl," he slurs as he walks past Emily with his arms held out for me. "C-con-congratuslations!"

"George!" Mama snaps angrily. "Your eldest daughter is about to leave, and you are dru—"

"It is ok, Mama," I declare, cutting her off, "I didn't expect to have the same emotional farewell that he had bestowed upon Emily. Indeed, this is marginally better than the goodbye I *was* expecting."

"Elshie?" he slurs once again, looking entirely confused over my admission.

"Thank you for everything, Mama, Emily," I tell them as I

kiss each one of them on the cheek. "I shall be in touch, Mother, and I shall see you, Emily, in a few days' time."

"Elsie, are you ok?" Edmund asks as he appears in the doorway, looking concerned.

"I am perfect, thank you," I smile sweetly for him; he is the one taking me away from all of this. But then I step towards my father, trying to ignore the smell of liquor and the swaying of his legs. The man cannot even focus on me.

"Father, I thank you for the years we have shared together, even if the majority of our meetings were fleeting at best. I am sorry I never captured your heart as Emily did, but I hope I managed to present myself as a lady in our society should. Congratulations to you; you are finally free of me. Goodbye."

"Elsie?" Mama whimpers, so I offer her a solitary nod of my head before taking Edmund's outstretched hand so I may leave this place for good.

Chapter 12

Edmund

My wife has been quiet for too long; I am worried about her, about what I should do to make it better for her. My mother has always used distraction to help me forget about my woes, so with nothing else up my sleeve, I reach for her hand and bring it to my lips.

"Talk to me, Elsie, tell me how I can help," I whisper, for she has already jumped in surprise over my touch. "Remember we are friends, first and foremost."

"I am sorry, Edmund, I should not be so melancholy after we have just wed," she sighs, leaning against me for comfort. No one is here to stop her, no one has any say over us anymore; the rings on our fingers say as much. The realisation has me wrapping my arm around her delicate shoulders whilst inhaling the scent of her hair. She feels so soft.

"Don't you see, Lady Barton, we have all the time in the world," I tell her, contemplating that thought myself. "If you need to feel sad today, then feel sad, Elsie, and know that I am here for you. We can feel happy another day."

She remains quiet and still, seemingly taking comfort in me. It brings a sense of pride I have never felt before, an affirmation that I am now a man, a husband, and a good person. I smile about that. I also begin to think she has fallen asleep, for the only thing I can feel and hear is her deep breathing. I vow to be the man she deserves, the man her father failed to be for her for reasons unknown. George isn't a bad man, but it is fair to say that he is foolish in many ways.

"Edmund?" she murmurs, still lying somewhere between waking and sleeping.

"Yes, Elsie?"

"I think you've always been there for me."

"And I always will be."

Elsie

I wake with a start; the horses have jolted the carriage with a sudden halt. Less than a moment later, I realise I am completely draped over Edmund, drooling and no doubt having snored the whole way here. I move back as soon as possible, smooth down my hair and try to wipe my mouth with the back of my hand without him noticing. I fear I do not succeed in this feat; however, Edmund is nothing if not a good friend and a perfect gentleman, so he pretends not to notice.

"Are we here already?" I ask whilst trying to make out what I can see in the darkness. "I thought it would be light again by the time we arrived."

"We are stopping here tonight," he replies. "It's an inn, one I have stayed in many times before. Do not worry, it is extremely respectable here, and I have reserved two rooms."

"Y-you did?" I ask, whipping my head around to face him again. "I thought, as man and wife, we would be…er…that is to say…"

"And I would love nothing more than to share my bed with my wife, but I refuse to do so in such an establishment. I do not want you to feel pressured or embarrassed in a strange place," he explains, sounding very reasonable, and dare I say, sweet. His words make complete sense and yet…*it's our first night as man and wife*! Should it not mark something? Set a precedence for how our married life will be?

"You are right, Edmund, of course you are, and I thank you for your consideration of my feelings," I reply with a smile that feels unnatural.

"Elsie," he says quietly, leaning in close so he can brush his fingers against my cheek, which calms my anxieties a little. "Do not read into this, I am by no means rejecting you."

"It is fine, Edmund, really," I rush out with a lump of emotion forming at the back of my throat. He has rejected me, even if he has not meant to, it is still exactly how it feels.

"Elsie –"

Before he can finish his attempt to reassure me, the carriage door is pulled open, and the footman is asking if we are ready to make our way over to the inn. Edmund tries to ask him to wait, but I am more than ready to leave this enclosed space where I might break down and cry if I am not careful.

"Yes, we are!" I gasp, smiling with my teeth over the

reprieve.

"Thank you, Cedric," Edmund mutters from behind me as I step outside, accepting Cedric's hand as he helps me out of the carriage.

Edmund handles everything once we get inside, speaking assertively but respectfully, all the while I stand back, just hoping I can get to my room as soon as possible. I do not know what I was expecting, but it wasn't this, being left to sleep alone in an unknown room in an unknown inn in an unknown location. Just as I think this, Stanley seems to read my thoughts and yaps at me, causing the landlord to jump in surprise. He offers my darling dog a sneer before looking me over from top to toe.

"Is everything in order?" Edmund huffs as he hands over his coat and gloves.

"Yes, sir, your rooms are ready, your chamber is the same as usual, Lord Barton," he fusses over Edmund, who still isn't offering to look at the man in question.

"Then you can stop staring at my wife," he snaps.

"Your wife, Lord Barton? Please excuse me, I had no idea you had married," he says, now beaming at me. "Why, congratulations!"

They shake hands all the while I look on with curiosity; this man is embracing him like an old friend.

"Forgive me, Elsie, Bernard has been giving me room and board for years," Edmund says as he offers me his arm. "He used to do the same for my parents when I was a small boy."

"I remember those days as if they were yesterday! Edmund was always the quiet one, whereas Stephen, your older brother, was always flirting with the maids. He was a real character that one." His face turns solemn over the mention of Stephen. "Such a shame what happened to him."

"Indeed," Edmund says, now offering Bernard a smile, even if it is a sad one. "Bernard, I am going to escort my wife to her room, please make sure we are not disturbed until morning."

"Of course, and may I say, you are a lucky man, Edmund," he says with an affectionate wink, causing me to feel a warm blush creeping all over my face and neck.

"Thank you, Benard," he replies, "but I am more than aware of how lucky I am to be able to call this young lady my wife."

I smile in thanks to Bernard just as Edmund begins to lead us down a dark corridor that is adorned with guild-framed paintings of various landscapes in the countryside. We do not speak until we arrive outside of a door, which he unlocks so he can show me inside. Once the door is closed, I turn abruptly to face him. The room is adequate in size, decorated in deep reds and dark woods, and with a fire crackling to keep the chill away. A four-poster bed with fresh linens and the promise of a comfortable night sleep sits in the middle of the room and I wonder if it would be big enough to hold us both. Though, from the look on Edmund's face, I think I am unlikely to find out the answer to that question.

"Is the room to your liking?" he asks as he walks over to stoke the fire.

"Yes," I reply quietly, "the bed looks more than ample for me."

My words cause him to stop and look over at me with concern. I offer him a smile, but still, he says nothing. Instead, he walks over with cautious footsteps and takes hold of my hands, which he kisses, one at a time.

"Edmund, I—"

Before I can finish my sentence, one that was going to reassure him that I understand his reluctance to stay with me, he places a hand to my cheek and kisses me, just as he did when he had stolen into my room. It consumes both my mind and my body, and I have a feeling of wanting more; so much more. Though, before I can fall any deeper, he forces himself away from me, panting and looking…*hungry*. I have only seen a hint of this on a man before, when Tobias gazes upon Emily. It sets my heart racing with excitement.

"Not now, not here," he says with a heavy breath, almost to himself.

"But—"

"I have vowed to give you everything you deserve," he whispers, "and I shall forever regret it if I make our first time like this."

"Edmund," I sigh, unable to express the words that are clouding my head – *take me, make me yours!*

"Sleep well, Lady Barton, and I shall see you first thing in the morning," he says before kissing me chastely on the cheek.

"Goodnight, Edmund," I murmur as he practically runs from the room, leaving me feeling even more confused than ever. Is marriage meant to be this hard already?

Edmund

It was both hard and easy to leave my wife to her own bed. Hard because there is no denying, I would give anything to show her how much she is desired, but also easy because I am no longer the 'calf' Tobias so enjoys mocking me with. I know how to do things properly and how to be patient for the greater good. And Elsie Rothschild is the greater good...Elsie Barton, that is. She is now my wife, my greatest responsibility, and most desired possession. And I am hers.

Dawn brings the sound of birds singing at the top of their lungs amongst the trees behind us. I have always loved to hear them bringing in the new day, and with it, a reprieve from all the worries from the day before. My anxieties began early in life, and with them, an inability to sleep much past an hour or two. And during that sleep, I am often plagued by nightmarish visions of someone screaming, crying, and of someone grabbing me. As a child, I regularly dreamt of being left in the middle of a forest full of naked trees and an icy chill blowing all around my malnourished and unkempt body. My yells for help were left unanswered as I succumbed to hunger and bitter coldness. At times, I could hear a woman's voice calling for me, my mother, I had thought, but she never came, never revealed herself to me. And so, I was left abandoned. A confusing thought seeing as I have the most loving and caring parents one could ever hope for.

Growing up into a man, my dreams morphed into fears of losing my brother. We'd be out on one of his adventures, but it would soon turn dark and with that icy wind returning to warn me of an impending tragedy. He was always wild, throwing himself into whatever escapade he could find. I envied him for it, for his ability to cheat death and not even get into any bother with my parents. Perhaps it was because I was the baby of the family, but my mother had always treated me like a fragile ornament. Stephen was able to gallop across uncharted territories whilst I was practically tethered to my father's horse. My brother saw to it of course, that I was able to straddle the boundaries of safety and danger when no one was looking. I loved him for that; I loved him for many reasons.

Just before his accident, I was plagued by visions of him falling into an abyss, grasping for my hand, begging me to help him, but I could never reach. I was right back to screaming for someone to come and help me, but just like my earlier nightmares, no one ever came. He would sink beneath a black shroud of death just before I came to in a puddle of sweat and shortness of breath. When I first heard of his fall from his horse, I immediately blamed myself for not warning someone earlier. I could have begged him to stay in that morning, told my mother, or gone with him myself.

Over the years, I started to let go of my guilt, right up until I began having dreams of losing Emily. In those dreams, she was always running from me with her infectious laughter, just as she did when we were small and playing chase. Just before I caught her, she would vanish, and my arms would wrap around thin air. I would be left alone, small, and helpless in that forest of lifeless trees, thick fog, and an icy grip of loneliness. A mere few months later, she was married, and I was heartbroken.

Last night was the first night I actively tried not to sleep; I was too afraid I would dream of my new wife being stolen away from me. I could not bear to lose someone so close to me again. The very idea I can predict future tragedies is positively absurd, and yet, what *if* it is possible? What if I dream of her and weeks later, she is taken from me? Surely, it is best not to risk sleep, to not risk endangering what I hope to have with her.

"My Lord," Cedric says after he has knocked on my door, just as I had instructed him to the night before. His voice has me stretching away my fears and rubbing my eyes so I can at least focus on him when I eventually open the door.

"Morning, Cedric," I greet him once the door is open, "are we nearly ready to go?"

"Yes, My Lord, though there have been no signs of life from your wife's chamber," he says shyly. "Shall I send one of the chamber maids to wake her?"

"That won't be necessary, Cedric, thank you," I tell him as I reach for my jacket. "I believe I earned that right when I married her yesterday."

I laugh, patting him on the shoulder as I walk past his hunched over frame, trying to hide his smile over my reply. I listen to him shuffling away in his boots that had needed replacing a few years ago. I make a mental note to have some made for him. My father had warned me against such grand gestures, explaining how my generous nature would be taken advantage of. However, Cedric has served my family for decades; it is the least one can do for a loyal and hard-working employee.

When I reach Elsie's door, I place my ear to the timber and wait to hear some kind of movement. After a few moments of silence, I decide to try the handle, which to my surprise, opens without effort. She did not lock her door; I will have to have words with her about that. I can only assume she did not think on it, having never had to up until now. However, her safety is now my responsibility, and I will make it known that she is not to place herself in unnecessary risk. I lost Stephen to folly; I refuse to lose her.

Once inside, I take some time to indulge in the beauty of my wife, lying completely still in her white night dress and with her rich brown tresses fanning out over the white cotton pillowcases. The sight takes my breath away, even more so when I remind myself that she is mine, all mine.

"I won't lose you," I whisper as I perch on the mattress beside her sleeping body. "Yesterday exhausted you more than I thought it would; your father no doubt having played a part in that," I utter softly, stroking back her hair that feels soft to touch. "I vow to make him see, to make him appreciate just how amazing you are, Elsie Barton."

I lean over her face, studying every detail and committing it to memory. She is perfect, perhaps too perfect for me, but I have her all the same. I enjoy seeing her natural, her hair flowing without pins or combs to set it in place. I cannot help but follow it with the back of my hand, then watching as it moves underneath my fingertips. I lean even closer, taking in the scent of her soap, the rise and fall of her chest, the pulse in her neck, the sensation of her breath blowing against my skin as I move my lips closer towards her parted ones.

"I denied us last night, my love," I tell her, "but I need you, all of you."

I feel so very desperate, knowing her womanly curves would feel so good against me. She asked me if I enjoyed the physical act of love and I had felt ashamed and awkward. I had told her the truth when I said that I did, but that it had also lost its appeal when I began to realise the women had meant very little to me. It was love that was only skin deep. With Elsie, I could fall into an ocean with her. But I would never take what was not offered, would never give what wasn't desired.

"Edmund?" I hear her emit through her soft lips, her mouth sounding dry, and with her eyes still closed. It gives me ample opportunity to retreat away from her.

"Lady Barton," I reply with a smile upon my lips. I watch

as she flutters her eyelids, trying to adjust to the morning light.

"Edmund…" she barely whispers, her eyes solely fixed on mine. I grab hold of her hand as she reaches out for me. This moment has me believing we will be every bit as great as Tobias and Emily. This is *our* love story.

"How did you sleep?" I ask softly, her senses still acclimatising to her waking.

"I dreamt I had married Lord Boreham," she says with a confused look on her face, "he came to me in the night and he…"

She emits a groan at the same time as lifting her free hand to her head and rubbing it, as if trying to wipe away that nightmarish scene.

"Do not think on it a moment a longer," I try to reassure her. "I am here to let you know it is time to get ready. We will arrive at Hardy's estate by lunchtime if we make a move soon."

"Oh, yes, of course," she says in such a way, I instantly know her moment of vulnerability has vanished and her mask of the woman who she thinks she needs to be is back in place. I would choose the real her over her mask without question, but she is not ready to believe that yet. She will though, and soon.

"I shall leave you to dress and meet you in the dining room; you must be starving," I tell her as she gets to her feet to begin ordering her clothes. She nods her head but continues without pause.

As she walks past me, I reach out to grab her wrist and pull her against me. Her wide eyes and natural flowing hair have me staring for a moment, wishing to kiss her as we had when I had snuck inside of her room in London. Her emerald-green eyes move to focus on my lips, which pleases me beyond words; she wants me too.

"Elsie, you must always lock the door when we are apart; I should punish you for leaving this room open last night."

"Punish me, Edmund?" she says with a hint of nervous laughter. I merely pull her in even closer so her body is now flush against mine; it feels as good as I hoped it would…better.

"Punish you," I whisper straight inside her ear, enunciating each word with a hint of mischief behind them.

"A-a-alright," she stutters just before I kiss the soft skin beneath her earlobe, the sensation causing her to shudder.

"Good," I whisper. "Your safety is my priority, Lady Barton. Wear your hair down today, will you?"

"Of course," she replies, "whatever my husband desires."

"And on those parting words, which I will be sure to remember, I shall take my leave."

Chapter 13

Elsie

Edmund and I have been travelling for what feels like an age, talking of everything and nothing. Though pleasant, I am now feeling extremely confused. In fact, I have been close to screaming more than once during this long and tedious journey. Edmund, the boy who made me feel so inadequate, the man who became my friend, and now the husband whom I have no idea how to be myself around, is driving me to distraction. It is no surprise I do not feel myself around him; I have reverted back to the version of Elsie who I have always portrayed to the outside world. I wonder if I shall ever feel comfortable in my own skin. The way he is talking so excessively, as if trying to avoid any moments of uncomfortable silence, I have to wonder if Edmund thinks the very same thing about himself. Are we just two lost souls trying to find themselves in a world full of masked appearances?

"Elsie, do you think—"

Edmund's words are cut off by the sudden halt of the carriage, which sends us both flying from our seats. Edmund tries to reach out for me, but I still manage to hit my head on the edge of the seat opposite. A sharp pain spreads across my forehead, quickly followed by the sensation of warm liquid oozing down my face. In fact, when I finally realise we've stopped falling, I feel quite dizzy. Even the noise of the horses whinnying and stomping about on their hooves sounds distorted. I try not to cry, but the shock of everything causes my eyes to stream with tears.

"Good God, Elsie, you are bleeding!" Edmund cries, sounding panicked. "Can you speak, Elsie?"

"Mm," I groan, lifting my hand to investigate the wound. "What happened? Has someone attacked us?"

"My Lord!" a panicked voice shouts from outside. "Lord Barton, are you and Lady Barton alright? One of the horses was spooked by a passing stag. I am sorry, the driver couldn't—"

"Do not worry, Cedric, I am sure you both did all that you could, but my wife is hurt," Edmund informs our worried looking footman, who is now poking his head through the door, his face pale with shock. "Please, grab one of my shirts from my luggage."

"No, Edmund, it will spoil," I slur. "It cannot be that…"

The wooziness in my voice surprises me, and with one fearful look from Edmund, I give in and let Cedric carry out Edmund's instruction without further argument.

"My God, Elsie, less than a day married, and I've already failed to protect you," he says with such concern in his eyes, I end up smiling with some relief. "Are you laughing at me, Mrs Barton?"

"Yes," I indeed laugh, and it feels good. So good, I indulge in it for longer than I initially meant to. "So serious, Edmund, the boy who used to encourage my sister with her wild antics because he was so head over heels in love with her."

The comment has us both stop smiling, and I instantly regret having said anything at all. I never meant for it to turn the atmosphere awkward. For a moment, I think he is going to turn angry, or leave me alone in this carriage to feel guilty over my thoughtless words. But then he smiles, showing his teeth and crinkling his eyes with genuine happiness.

"What can I say, Lady Barton? We all have to grow up at some time," he says, holding one of his shirts to my head and with softness in his eyes. "To see the things we really want and go for them."

"And what do you want, Edmund?" I ask as I fall under the hypnotic look in his eyes.

"My wife," he says with a soft laugh that has me smiling with him.

"A very good answer," I tease. "Why do you keep calling me Lady Barton, or Mrs Barton?"

"Because if I do not say those words out loud, I am not sure I'll believe it," he says. "How lucky I am to have found you, Elsie, and to have you as my own."

I open my mouth to say something, though I couldn't tell you what exactly, just know I need to answer him in some way. However, before any words manage to escape me, Cedric opens the door with a ruddy complexion and a look of an apology about him. Edmund reluctantly turns to face him, no doubt hoping for an update on the state of the poor horses outside.

"The horses are well, but the driver doesn't want to risk driving them when they are still so spooked," Cedric says quite sensibly. "Fortunately, My Lord, there is a tavern about half a mile from here. It shouldn't take you and Lady Barton long to get there on foot."

"A good idea, Cedric," Edmund replies as he turns back to

study the gash on the side of my head. His face wincing over the sight of it does not reassure me at all. "I shall carry you, Elsie; you cannot travel as you are anyway."

"Do not be so silly, Edmund," I huff, "my legs are uninjured, I can walk myself."

"What was it you said this morning? *Whatever your husband desires*?" he teases. "Then, it is my desire for you to do as you are told. Let me help you from the carriage, and no arguments."

Edmund carries me the entire length of the path that leads us to a modest-looking tavern, and though I enjoyed the theatrics of it, as well as feeling close to him, I am more than happy to stand on my own two feet. Edmund is muscular and lean, so there is no room for comfort within his arms. Besides, my head has stopped bleeding and I no longer feel as though I might faint. I am mostly in need of water and somewhere to rest a while.

Fortunately, Edmund puts me on the ground before we walk inside to face whoever is on the other side of the door. Hopefully, there won't be many people, for my dress is completely ruined and I can only imagine how bad my head looks. My husband offers me his hand, which I take without question, taking comfort in the feeling of his new wedding ring against my skin. I indulge in the fact that I no longer have to fear being seen with Edmund without someone's watchful eye on me.

Having said that, as soon as we walk inside, the landlord, a lanky gentleman with a face covered in grey whiskers, stops in his duties and stares with a perplexed expression on his face. It's unsettling, so much so, I pull back on Edmund's hand. He immediately turns to face me with a reassuring smile.

"No need to fear anything, Elsie, he's probably a little

taken aback by your wound."

"Is she alright?" the poor man gasps as he points with his towel towards my head. "What on earth happened?"

"An accident with our carriage," Edmund explains as he pulls us towards an empty table. "Might we trouble you for some water, and perhaps a glass of Brandy for the shock?"

"Of course; please, sit down," the man flusters as he sets to making up a range of drinks. His kind nature shines through his concern for me, a complete stranger, which has me feeling infinitely more relaxed. "I can send one of the chamber maids for the doctor. He lives less than a mile away."

"Oh, there is no –" I begin, but Edmund cuts me off with a stern look that tells me my protests will be futile.

"That would be very good of you, my wife needs looking at, even if she doesn't think so herself," he says, grinning at me when I roll my eyes. "My driver is settling the horses as we speak. If you serve food, we would be most grateful for a meal before we attempt to travel again."

"Of course, I'll put together a basket for your driver too," he says, placing the drinks down before us.

"Thank you so very much," I tell him, to which he smiles and shuffles off to a room out the back, leaving Edmund and I alone. "Edmund, my head has stopped bleeding now, there really is no need for a doctor to come and tend to it."

"Nonsense," he says before studying it for himself. "I am afraid there is quite a bit of blood in your hair, but otherwise, the cut is hidden. How does your head feel? Dizzy still?"

"No, I am fine, really."

"Good," he whispers before kissing my hair where I had hit it. It feels intimate, even more so than when he had kissed me in my room. A sensation of butterflies ignites inside of me, and I realise I am falling into much deeper emotions for him. "Hopefully, I'll have you at Hardy's estate by nightfall. You will have an early night and plenty of rest tomorrow."

"Oh, Edmund, do not fuss, we are supposed to be on our honeymoon," I dare to say out loud, "doing what couples do on honeymoon."

"All in good time," he simply says, pulling away completely.

Oh, I did not expect that answer, and I did not expect to feel so much pain from his refusal of me. In fact, I would confidently say it hurts more than hitting my head against the edge of the carriage seat. By the time the landlord lays out a feast of cold meats and other such tasty morsels for lunch, my head is hurting again, and I no longer feel the relief I had felt when Edmund had acted so concerned for me.

Chapter 14

Elsie

After I was given the all clear from the doctor, we resumed our journey to Kent, though we barely spoke at all. Something changed in Edmund, and I no longer feel desirable. In fact, I am left feeling more confused than ever.

When we arrive at early evening to the sight of Emily and Tobias resting by the fire in their living room, I am not at all surprised to see them there. Apparently, Tobias had lasted as long as he could in London, amongst my family and societal pressures, and had deemed it necessary for them to return. Emily apologised for not giving us more time to be by ourselves, but Edmund told her not to worry, which in turn, only made me feel worse.

"And will you be sharing a room?" Emily asks with a pointed look at me, but it is Edmund who answers for us both before I even have a chance to say a single word.

"No, not tonight, Elsie needs her rest," he replies, pulling back my hair to reveal my cut. "I am sure she would sleep better in her own bed."

"Of course," Emily utters, though her expression when she looks at me says she knows how hurt his rebuttal has made me feel. All I can do is nod, for I am too afraid I might cry or scream if

I open my mouth to reply. "Molly will show you to your usual rooms."

"No need, I know where I am going," I reassure her, sounding cold and formal.

"I shall accompany you," Edmund says, offering me his arm, but I step away to make it quite clear I do not need, nor want, his company. I am thoroughly exhausted from having my emotions toyed with.

"That isn't necessary," I tell him without room for argument. "And besides, it looks as though Monty is going to escort me. I am sure he will be happier in my company, especially when you have other distractions to keep you amused."

I left him looking dumbfounded as I made my way to the door, closing it shut after Monty, so my husband knows without question, that I do not want him to follow me.

Edmund

"Oh, dear," Emily says with a painful-looking wince all the while I stand there, gaping my mouth open like a fish.

"Well done, Barton," Tobias says with amusement from his chair in front of the fire, "you have surpassed even my expectations. I thought it would be at least a week or two before you managed to bungle your marriage. Not only that, but you've now deprived my wife and I of our loyal companion. He always seems to know when a damsel in distress is in need of his comfort."

"What in God's name did I do?!" I finally cry, scratching my head as I gesture towards the door from which Elsie has just stormed through.

"Tell me, Edmund, and I do not wish to be indelicate, but have you and my sister…erm…that is to say…" she begins, but pauses in order to step closer and lower her voice, "…*consummated* your marriage yet?"

"Of course not!" I declare indignantly. "I wouldn't dream of doing such a thing in an inn where anybody could stay. I want it to be special; she deserves no less!"

Tobias simply chuckles to himself whilst shaking his head, whereas Emily remains standing there with that wince still upon her face. However, I am none the wiser as to why Elsie has lost her temper with me.

"I have been with women in such establishments, and I would never want to repeat that with my wife. It should happen somewhere private, respectful, and personal. Was it wrong of me to want such a thing for our first time?"

"No! No, no, no," Emily gasps, "it is very sweet and gentlemanly of you."

"Then why are you looking at me like that? And why is Lord Romance over there laughing to himself?"

"I am exceedingly romantic," Tobias utters, "in private."

"That you are, darling," Emily says with a healthy blush, but also with a huge grin on her face. "However, Edmund, we are talking about you, and I think you may have been too sweet for your own good. You see, I am going to guess that you haven't explained this thoughtful gesture to Elsie?"

"Well, not exactly, but I couldn't very well explain that I had had those kinds of relations with other women in rented rooms, now could I? I would never want to take my wife in such a way; she deserves only the very best."

"And I completely understand, but from Elsie's point of view, you've just rejected her," she explains with that same worried expression on her face. "Twice," she adds, pointing towards the door.

"One thing a woman does not take well to, is being rejected, Barton," Tobias says, looking knowingly at Emily who nods affirmatively.

"She had a serious injury to her head! I couldn't subject her to anything knowing she needs time to rest and recuperate."

"Yes, but Elsie can only see your rebuttal," Emily rushes to explain, "and she already fears being second best."

"Oh, dear God, that is not what I meant to make her feel at all," I groan as I sink into one of the chairs. "I have been trying to show how much I care about her all day, but I've only achieved the opposite."

"These are just teething problems, Edmund. You will get there, you both will," she says, placing her hand gently over my arm.

"Should I go up and see her now?"

"Best give her that rest you wanted her to have, then try again in the morning. The sun always makes everything seem better than they were the day before."

I release a long sigh and nod. Marriage is even harder than I thought it would be.

Elsie

Sleep evades me, and after tossing and turning for what has felt like hours, I can take it no more. I step out of bed and retrieve my robe. I need air, cooling fresh air, so I make my way downstairs and step outside the front door. It is dark but the moon is full. I just need to walk my way out of my anxious and frustrated thoughts.

Now that I am out here, in the dark, the silence, I can better understand why my sister enjoys the outdoors. I never much indulged in its pleasures when I was younger, for I was always deemed to be the more responsible one. The eldest must set an example for her younger sibling, as well as represent the family by her actions. Emily, although a daughter of a viscount, was afforded a level of freedom that I was not, especially when she was so obviously our father's favourite child. Running around the countryside never even occurred to me back then, and even if it had, I am sure my poor mama would have chastised me even more so than she did Emily. She needed at least one easy child.

However, in a state of deep thought, my strange affliction of insomnia is now causing me to wander from my sister's house, away from my husband, and in search of something I cannot even name, for I do not even know what it is.

A small, rickety bridge grabs my attention, it having a slither of moonlight hitting at just the right angle. It looks as if a painter has arranged the scene for his latest masterpiece, and so I must go to it. The water sets my tense muscles at ease a little, almost clearing my head of all the troubling thoughts that have ailed me since marrying my sister's former admirer. To be a poor conciliation prize to both my father and husband is enough to trouble any woman's mind. I try not to feel ugly emotions such as jealousy, but it is a strong ask when I have tried so hard to be what society deems to be the perfect lady, only to see my sister now living the life I was brought up to believe would be mine. It makes me feel wicked, superficial, and utterly miserable.

"Oh..."

A moan escaping through the trees across the path from me interrupts my daydreaming. It is so fleeting; I almost start to believe I imagined it. However, the sound of carefree laughter soon follows, one I recognise almost immediately. Emily, when she was reading books no lady should have any business reading, and when she was only fifteen years old at that. I know I should ignore it, turn around and return to the house, however, I cannot deny how curious I am.

Like a greedy thief, I creep amongst the trees and undergrowth, being careful not to step upon a twig that is likely to snap and give away my position. I then take refuge behind a bush. When my eyes finally manage to focus on the scene that is barely a stone's throw away from me, I am taken aback by the sight of my sister and her husband lying naked beneath a large oak tree, with only a thin blanket to shield their modesty. Tobias, my brother-in-law, cages her beneath his broad body, with that same painter having bathed each and every one of his muscles in silvery moonlight. Her hands are braced against his shoulders and her leg hooked around his. Their hips look to be massaging against one another, causing her to pant and roll her eyes before closing them altogether.

"My beautiful wife," he gasps, "the stealer of all my thoughts!"

"Thoughts?" she giggles with a long moan at the end.

"So many thoughts...ahhh..." he trails off as she seemingly pushes him over and onto his back, so she is now on top, gyrating against him.

"Oh, my!" I gasp to myself as I watch his hands move to hold onto her naked breasts, quite clearly enjoying what she is doing to him. It is such a sight; I have to turn away. My breath has quickened, and my heart is thumping so forcefully, I fear it might leap right out of my chest.

"Lustful thoughts?" she whispers between pants.

"Ridiculously lustful thoughts!" he laughs before emitting a moan that sounds as though he is half in pain, half in rapture.

"I am…I am…" she cries out before she too, emits a moan similar to that of her husband.

A silence ensues before they seemingly fall into fits of laughter. The sound of their kissing leaves me no choice but to turn and face them once again. Still naked, bar the sheet wrapped loosely around the parts that truly matter, I watch as he leans over her, brushing away her hair while looking so adoringly into her eyes, so happy with her, I cannot help but feel that ugly pang of jealousy once more. The way they are looking at one another is so beautiful, I have no words with which to describe the scene that will do it any sort of justice.

"Emily, I love you more than anything," he whispers with a smile I do not believe any other person has ever seen on him. It is all for her, just her. "You and James."

"And Monty?" she asks with a teasing smile. He laughs, then kisses her forehead with so much tenderness, I must confess, for a moment, I wish it were me lying there with him.

"Of course, my love, and Monty," he whispers, turning serious again. "I love you."

"And I you," she says, pushing back his own hair with affection.

It is too much to bear, too much to watch without the need to scream in frustration. With as much care as before, I turn and run far away from all that it is that I so desperately crave for myself.

I run back to the house where my husband lies sleeping. I am sure that if he had borne witness to what I had just seen, he too would be feeling beyond frustrated, wanting nothing else other than to be there with Emily instead of Tobias. As for me, it is not the man beneath the tree that I want, more the relationship that my sister shares with him.

A loud knock wakes me from a slumber I had worked hard to fall into. I feel so awfully rotten, I almost wish I had not fallen asleep at all. Memories of my sister and her husband coming together on that forest floor has me snapping my eyes shut once more. I am sure I must look frightful and am in no fit state to welcome anyone into my room.

"Elsie?" Edmund calls for me, thankfully remaining on the other side of the door. He is the very last person I wish to see right now. "Elsie, are you well?"

"No," I shout back, behaving very unladylike, but this is surely preferable to him coming in to see me looking so frightful. "I am very unwell, Edmund, might I see you later?"

A silence ensues and I begin to relax in the knowledge that he is going to leave me well alone, though I will not fully set myself at ease until he has made it clear that he is leaving.

"Elsie, I am coming in!" he announces, and bursts through the door before I even have a chance to argue. As always, he looks the epitome of handsome, whilst I try to cover my face with the sheet pooled all around me.

"Edmund!" I all but shriek in shock. "What on earth do you think you are doing?"

"Checking in on my wife," he says, as though I am completely clueless, "as any other good husband would."

"A title by name," I tell him with an air of bitterness, "you and I both know this is not a real marriage."

"Elsie…" he begins, but I cut him off, thinking of how Tobias had looked so lovingly at my sister last night.

"It is quite alright, Edmund, you do not need to check in on me, I will manage as I always have."

"And how is that?" he asks as he edges towards the bed.

"Alone," I answer simply, dropping the sheet to gaze out of the window where I see Emily taking a turn with Monty and her faithful maid. "Have you seen my sister this morning?"

"Not yet, no," he replies cautiously, before dropping to perch on the edge of the bed, where it dips beneath his weight.

"She is looking especially beautiful today," I comment, one that earns me a sigh, "as she always does."

"I am sure her husband appreciates the fact," he says quietly, "though, beauty runs in the family, so it is of no surprise."

"Please do not be charming with me, Edmund," I sigh before finally chancing a glance at him. His expression reveals his pity for me, or for himself, I am not entirely sure. "I know who I am and who I am not."

"Who you are is my wife," he says resolutely, "Lady Elsie

Barton."

"Do you still love her?"

"Elsie," he exhales audibly, "I have already told you the answer to that question!"

"But now that you are here, gazing upon her every day, surely you cannot feel nothing after having loved her for so long?"

"Elsie, I cannot do this anymore," he says, getting to his feet, "I am not in love with Emily!"

"But you are not in love with me either," I tell him, stopping him dead on his feet. We stare at each other for a moment or two, as if completely lost for words. "I saw them together, last night."

"Who?" he asks, looking completely confused by my rambling.

"Tobias and Emily," I admit, the awkwardness of the conversation now causing me to begin fiddling with the sheet beneath my fingers. "They were doing what I presume a wife and a husband are meant to do."

"Oh!" he gasps, walking back over to sit with me on the bed. "How…where…you did?"

"Yes, in the woods." He looks even more confused by my explanation, so I simply shake my head, telling him not to question me any further on it, for it matters very little.

"And what did you think?" he utters at the same time as my cheeks suddenly flame up through embarrassment.

Edmund

"I could not help but feel envious."

"You did?" I ask, sounding more than a little shocked.

"For the emotion," she quickly clarifies. "To have someone look at you the way they did one another, well, I can imagine it is everything to that person."

"I would not know that part of it; it has only ever been a physical act for me," I try to reassure her. "It is why I gave it up some time ago."

"And do you miss it?" she asks, turning to face me so our fingers are but a few inches away from one another. I eye her delicate ones, still fidgeting with the sheet, giving away her anxiety.

"It is hard to say," I answer, edging my fingertips towards hers. She does not flinch or move away, simply stays quiet while I think of the words with which to answer her. "I miss the feel of a woman, her softness, her caressing me, but do I miss giving someone I do not know a part of me I cannot get back? Then, my answer would be no."

"I am not sure I understand," she says as I take a chance to close the gap between our fingers and touch her. She takes a deep inhale and I find myself enjoying the sound.

"Perhaps you need to have done such a thing to know," I try to explain.

"Perhaps," she whispers. "There is just one problem."

"Yes?" I urge as I lean in close to where her lips are parted and her cheeks are glowing.

"The only person I could do such a thing with, would be

my husband," she still whispers, and I feel an overwhelming lust I have not felt in a long time; too long. I move in even closer, wanting to kiss her, to kiss my wife. "And my husband is y—"

Before she can finish, I take a chance and place my lips against hers. I cup her cheek, pulling her that much closer to me so I can kiss her with an intensity I have been holding back for so long. I can admit to playing hot and cold with Elsie, for I have feared rushing my wife into something that is still so new to her, but in this moment, I cannot stop myself. My thoughts only centre around her, tasting her, holding her, even making love to her. I am still so confused over the intensity of how much I have fallen for Elsie, and I am so desperately afraid of hurting her. Love has burnt me badly in the past, and though I no longer feel the same way about Emily, I do remember the paralysing pain it caused to not have her return my affection.

As I part her lips with my tongue, seeking entrance to her beautiful mouth, she emits a small moan of desire and braces her hands against my arms. But she does not push away. In fact, she soon kisses me back, exploring this new level of intimacy. As our kiss deepens, I take an even bigger chance and begin to push her back towards the mattress, all the while I move my body over hers, caging her in beneath my arms. As my hardness begins to throb with a need for her, she emits a small gasp and pulls back, igniting a sting of rejection I thought I had long left behind.

"What was that?" she asks.

"I am sorry," I cry, still holding onto her but only because I am unable to move. "I thought you understood what...I mean, I thought Emily...Oh, God!"

I jump up and away from her while she looks back at me with utter bewilderment.

"Edmund, I just wanted to know—"

"No, you are right, this was foolish of me," I fluster as I get to my feet, readying myself to run far away from her anxious expression, one I have caused with my lustful needs.

"No, wait—" she calls out as I march away, closing the door behind me for fear I might be pulled back in to face her.

Once I am far enough away to not be heard, I slip to the floor and take in deep, panic-stricken breaths, willing myself to calm down. I am still ashamed of my past, of what I did to Emily, and how rejected I had felt afterwards. I cannot place that burden onto Elsie, another innocent young woman who requires nothing but love from a gentleman who deserves her. It is a pity I am not that gentleman.

Chapter 15

Edmund

The air is cooler than yesterday, much like my mood after this morning. Still, it does not slow down young Monty, nor Emily for that matter. We're walking across the grounds of her estate with Marley and Ethel in tow. They seem pleased to have been given a reprieve from their colicky baby brother and their thoroughly stressed-out mother. They bicker but show a mutual affection for one another, much like Emily and I once did, before I realised I loved her more than a friend.

Just as Emily had, I always believed Elsie would be married before her, leaving her younger sister free to marry whomever she liked. Fate, however, had other ideas. Better ideas, you could argue. When I look at her and Tobias sneaking love-filled gazes at one another, I know they were destined to be together. She would never have looked at me like that. Perhaps no one ever will, which is a sad thought to stomach.

"Penny for your thoughts," Emily says to me, smiling with her teeth and wild hair hanging around her shoulders.

"Perhaps they are worth more than a penny," I tease, and she laughs at me.

"Well, then, might you tell a friend what is troubling you so?"

"It is…*delicate*," I try to explain, for it is not a subject one should be bringing up with just anyone, especially a Duchess. However, Emily is my friend, first and foremost, so perhaps she is the perfect person to whom I should open up.

"Might it involve my sister?" she assumes rightly.

"But of course," I reply, "you Rothschild girls have always plagued my thoughts."

"*Plagued*? Such a harsh word, Lord Barton!" she tuts at me, and I laugh over her playfulness.

"Do not 'Lord' me, *Your Grace*!" My teasing is rewarded with a gentle nudge of my shoulder.

"Seriously, Edmund, what is causing you to furrow that brow of yours? It is causing a crease so deep, you could lose a penny inside of it."

"If I explain the cause of my worry, I hope you will not take any offence from it," I try to explain, but it only causes her to stop and look at me with obvious curiosity.

"Well, now you must tell me," she says, crossing her arms in front of her, "I am much too intrigued to let this go." I pull a face that conveys my unease, but she simply takes hold of my hand and smiles. "You know you can tell me anything, Edmund, and I will only offer you my advice and friendship."

"Oh dear, this is where it gets a little awkward," I begin with a wince. "You see, she caught you last night, you and Tobias…out in the woods?"

"Oh? Oh!" she says with a set of wide eyes. She then shocks me by bursting into laughter so loud, I end up chuckling with her. "Forgive me, Edmund, that tree holds a special place for Tobias and me, we could not help ourselves. We also thought it would be less risky. We assumed our guests could not possibly hear us if we were out in the open, far away from the house."

"I truly am happy for you both, and I am glad you enjoy that side of your marriage," I mumble awkwardly, "however, it has made Elsie feel rather bereft of such feelings. I know she is hoping to hear how I truly feel about her, those three little words every lady is wanting to hear."

"And you? How about what you are after, Edmund?" she counters with a bounce in her step.

"You know I have always wanted to marry for love and…" I trail off as I flap my hand around in the warm air, attempting to skirt around the issue. She merely laughs at me again.

"But you do not love her?"

"It is not that," I rush out to try and explain, "more a case of not feeling like I deserve to feel that way about her. One rebuttal from a Rothschild was enough to push me off course and nearly ruin you, Emily."

"Dear Lord, Edmund!" she scoffs. "That is one of the most ridiculous things I have ever heard! For one thing, before I was married, I had no intention of seeing any man in that way. I was still childlike and content to be so. You saw what Tobias and I went through before we discovered our true feelings for one another. And as for the business that followed, well, that was unfortunate. But there was no wrongdoing on your part. If it is what you needed at the time, then why not? You did not believe you were hurting anyone."

"Your logic makes sense to a rational man, alas, I do not feel at all ready to be rational about it," I admit. "I am trapped in a prison of guilt and self-loathing. How can I possibly offer someone else love and adoration when I feel so little towards myself? Elsie deserves a man who is sure of himself, who trusts himself to be everything she needs and more."

"Even if that is true, it is you who she has," she says, linking her arm through mine. "So, you can either torture both her heart and yours, or you can step up and be that man."

"What if I am never able to allow myself to say those words to her?"

"It is a possibility," she says pensively, "but a certainty if you never try."

We walk along in silence for a while, contemplating those words, and it strikes me that I truly have changed my feelings for Emily. I feel nothing other than friendship; I am finally free of those punishing thoughts of her and I one day being together. She is deeply in love, and I am deeply in limbo. A purgatory in which I am forcing myself into, but for how long?

"Penny for your thoughts," she asks again, this time with a wink and a grin.

"I was just wondering when my best friend became so smart," I tease.

"You wicked brother-in-law, I have always been exceedingly smart," she pouts whilst nudging me again. "Much smarter than you it would seem."

"Actually, on this occasion, I will agree with you."

Elsie

After tea, I take myself to a room far away from the hustle and bustle of serving staff, hoping to avoid conversation. I do not wish to talk to anyone after feeling so humiliated this morning. My husband has only confirmed my suspicions; that I am not worthy of his love or affection. Only Emily can be honoured with those things from him. Our story is rather like a Shakespeare play, a tragic comedy to make you both laugh and cry.

With that sad realisation, I have decided to dedicate this stay in my sister's house to search for some other purpose to my life. After all, I had already resigned myself to spinsterhood, and to tend to my studies of music and art. Perhaps I could lend a hand to those in need of help, much like Emily did when she was banished from London. It will be a simple life of tepid warm emotions, but a peaceful one. I can be just as happy as Emily, if not more so. After all, Lady Elizabeth appears to be one of the most contented ladies I know. In fact, I shall tell Edmund that he has my blessing to court other women, to take on lovers and leave me be, far away from the city so he can conduct his affairs as he sees fit.

Just as I make this decision, cementing it firmly in my mind, I come across a beautiful grand piano sitting in the middle of a sun-drenched room. It is as if some greater force is sending me a sign to continue with these endeavours. My fingers twitch with a need to stroke them across the white and ebony keys, to let my passion flow against something tangible. Something I can grasp and wield to my own wants and needs.

I waste no time in pacing towards the stool, adorned in crimson red velvet, where I take my place before this most beautiful of instruments. The first few notes are meaningless, as if greeting an old acquaintance with nothing in particular to say. However, as I stare out the window, I notice Edmund and Emily walking along like they used to when we were younger, when I was left alone to be the sensible one. The *boring* one. I begin hitting the keys with venom in my blood, knowing I will never mean what Emily does to him. I am second-best, always. I use the entirety of the keys, slamming the notes as if they have personally offended me. My melody is dramatic, something akin to a thunderstorm, black in both colour and mood.

As I hit the end notes, I indulge in the sensation of my heart thumping behind my ribcage, and my breathing being short and shallow. I open my mouth to scream, but something shifts in the air, and I realise I am no longer alone. Seeing as my husband is indulging himself in the company of the real woman whom he desires, it must be Tobias, my brother-in-law. I audibly sigh, knowing he will have something scathing to say that will only have me feeling even more wretched. Though, at least he might give me the opportunity to release my temper, even if he is not the real cause for it.

"Such an angry piece of music, Elsie," he declares as he steps into view. "Though I must admit I enjoyed it. Your sister rarely plays in front of me."

"Good afternoon, Tobias, your piano is exquisite, but I must warn you, my mood is as dark as the music I just forced it to play."

"Evidently," he says, causing me to smile, even though I do not want to.

Nothing else is said for a few moments so I begin playing, only this time, my melody is slower, brooding, and ever so much softer on the ear. Tobias sits casually in his chair, seemingly enjoying my playing; at least someone appreciates my efforts.

"Do you know when I first started to respect you, Elsie?" he says out of the blue, causing me to cease playing for a moment or two, if only so I can try and make peace with his words.

"What a question to ask someone," I sigh as I take up my playing again. "It still astounds me that you are a duke when you utter such insults, as though it is perfectly reasonable to do such a thing."

"Oh, I apologise," he says with a smile that my sister finds endearing, but only causes me to roll my eyes, "did you want to engage in meaningless chit-chat before getting to the point?"

"Firstly, no you don't, you never apologise to anyone other than Emily. Secondly, do I really want to know this point you are trying to make?"

"You are quite right; I don't apologise for bypassing social etiquette when we both know it is not necessary. But as for the point, I should imagine you do. As an outsider to your situation with Edmund, and as someone who believes in being useful over protecting somebody's feelings, I can tell you what you need to do to get to the truth of the matter with your husband."

I am almost afraid to ask him to elaborate, though, and it pains me to admit such a thing, he is right. He will know more than me when it comes to navigating the male mind. As much as I hate to say it, I do need the great Duke of Kent's advice. I can also admit that I don't desire to waste time by talking about the state of the weather or how well the apple blossom trees are looking, or any other such nonsense I am supposed to talk about when in the company of a duke. Besides, Tobias is not what one would describe as a 'normal' duke, which I am actually thankful for at this moment in time. What I am not thankful for is the expression on his arrogant features when I turn to face him, as though he knows exactly what I am thinking.

"I am listening," I murmur, hating every moment of having to concede to his arrogance.

"Whilst I would love to revel in this moment, Elsie, I cannot bear to waste energy on vanity."

"I thought vanity was positively mandatory for a duke," I reply with my own smile as I continue playing.

"The first time you had my respect was when you lectured me about sending Emily away, when you showed no fear of breaking your obedient, lady-like persona, because you knew your sister needed the real Elsie Rothschild more. I will happily admit, I like the true Elsie Rothchild, she is far more interesting than the debutante you have been trained to be."

His words finally cause me to stop playing and truly listen. In fact, I feel suddenly overcome with emotion, to have someone as insensitive as my brother-in-law tell me that the real me is better than who I am expected to be, is enough to bring tears to my eyes.

"So, what do you suggest I do when it comes to Edmund?" I ask, refusing to look at him for fear he will see my tears.

"Avoid the meaningless talk, the expected coyness of a lady, and be brutally honest with him," he says as he gets to his feet. "Demand what you want, be it answers, action, or both. Just as you did with me."

"I don't think I got anything from you if I remember rightly," I reply with a breath of laughter, remembering it as if it were yesterday. "You sent me packing just as you had with Emily."

"Just because you did not see how I responded to your demands, does not mean I didn't act upon them," he admits. "Had it not been for you coming to reprimand me that day, I do not think Monty would be with us today. And I would not have begun to see through the lies that were being told to me."

"Oh," I reply with surprise over his admission. He simply nods to confirm everything he just said. "And I suppose without Monty, you almost certainly would not have won my sister around."

If I look close enough, from a certain angle, I can see a hint of a smile on his face.

"Don't procrastinate, Elsie, do it today."

"Tobias?" I call out before he walks away, and he stops with his back to me. "Thank you for taking my advice back then, you make my sister very happy. I only hope to be just as happy one day."

"That depends on you as much as it does Edmund," he says, "do not keep everything bottled up inside as I once did. You were witness to how badly that can turn out."

"If your advice works, I shall deny all knowledge of this conversation," I tease.

"If you mention this conversation at all, *I* will be the one denying all knowledge," he replies with that tiny hint of a smile before walking away.

After a moment's pause to think, I close the piano and make my way over to the doors that lead onto the garden outside. Dark clouds have rolled in, making a blanket of grey across the sky that was bright blue only this morning. It feels ominous, so much so, I half contemplate putting off this conversation with Edmund until the sun is shining again. But then I would have to live with Tobias poking at me to have it sooner rather than later. Besides, I have gone and worked myself up for it now.

As I approach my sister and husband walking back over the field and through the garden gate, I try not to see how happy they are in each other's company. However, it is extremely difficult, and only has me feeling all the more angry.

"Elsie!" Emily beams.

I love my sister, I really do, but why does she always have to be so appealing to every man she comes across. She exudes happiness whereas I only seem to come over as stuffy and disinterested.

"Emily, Edmund," I greet them stiffly. "Might I have a word with my husband in private?"

"Of course," she says, giving Edmund a knowing look, then a smile for me. It more than gives away who the subject of their conversation has been. She pats my shoulder before making her way back to the house with Monty in tow.

I watch as she gets further and further away before turning to face Edmund again. This is not a conversation I would like to have in front of others.

"Elsie, I am so glad to find you, I wanted to –"

"Edmund, I refuse to draw this out a moment longer," I tell

him resolutely. He looks taken aback by my tone, but his perplexed expression will not stop me from having my say; it is long overdue. "I need to know what kind of marriage you are after; the constant change in your attitude towards me is much too much, and I refuse to allow anyone to play about with my emotions. Emily once did that with Tobias, and though it worked out well in the end, I am not Emily. I will never be Emily, so trying to turn me into her is futile."

"I know you are not Emily," he says, sounding hurt over the insinuation. "I do not want you to be Emily. I am sorry if you thought I was ever trying to do such a thing."

"Good," I reply with a firm nod of my head. "Because if you are still in love with her, or you are hoping I might be a good substitute for her, then I think it best we make the necessary arrangements for this marriage to be one for appearances sake and nothing more. I will not live in her shadow a moment longer."

"Elsie, when have I ever made you think that you are somehow lacking in comparison to her?" he asks, now beginning to sound just as angry as I am.

"Frequently…as a child. Even so, you never once looked at me when she was still an option," I argue whilst crossing my arms like a petulant infant.

"Elsie, I cannot make changes to how I was in the past, I can only say that I am now a man," he laughs, which only makes me feel all the more vexed.

"Do not laugh at me, Edmund Barton!" I snap, throwing my arms down by my sides. Fat drops of rain begin to fall from the sky, and a sudden chill hits the air; it feels as if the weather is flowing through me.

"I apologise," he says gently, stepping in closer towards me and looking right into my eyes. "Let us get inside before it really starts to pour."

"I am quite content outside; I will not put this off a moment longer, I can't!" I fluster, now pacing from side to side. "You cannot make me; Lord Boreham never would have made me doubt his feelings for me."

"Lord Boreham would have had you locked away in silence for the rest of your life. You would have been a pretty thing on his arm and nothing more."

"But I wouldn't be left feeling so…so…" I close my eyes tightly, ball my hands into fists, all the while feeling as if I could scream at any moment. "Undesired!"

"Elsie," he says, grabbing hold of my arm before I can stomp away. I refuse to open my eyes, even when his other hand reaches for my wrist, so we are now face-to-face, and getting soaking wet in the heavy rain. "Elsie, look at me."

"No," I gasp, shaking my head, if only to convince myself to not give into him until I have some sort of answer that I can accept.

"Lady Barton, open your eyes for your husband!" he demands, pulling me towards his body, his breath now fanning my face.

"No, not until—"

Before I can finish my sentence, he pulls me against his lips and kisses me. My face instantly relaxes as he parts my mouth so he can kiss me more deeply, just as he had in my room. My hands are thrown around his neck so he can wrap his own around my body, with one of them moving up to the back of my head which is now thoroughly wet. It becomes so rapidly wet, my hair soon becomes stuck to my face and neck. His tongue moves against my own with such a pressure, it feels as if he is finally letting go of all his gentlemanly restraint and showing me what he really wants from me. I emit a moan at the same time as my entire body slumps against his, to the point whereby I think if he were to let go, I would melt onto the ground. He moans too, and I feel the same hardness below that I had felt in my room earlier today.

"Time to make you mine, Lady Barton," he whispers with his lips still so close to mine.

"Here?" I ask, just loud enough to be heard over the rain.

"And risk another man seeing you in a manner that is only reserved for me? Never!" he says before bending to pick me up so he can carry me back to the house.

We look at one another virtually the whole way there, through the house, up the stairs and into my room. He does not show any strain and when he finally places me back on the ground, he shows no sign of having exerted any energy whatsoever. Edmund is strong, so much stronger than I ever thought he was.

"You are shivering," he says softly while turning me away from him so I can see the rain still pouring outside, the garden caught in a waterfall of wind, rain, and grey skies. "I know how to warm you though."

His lips brush the side of my neck, and it begins to heat me up already. His fingers start caressing my neck, then trail down my wet skin until he finds the fastenings of my dress, which he begins to undo without any need for assistance. As he pulls it down over my arms, his warm fingers trail over my skin, leaving goosebumps in their wake. Next, he removes my stay, releasing me from its confines to leave my true self to be exposed. My skin is covered in small bumps that are a combination of cold and excitement. He kisses my neck again, moving along the entire column and shoulder, allowing me to indulge in his touch. His fingers move to the swell of my breasts, touching softly before he reaches my peaks that feel so hard, they verge on painful. My breathing intensifies and my heart pounds between my ears, but I want it; I want him to claim me like I am more than the mask I wear. This is for him and me, *only* him and me.

"Turn around for me, Lady Barton," he whispers against my ear, and I smile.

When I face him, he is already beginning to remove his wet jacket, but I stop him with my hands.

"Please, let me?" I ask, to which he smiles his silent answer.

Taking my time to study his breathing, his facial expression, and the way his body flexes beneath his wet layers, I remove his jacket over his shoulders. In fact, I remove each piece of clothing in much the same way until at last, I get to take in his naked torso. Flawless, smooth muscle stares back at me and I marvel at it.

"Do you approve of me as much as I approve of you, Elsie?" he whispers before cupping my face between his hands and kissing me chastely on my parted lips.

"I want to see more," I reply, looking down to the waistband of his trousers, wondering what lies beneath.

"And you will, but not before I see you," he says, bending

upon his knees as he begins to unfasten what is left of my clothing. I should feel nervous, but I cannot, not when it is Edmund looking up at me. Instead, I feel impatient for all that he has to offer me.

Before he releases my final petticoats, he closes his eyes and kisses my stomach, and my hands sweep through his damp hair. As the fabric of my final layer drops to the ground in a pool of damp cotton, he leans back to take in all of me. He says nothing, just stares. Does he like what he sees?

"Exquisite," he murmurs as his hand reaches to sweep through my curls below. I gasp over the sensation but still want more, so much more. I am not left waiting for long. His fingers move through me, and I quiver. However, then he does something completely unexpected, something Emily never warned me about. He begins kissing me right where he has been touching me. I open my mouth to protest, but then he looks up at me with those beautiful brown eyes, and it is enough to reassure me and to trust what he is doing. As I close my mouth again, he holds on tighter to my hips and shuts his eyes to continue his kissing.

It is strange at first, and I question what it is I am supposed to feel from this, but then he flutters his tongue over a bundle of nerves, and I gasp over the deliciousness of how it feels. I sense him smile against me, as though he has found a weak spot that will have me falling apart around him. I wobble on my feet, losing hold of my centre of gravity as he works against me, so he lifts my leg and places it over his shoulder, which only causes his movements to feel all the more intense.

"Oh…oh, Edmund, something…something is building within me," I say, sounding pitched and not quite myself. But something is indeed coming, building to a peak, of which I am not sure I will recover from if I reach it.

"Let it go, my love, it is beautiful," he says before returning to his work.

"But…but…"

My words are instantly lost as a release of something entirely euphoric hits me.

"So sweet, Elsie, all of you is so sweet," he says as the sensation ebbs away and I am left feeling dizzy from it. He moves away before getting to his feet and kissing me with a reassurance that what just happened, was supposed to happen, and happen without shame. "You look beautiful, even more so than usual."

"I-I do?"

He kisses me before lifting me inside of his arms again, his eyes holding me captive until he lays me down upon the bed. I watch him stand before me and slowly remove his boots and trousers, so I am able to study all of him. When I see what is hard and waiting for me between his legs, I get my first bout of nerves. Emily informed me of how we are supposed to come together, but looking at him has me questioning how I shall ever take something like that inside of me. He runs his hand along the length of it before moving towards the bed.

"Here," he says as he takes hold of my hand and wraps it around him. It feels soft to touch; rigid, but soft. I look into his eyes as I explore him, questioning my actions, though he only looks all the more excited by my touching him. I can see how much he is enjoying it.

"I am nervous," I admit, "I'm not sure if I will do it right for you."

"Elsie," he begins as he climbs onto the bed and lies

between my legs, so we are staring into one another's eyes. "This is about *us*, not me. I have never been with a maid before."

"You haven't?" I ask with shock in my voice.

"Believe it or not, my darling wife, I have only been with two women, and both were ladies who were well used to the male body."

"Oh," I reply sheepishly. "I assumed you had been with a number of women. Did it hurt them?"

"No," he whispers as he leans in to kiss me chastely on my lips, "but you might find it does the first time…or so I have been told. But I shall be as gentle as you need me to be. I love you."

My eyes bulge and my mouth gapes open over his words, to which he smiles.

"I have been afraid to tell you for fear I was undeserving of you, but you are right, I am only hurting the both of us by denying what I so dearly want with you."

"How can you be sure that you…you love me?" I ask.

"Because you chose me, Elsie Barton, you chose me, and no one has ever done that before. When you took my ring with that smile on your face, when you blew caution to the wind and kissed me in your room, I knew I was supposed to be with you; never your sister or anyone else, only you. Ever since that first kiss, everything has only become that much clearer to me; fate was pushing me towards you, and only you."

"Edmund," I whisper as I touch his handsome face. He kisses my fingers before leaning in to kiss my mouth, making it deeper as his hardness presses against my nerves below. "Do it,

Edmund, make me yours once and for all. I can think of nothing I want more."

As he kisses me again, his hand moves down to position himself before he finally pushes inward. A stinging sensation has me gasping with pain and he stops. He looks at me and strokes my bottom lip with his thumb, then moves his hand to move across my face in gentle strokes.

"Relax, Elsie, relax and let me take care of you," he whispers. I take a few deep breaths before nodding and he moves in further. "Keep looking at me," he says as he pushes in, and I breathe deeply. I keep staring into his brown eyes and it helps; I feel entirely safe with him; he has my complete trust.

"I feel so full," I tell him with nervous laughter.

"I am completely inside of you, and it feels so right," he says before kissing me again. I reach up to kiss him back, so he wraps his arms around me. As our kiss deepens, he begins to rock his hips against me, his hardness moving in and out, opening me up bit by bit. We move like fluid, and I can no longer tell where I end, and where he begins. We are finally one.

Soon, we are moving together, fast, and deep, and I kiss him with a need for more, to reach that peak again, only this time, we go together. His breathing is quick, as is mine, and when I stare into his eyes, I cannot remember seeing anything quite so beautiful. He catches me staring and smiles.

"Jump with me, Elsie," he says as he reaches his hand down between us and begins touching me again. It is too much, too intense, and I fall without realising I was even close. But from the moan that escapes his lips, deep and guttural, he has fallen with me.

His thrusting against me slows before he stops altogether and rests with his forehead against mine. We slow our breaths and I feel a sense of belonging like I never have done before.

"Hmmm, I am in love with my wife," he laughs against me, his eyes still closed, but his expression ridiculously happy. "I never thought the day would come when I would be making love to a woman who is not only my wife, but someone I am in love with. So, so in love with."

His eyes burst open and the amber in them almost sparkles.

"Me?" I whisper.

"I have no other wives." He smiles before kissing me and I laugh with relief and happiness and everything I thought I'd never have. "Yes, of course you, Elsie."

"Say it again," I plead, "say you love me and only me again."

"I love you so much, I am not sure how I will ever leave this bed," he declares, and I indulge in the sublime happiness that has me laughing again.

"And I love you," I finally admit. "The boy who made me cry on my sister's birthday; I love him."

"He was a foolish boy, but I promise the man before you more than knows how much you are truly worth," he says before wrapping me up within his strong arms. "Elsie Barton is mine; all mine."

I smile against his chest, finally feeling like the true me can be happy. As long as this man loves me, I don't need anything else. Just him.

Chapter 16

Edmund

"Do you know, I am quite tired," I declare in the drawing room after a delicious dinner with Emily, Tobias, and my beautiful wife. I theatrically stretch my arms high into the air and feign a loud yawn that fools no one, least of all Elsie. Her cheeks glow brightly, almost as much as the candle flames. "I think it might be time to retire to bed; how about you, Elsie?"

"Nonsense," Tobias intervenes with a devious smile on his face. "You can at least have one more drink with me. And I know Emily has been meaning to show Elsie her newest piece on the piano."

"Stop it!" Emily giggles, nudging her husband, which only causes my poor wife to heat up with embarrassment even more. "Do you not remember our honeymoon period?"

"I recall we spent it hating one another," Tobias replies with a shrug of his shoulders.

"You know what I mean," Emily tuts, "stop being so cruel."

"Only if you are feeling tired too?" he says with a quirk of his brow.

"I am always tired, Your Grace," she says with a smile that always makes me feel as if I am intruding on a personal moment between them. When I look away, I see Elsie smiling in much the same way as her sister, encouraging me to get to my feet and escort her to bed…*our* bed.

Elsie

I will never get used to the way my husband looks at me when we are connected like this. My sister was right, this act we perform is nothing short of beautiful, and I relish it each and every time. Finally, I have someone who looks at me the way Tobias looks upon Emily, the way my father looks at my mother, the way every hero looks upon every heroine in every love story. And I look back at him in exactly the same way.

As his hands grip hold of mine, his body thrusts deep and slow inside of mine, all the while my hips arch to meet him more urgently. My mouth begins to gasp for breath as a deliciously torturous sensation begins to ebb and flow through my body. Edmund smiles at me with arrogance, knowing I am about to explode with pleasure at any moment.

"How did we go so long not knowing how much we mean to one another, Elsie?" he pants, his hips slowing so as to prolong our intimacy.

"I could answer, but I am afraid it would spoil the moment, Edmund, and your body feels much too good for me to risk that."

"Always so smart," he laughs before cupping my cheek and kissing me so deeply, I forget what we are talking about and release without even giving my body permission to. I pull back to emit a gasp of intensity, my eyes remaining on his handsome face as he takes pleasure in my reaction to him. "That's it, my love, that is what I love to see."

"Edmund…" I call out, sounding pitched and breathless.

His hands suddenly grip hold of me to the point of pinching my skin while his body convulses against mine, releasing a heat that spills down my thigh. It takes him a few long moments to recover, and it is only when I laugh against his spent body that he eventually rolls off to one side. He looks at me in such a way, it chips away another piece of doubt. I chose him, and maybe he did choose me after all.

"I love you, Elsie Barton, always," he says, stroking my cheek.

"Suddenly, I cannot wait to be in Witney," I admit, "building a home of our own."

"Well, it just so happens I received a letter this morning from Phillip," he says with a beaming smile. "The roof is finally watertight, so we can return as soon as we are ready." He leans over my chest to kiss me with equal parts passion and adoration. "Are you ready, Lady Barton?"

"Yes," I whisper before kissing his soft lips one more time. "I am ready to follow you anywhere, Edmund."

Elsie

My sister is trying her hardest to not look too relieved to be having her house and husband back to herself. Edmund and I are packed up and ready to finally begin our new lives together in our own home. I laugh at her, for truthfully, I am relieved too. Although I have enjoyed our honeymoon period, and I have more than appreciated having my sister's house in which to work out how much we really mean to one another, I am more than ready to take the next step with Edmund.

"I expect you to write as soon as you arrive," Emily says with mock sternness to the both of us.

"We will. Perhaps not straight away, but soon, I promise," Edmund says with a mischievous glint in his eye. That look tells me he will be taking me to his private quarters as soon as is humanly possible.

"Of course, brother-in-law," Emily replies, sounding both cheeky and unsubtle. "My sister is a lucky lady. Though, so are you."

"Believe me when I say I am more than aware of that fact," he says with the softest expression; one that has me inwardly swooning. "However, we must depart. I believe your husband's eyes are in danger of rolling right out of his head if we do not leave soon."

"Oh, come now, Barton, I have a cold exterior to uphold, one that only comes down for my wife and son. However, I will say this, it has been mildly entertaining to have had you here. Particularly Elsie's forcing you to finally mature into a man."

"Thank you, Tobias, I think," Edmund laughs as they shake hands.

"Treat your new wife well and you will be happy, trust me," he says before bidding Elsie adieu.

"I agree," Emily adds, "you are only as happy as your wife is. However, I know Edmund, he will see you right, sister."

"I know, for I have known him as long as you have, Emily," I reply before she grabs hold of me in a tight embrace. "Give James a tight squeeze from me when he wakes."

With nothing further to add, we embark the carriage and

make our way down their extensive driveway. My husband holds me tightly, and I feel a comfort I know I can never better. I already feel at home because I have him by my side.

Edmund

I have to concede I am an awful host to my new wife when we first arrive, for I do not even bother to show her around the property before carrying her off to our bedroom, where I keep us busy for several days. We only leave to eat and to at least pretend we are going to do something more productive. However, every time we reach the staircase, I abandon my tour and lead her back to where I have my wicked way with her. Though, she does not complain, and even looks a little forlorn when she thinks I am going to break with this new tradition of ours. Life is bliss and it is all thanks to her.

It isn't until a week has passed that we decide to properly acquaint ourselves with the staff and our surroundings. I am but a little ahead of Elsie when it comes to knowing my new estate, but I am sure we will have fun learning about the ins and outs of running such a place together.

"Phillip," I call over, still sitting at the head of the table where we have just enjoyed breakfast together. He immediately shuffles over with a serious expression and a sharp nod of his head. Elsie brings her hand up to her mouth to cover her smile. It feels a little like we are playing at being adults, this being our first time living away from our childhood homes with one another.

"Yes, My Lord?" he replies.

"Perhaps you could arrange for my wife and I to have a proper tour of the place," I tell him, to which he dutifully nods his head. "And a proper introduction to the housekeeper and staff."

"Of course, My Lord," he replies, "I shall ready it as soon as possible."

"Wonderful, we shall meet you in the entrance hall." I smile at him, but he remains looking emotionless. "Whenever you are ready, Phillip."

As soon as he has shuffled out the door, I cannot help but laugh with Elsie.

"I think you are going to have to work your charm on him," Elsie finally says when we have managed to stop our giggling. "He hasn't quite worked you out yet."

"Come here," I whisper, looking at her like I so often have over the last few weeks. She makes a show of rolling her eyes but the way she rushes over to where I am sitting tells me she is just as keen to have me wrap my arms around her. And I oblige as soon as her legs hit my lap. "Do not forget you will have the housekeeper to deal with. If she is anything like your mother's housekeeper, then you are in just as much trouble as I am."

"I have already met her," she says with a haughty smile and a kiss upon my lips, which I take deeper before forcing myself to release her. We must not give into our lust today; tonight, however, is a different matter.

"You have?" I ask, still staring at her swollen lips.

"Mmhmm," she confirms with a nod, "she came to introduce herself when I met Lucy, my maid."

"Where was I?"

"Still sleeping," she replies. "I took the opportunity to get dressed in my own room."

"Your *own* room! Your room is *my* room," I gasp with feigned insult. "Do not think you will be sleeping anywhere but with me, Elsie Barton."

"Relax, husband, it is merely somewhere to keep my clothes, my personal belongings, and whatever secret items I wish to keep from you."

"There will be no secrets between you and I," I whisper, kissing her again. "But what was she like?"

"So far, extremely nice," she says with a superior expression. "And she seems to love me already."

"There is no need to sound quite so haughty about it," I tease, "I will have Phillip smiling at me before the week is out."

"We'll see," she says before getting to her feet and holding out her hand for mine. "Come, let us go and explore!"

The house is beautiful, especially now there is no mould spreading across the ceilings. The builders have done an excellent job; it was money well spent. I still cannot understand why my cousin decided to leave this place to decay and ruin. Elsie is more than awestruck when she walks through the various rooms which will take some time to memorise. It isn't much smaller than Tobias' estate, and I still haven't been around all his rooms. After a while, she even begins to look a little overwhelmed, so I decide to call it a day and break for tea. We have the rest of our lives to get used to this place; it need not be a chore to get around it all.

"Shall we break for tea on the lawn?" I suggest.

"Wait," Elsie says suddenly, "can we see behind this door?"

She motions to an old oak door that is a little shabbier than the rest; it has been well used. I smile at her, for this door is intriguing. Who used it so much, and why?

"What is behind this door, Phillip?" I turn to ask my frowning butler.

"Er…that was your cousin's study," he says, looking a little worried. "No one was ever allowed inside. I have walked in there perhaps once or twice to see if it too, needed repairs. Other than that, it has been left as it was."

"Oh," Elsie says with curiosity in her voice, "that is very respectful of you, Phillip. Perhaps we should leave it too?"

"Nonsense," I reply, readying myself to laugh at the two of them. "Dear old cousin William is dead. I am not going to have some shrine left to rot inside of this place. We want to have a family one day, and I won't have our home being a place of morbid sentiment or fear."

"Very well, My Lord," Phillip utters, though I cannot be sure if he approves or not. I suppose it is not his place to say. He then takes out a large metal ring with many keys rattling together, all of them different in shape and size.

The door creaks open to reveal a musty odour and a room full to the brim with books, papers, journals, and…pictures. Lots and lots of pictures, as well as the paints and tools needed to create these works of art. It looks like half a study and half an artist's studio, all merged together in a messy and careless manner. I never knew my cousin was an artist. Though, in truth, there is much I didn't know about my cousin – why did he never marry? Why did he stop seeing my family? Why did he become such a recluse?

"Edmund, look at these, they are breathtaking," Elsie says as she looks through a pile of parchment drawings and canvases.

"I have to admit, they are," I agree before turning to look at Phillip again. "Was it widely known that my cousin was an artist?"

"No, My Lord," he says, resting his hands behind his back. "Though, *I* knew he was extremely keen on his hobby. He spent many hours in this room. In fact, this is where he was found when he…died. His hand was resting upon the drawing that is still sitting on top of the desk over there."

I waste no time in marching over towards the desk in question, where half a drawing is sitting, forever remaining unfinished. The subject looks familiar. All the pieces look familiar, for they are all of the same woman. The woman that is hanging in pride of place on the wall opposite. It takes up most of the space, but is so incredibly beautiful, it almost does not look big enough.

"Who is she?" Elsie asks before I can even get the same words out of my own mouth.

"I am afraid I do not know," Phillip replies, almost too quickly. I immediately suspect that he is not being entirely truthful with us.

"*Annie*," Elsie says from where she is standing at the corner of the painting on the wall. "It says 'Annie', just above his signature. I thought your cousin remained unmarried?"

"That is correct, Lady Barton," Phillip says. "Refused every attempt his parents made to try and match him."

"Do you suppose there's a story here, Edmund?" Elsie turns with excitement on her face.

"I believe there must be," I grin back at her. "Phillip, perhaps we could go to the town to meet some of the local inhabitants this afternoon? See if it might shed some light on the mystery of who 'Annie' is."

"Y-yes…of course, if that is what you wish, My Lord," he replies, looking as if he would really rather not.

"Excellent," I declare, telling him that is exactly what I want to do, whether he approves or not.

"If you look closely, Edmund," Elsie says, turning her head to the side with a frown, "her face…there is something extremely familiar about it."

I smile at her sweet expression before looking into the eyes of this mystery lady. They are richly brown, the same colour as my own. My smile morphs into something else, something I am not sure feels altogether comfortable.

Elsie

A few hours after the discovery of 'Annie', Edmund and I are casually walking through the town, greeting many of the people who work on the estate, as well as their families. We are eyed curiously but otherwise, everyone appears to be friendly and unperturbed by the new 'Lord of the Manor'. It helps that Edmund greets each and every one of them with a beaming smile and a genuine welcoming attitude. He has always possessed the ability to charm anyone to his will, from all walks of life. He never comes across as haughty, and I cannot ever recall him being rude, not since Emily's birthday party when we were still very small children.

"Ah, and this is Ruth Langford; she is perhaps one of the most educated inhabitants of the village," Phillip announces. The small woman jumps with surprise when Phillip booms from behind her. She turns with a smile upon her face and places a hand to her chest. She is of a similar age to Mama, and I automatically feel comforted by her presence.

"You speak much too highly of me, Mr Benfield." She laughs breathlessly from behind her gloved hand. "I *am* Ruth Langford, however."

"Good afternoon," Edmund says as he removes his hat politely. "I am Edmund Barton, and this is my lovely wife, Elsie Barton. We have just moved into the Colten estate, it had belonged to my cousin—"

"William," she says, now staring at Edmund as though he is a ghost. I even see her fingers twitching to reach out for him. They stare at one another for a moment or two, and if I am not mistaken, she looks as if she might be getting ready to burst into tears.

"Are you alright?" I ask from the side, distracting them both from staring at one another.

"Erm, yes, I am so sorry," she says, now bowing her head. "I did not realise I was in the presence of a lord and lady. Forgive my poor manners."

"Don't be silly," I nervously laugh, staring at Edmund with wide eyes that are telling him to do or say something to reassure this woman.

"How did you know William?" he asks, ignoring my unsubtle gestures.

"I didn't…I mean…not since childhood," she replies with a red hue spreading over her cheeks.

"How fortunate to have met you," I exclaim, forgetting the awkwardness of just now, "we have a mystery on our hands. Would you happen to know who 'Annie' is?"

Edmund

It is at this point I notice Phillip looking down to the ground, shuffling his hands as though something awful has happened. Suddenly, I do not want to find out who Annie is, neither do I want to be here, with this woman who obviously knows something about my cousin that I am not privy to.

"Come along, Elsie, I fear it is getting late," I tell her, hoping she notices the anxious tone of my voice.

"Edmund, we're just about to get some answers," she says with a furrow of her brow, "and besides, Ruth is—"

She turns to look at me, still gesturing towards the woman in question, but when she sees my pleading expression, she simply nods her head and smiles.

"Perhaps you are right," she says with another reassuring nod of her head. "However, I would love to hear more about the town. Would you be willing to come for tea tomorrow?"

"That would be lovely, though, I insist you come to my house," Ruth replies, looking a lot more relaxed over the change of subject. "Mr Benfield knows where I am; perhaps he could escort you here. Shall we say, eleven o'clock?"

"I look forward to it," Elsie replies sweetly.

Hours later, in the privacy of my cousin's study, I find

myself staring at his painting. The woman's eyes hold me captive with all the unanswered questions that have come into my head since the moment we stepped in here.

Who are you? And why do you make me feel so uncomfortable?

Chapter 17

Elsie

"Your home is beautiful," I tell Ruth, for it truly is. Her garden is just as breath-taking as the grounds on Edmund's estate. It is on a much smaller scale, but it is no less alive with a mixture of scents, colours, and the sound of buzzing from various insects. It all invades my senses in the most delicious way. And as for the company? I have never met a more aimable person. She reminds me of Elizabeth, but with a much softer tongue. I can tell we are going to be great friends.

"Thank you, I do love to tend to the garden," she says whilst pouring tea, her hands looking too delicate for those of an avid gardener. "I suppose Maybrook House has many gardeners to tend to the extensive grounds. I remember the rhododendrons being especially beautiful at this time of year."

"It is more than likely, though I cannot say, I have yet to see anyone beyond the household. We only arrived a few days ago," I explain, indulging in my first sip of tea. "We have been staying with my sister and her husband in Kent."

"You seem very happy with Lord Barton," she comments, and I smile because I am. "A marriage of true love?"

"We grew up together, though it was my younger sister he favoured, right up until she was married last year. It has taken some time to convince me that he has now relinquished those feelings and instead, bestowed them upon me."

"Perhaps it was fate?" she says with a teasing smile, and I laugh.

"Fate," I repeat, thinking about it. "Funny, I have never put much stock in such beliefs as 'fate'. I cannot deny, however, it has taken a series of unusual events to get us here. So perhaps you are right."

"I suppose some things occur through fate, whilst others happen through outside manipulation," she says rather cryptically, looking off into the distance, as if caught in a dream. "Apologies," she eventually says, as though forgetting herself, "I read a lot of philosophical texts and my mind wanders without me meaning it to. Please, ignore my ramblings."

"Sounds fascinating," I comment, "I would love to read some of these *texts* myself, one day."

"Oh, in truth, they are rather tedious most of the time," she smiles. "I often have to spend many hours wading through all the waffle of professors and so-called experts before I get to the parts that truly matter. But what would I know? I am merely a woman."

"Quite," I reply with a knowing look. "Your parents must have been quite progressive to have let you study so extensively."

"My mother always wanted me to have a good education, and my father always wanted to please my mother, so that is how my studies began. *Fate* deemed I would take to studying like a duck to water. I practically consumed anything I could get my hands on. When Mama died, my father was already beginning to suffer from an affliction of the mind. He needed a lot of care. Since I was not married, nor did I have any hint of a suitor, I made the decision to care for him myself."

"Is it just you and him? In this cottage, I mean," I ask tentatively, for it is a personal subject.

"Yes, has been for decades," she says with a smile that tells me she is not sad or disappointed by it. I should imagine she was more than willing to give up on marriage in favour of a life dedicated to caring for her father, all so she could continue with her studies. "Before he fell ill, he had been a minister. He had savings as well as this house; we have been more than comfortable."

"You are happy to never have married then?" I clarify, thinking about Elizabeth and how she lives with some regret over the almost very same situation.

"Honestly? Yes," she says with a soft laugh, as though admitting to such a thing is somewhat shameful. "I never looked at boys and felt any sort of adoration beyond friendship. I often thought of marriage as a chore, a sacrifice, an irritation. Do you think that makes me sound wicked?"

"Not at all," I tell her truthfully. "I was beginning to think I would end up the same, though, I must confess, I have always wanted love and a family of my own. I am not sure I would have been as content without them. I am grateful that *fate* or whatever it was, finally brought Edmund and I together."

"Speaking of which, how is Lord Barton?" she asks with caution in her voice. "He seemed a little off-colour yesterday."

"Truthfully, he is not himself at all today," I tell her sadly. "He was missing for half the night. I think he was in William's study where there are countless pictures of the mysterious 'Annie'."

"I see," she says as she places her teacup down on the table.

"You know who she is, don't you?"

"I do," she replies with melancholy in her voice. "Annie died many years ago, and that is all you need to know. My initial reaction was only due to the fact that we were once very good friends. William too. I miss them, that's all."

"So, Edmund has nothing to worry about?"

"Edmund?" she says with confusion in her voice. "Of course not. Annie has nothing to do with him."

"Oh, Ruth, you have no idea how glad I am to hear you say that." I laugh softly; my head feeling a little dizzy with the relief. "I was beginning to worry. And now I can reassure him, and we can return to normal. Speaking of which, now that we are becoming more settled into our new home, I am going to need something to occupy myself. I was hoping you might be able to inspire me."

"Of course, I am happy to help," she says jovially.

"Thank you, Ruth," I tell her as I place a genuine hand of friendship on top of hers. "I hope we can become good friends too."

Elsie

Two months pass by in a blur of falling more and more in love with my husband, as well as making a great friend in Ruth. We have taken to reading books and discussing them at length, as well as exploring the local area where she points to all the places that hold special memories for her, including those that include William and Annie. She mentions another boy, Samuel, but only very rarely. I wonder if they had once been lovers, for she soon changes the subject if I try to delve any deeper about him.

Edmund appears to have let go of his anxieties over Annie and has stopped visiting William's study. It now remains locked, with Phillip keeping hold of the keys. I suppose it will need clearing out soon, but for now, it can be forgotten about. I do not wish to uncover any more secrets, and neither does Edmund.

It is now Sunday, and we are engaged in what lovers do when they are alone in bed together. As I move on top of him, our naked bodies connected in the most intimate way possible, I indulge in the sensation of his hands massaging my breasts while his hips thrust slow and deep. I could spend all day with Edmund inside of me, filling me up in the most delicious way possible.

"I never want to stop, Elsie," he groans, and I smile, for I feel exactly the same way.

"Then don't," I pant.

"I cannot help it, you feel much too good for me not to," he grins before his teeth clench together, trying to hold off his release. His thumb finds my sensitive spot, my weakness, and begins to circle it so I am left gasping for breath. "Come with me, Elsie, please!"

With a pitched noise that falls from between my lips without meaning to, I feel my release, with his following not long after. His hands squeeze at my chest, and I momentarily freeze in rapture. Within moments, Edmund grabs hold of my waist and pulls me to the side so he can rest on top of me, and kiss me in such a way, I do not doubt his love for me.

"How did I live without you, Elsie?" he whispers between kisses.

"I honestly have no idea," I reply with a mischievous smile. "What are you up to today, husband?"

"Besides this?" he teases before pulling at my earlobe with his teeth. "I need to go into the town. You?"

"I think I might stay here today; I have felt quite tired over the last week or so," I tell him truthfully. "Perhaps I have been overdoing things with Ruth."

"You are not unwell, are you?" he says with concern written all over his face, then places the back of his hand to my forehead. "Perhaps we should call a doctor."

"Don't be silly, Edmund, I am fine," I laugh at him as he wraps his arms tightly around me.

"Your health is far from silly, Elsie, you are my life!" he says, igniting such a feeling, the sting of tears has me wiping my eyes.

"And you are mine, but I promise you, I am just tired," I try to reassure him.

"I love you."

"And I love you, Edmund. Now go!" I order, pointing towards the door with a stern expression. His laughter tells me I cannot be doing such a good job of it, but at least he is no longer looking fretful.

Edmund

I cannot help but walk through the town with a spring in my step. My life feels as though it is finally falling into place, with a beautiful wife whom I love with all my heart, a grand country estate, and hopefully soon, a baby on the way. Elsie and I have been intimate virtually every day since arriving here, and her sudden bout of fatigue and sickness could be the result of our love making.

With a smile on my face, I look up to see a man who I now know to be Ruth Langford's father. I have never spoken to him before, though I am more than aware of his ill-health. With that in mind, I decide to make myself known, and to assist him back to Miss Langford's house, should he need rest.

"Good morning, Sir, it is wonderful to meet you on this fine day. My wife has been telling me so much about you and your family. She's been spending quite a lot of time with your daughter, Ruth Langford."

"Ruth? My Ruth? Oh, yes," he flusters, and I half wonder if he had forgotten who Ruth was when I first mentioned her name. However, then he looks at me for a few moments, as if studying my face, my stature, my very soul. "I-I...My God!" the old gentleman finally gasps, and with a paling complexion.

"I'm sorry, have I said something out of turn?" I ask with a confused furrowing of my brow. He looks positively green, though I wonder if this is a symptom of his condition. Perhaps I should run back to Miss Langford's cottage for some assistance. After all, he has no idea who I am. "My name's Barton, Edmund—"

"I know who you are, you're William and Annie's boy!" he declares, pointing at me with an expression of relief over finally having worked out as to where he knows me from. Alas, he must have me confused with somebody else. Surely, he must.

"I am sorry, I do not know who you are talking about. My parents are called Charles and Jane, and they reside in London."

"Such a lovely couple," he says with a sad look in his eyes. "Poor Annie, and William. He never got over what happened to her. Lived up in that big old house all alone, just mourning the loss of his one true love."

"You're talking about William Colten, my mother's cousin."

"Yes, of course, your father!"

"Papa!" an agitated voice comes from behind me. I turn to see Miss Langford walking up to grab hold of his arm.

"Please forgive the ramblings of an old man, Lord Barton, he rarely knows what he's talking about," she rushes out in an attempt to brush over this shocking revelation. However, his 'ramblings' have already reignited a fear that had taken hold the very day after Elsie and I had arrived at Maybrook House.

"Forgive me, Miss Langford, but his words were more than the simple 'ramblings' of a confused man," I reply with a less than friendly voice. "He knew my cousin, William Colten?"

"Why, my little Ruth was Annie's best friend," the older gentleman cuts in, looking as though he is lost in the memory. "She, Annie, William, and Samuel, all as thick as thieves once upon a time. Course, that all changed when he was sent away to school."

"Father, will you please stop?!" Ruth snaps. Unfortunately for her, the angry expression she is now wearing more than gives her away. She looks far too flustered for this revelation not to be true.

"Miss Langford, he does not sound 'confused' to me," I tell her with a harsher tone of voice; I will not be lied to. "Do you know something about my family history?"

"It isn't my place to tell you what your family obviously chose to keep from you," she says sadly. "Some memories are best left to rest."

"You have her eyes, you know," the old man says with a wistful look upon his face. "Poor girl; she was so in love with your father."

"Father!" Ruth practically growls at the old man.

"I have to get back to my wife, but this isn't the end of the matter, Miss Langford," I tell her with a distinctively cold tone, one to rival even that of Tobias. "I will not have a stranger knowing more about my family than I do, is that clear?"

"Yes, My Lord" she murmurs, looking to the ground with a contrite look on her face.

"Good day," I declare, tipping my hat before marching away in the opposite direction. I would like nothing more than to interrogate her further, but I cannot manage that right now without losing a hold of my senses. I have not felt quite so anxious since discovering Greyson's plan to use me against Emily and Tobias.

As soon as I reach the estate, I head straight to William's study to look at the portrait we had discovered when we first arrived. I stare at the woman's picture, focussing on her face, her eyes in particular. Do they look like mine? No, it's impossible! My mother is Jane Barton, the most wonderful woman in the world. And my father is Charles Barton, not William.

"Edmund?" Elsie says softly from the doorway.

"Elsie," I gasp as I turn to run into her arms, seeking reassurance from the one true and constant thing in my life. I take her in, all of her. Her smell, her skin, her comforting squeeze of my back. How could she ever have questioned my love for her when I need her so much?

"Edmund, whatever is wrong?" she asks with obvious concern in her voice. "Please, tell me; you're scaring me."

Her words convince me to pull away so I can show her that I am well, that she has nothing to fear. It is me who is questioning everything I thought I believed to be true. *Who am I?*

I lead her over to the desk and tell her everything, even though the very words have me feeling sick. For a moment, she says nothing, just stares at me with shock taking over her beautiful blue eyes.

"Edmund," she eventually gasps, "I do not even know what to say. They must be mistaken, surely?"

"I would have thought so too, but you said so yourself, this woman has something familiar about her. And look," I tell her, pointing to the corner of the painting to where the artist, William, has named the canvas 'Annie'. "What if the reason for my parents' falling out with William had something to do with this? And what if Stephen knew about it too?"

"We don't know anything for certain yet, let us take a moment to breathe," she says calmly, her hand palming my face to try and soothe me. I take her touch for all its worth; my mind is a storm of uncomfortable thoughts and I need her now, more than ever. "Tell me what you need, Edmund."

"My wife, a bed," I tell her with a smile, to which she laughs at me. I kiss her with a hunger that tells her what I need.

"Well, now, that I can give you," she says as she takes my hand to lead me away from the portrait that is now taunting me with the secrets it knows.

Elsie

It is not long until I am straddling my husband, letting him take what he needs from my body. His hands trail up and down my back as I move against him, his lips worshiping my chest with sweet kisses that have me wishing this moment could last forever. Here, we are connected, safe, and undeniably in love. I can make him forget his troubles while he kisses away my fears. Fears I am yet to admit to him. But the moment I feel my release with a moan that escapes without warning, I know I must tell him.

"Darling, these moments have me wondering how I ever lived without you," he says as he continues moving me against him. I smile over his words, even though I am still scared of losing this, all of this.

Before I can respond, he wraps his arms around me and pulls me underneath him so he can take me how he wants to, hard and fast, right up until he releases a moan of his own. How did I ever live without this? Without him?

When we finally come apart, lying side by side, I take in his relaxed face, his beautiful smile, and instantly know that this is the time.

"You look happier," I tease, but it is enough to make him laugh and kiss me. I love him all the more during these moments.

"I am always happier with you, though…" He trails off,

now looking a little concerned. "You look worried, Elsie. What are you hiding from me?"

I open my mouth to say something, but the words don't come. When they are finally out in the open, it will make them all the more real.

"You understand that withholding information from your husband is a punishable offence," he says with a boyish smile, which I cannot help but kiss. However, he pulls away with a stern look on his face. "You cannot get out of telling me that easily, Lady Barton. Talk to me, Elsie."

"I do not wish to put any more stress on you, Edmund," I sigh heavily, brushing back his brow that still holds a layer of perspiration. "You are already so troubled."

"Elsie Barton, how do you expect me to not worry about my darling wife when something is obviously vexing you?" he says, taking me into his arms and kissing my shoulder. "I am not letting you go until you tell me."

"I have stopped bleeding, Edmund," I finally admit. "Nothing since we got here, Edmund, two months!"

"Wait, are you telling me…?"

His hand drops down to my stomach with his brow furrowed and his mouth hanging wide open in shock. I give him a shy smile and a shrug of my shoulders.

"Are you telling me we are expecting our first baby?"

"I think so, yes."

"Oh, my God! I had suspected, but now that you have said it… Elsie, this is amazing news!" he laughs with a look of pure joy on his face. "I am going to be a father? And you will be a mother? Our own family!"

I nod my head before he wraps his entire body around mine and begins kissing me wherever he can. I laugh nervously, trying to enjoy this moment before I admit how terrified I am. I have always wanted a family, and to have it with someone I love as much as I do Edmund, it is like a fairy tale come true. And yet, I am fearful of what is to come; both the physical and the emotional side of having a child.

"I am scared, Edmund," I eventually admit with a hard swallow of fear. "I have wanted this ever since I can remember; a wife and mother were the roles I was brought up to have. But what if I am no good at it? What if I am too cold, too soft, too everything?"

"Firstly, you are already the greatest wife I could have ever asked for," he says, delivering a soft kiss to the tip of my nose. "Secondly, you will be the best mother you can be. The fact you are worrying about it is more than enough to convince me you will be just as great as a mother as you are a wife."

"You promise to tell me if I am not good enough? If I am making mistakes?" My nervous questions have him brushing my hair away and smiling with adoration.

"Even though I cannot see me ever having to do such a thing, I promise," he whispers. "But only if you promise to do the same for me."

"Thank you," I utter, still with my lip trapped beneath my teeth.

"Elsie, talk," he says, nudging my lip free.

"I am afraid of when the time comes to...for the baby

to…*come out*?"

"Oh," he says, looking more serious and understanding of my terror.

"Emily told me how much it hurt and how scared she was," I sigh sadly. "She also told me how Tobias' mother died."

"Elsie, do not feel ashamed for having such fears," he says softly, "I can understand why you feel the way you do. What women go through to bring life into the world is truly amazing. I cannot tell you it will not hurt but know that I will be there every step of the way. Even if I am ordered out by some stuffy physician, I will insist that I remain with you."

"Be there? Watching it all?" I ask, sounding entirely shocked over him offering to do such a thing. "You will be thrown out!"

"I would like to see them try," he replies indignantly. "You and I are in this together, and if I want to be there to support my wife, and to see the birth of my first child, then I will argue with anyone who tries to stop me."

"Edmund…" I whisper as I touch his face with pure adoration. He kisses my fingers before returning the same look of tenderness to me.

"Elsie, you are one of the strongest women I know; you could do it all on your own if you had to. But you will never have to find that out because we are in this together."

"I love you, Edmund," I whisper.

"And I adore you, my darling wife, and mother-to-be," he says before wrapping me up inside of his arms.

Chapter 18

Elsie

The following day, as I lay facing my sleeping husband, a deep frown etched between his brow, I decide to go and visit Ruth. I cannot sit by and let Edmund sink further into the depths of anxiety and confusion. If she is privy to information about his origins, he deserves to know that information too. I have never understood the reasons people give to keep others in the dark. If only people were honest, half the world's problems would vanish within an instant.

I kiss Edmund's cheek one more time before climbing out of bed to get dressed. I automatically look down to my stomach, where I only now begin to notice a small bump beginning to form. A mixture of excitement, disbelief, and worry runs through me, so I look at Edmund to try and strengthen my resolve to push it all aside and instead, focus on my mission. He rolls over and reaches out to where I was just lying next to him. His frown only deepens the longer his hand cannot find me.

"Elsie?" he mumbles, making me laugh softly over the muffled questioning in his voice.

"Shh, go back to sleep," I whisper as I bend to meet his face with a chaste kiss.

"Whatever are you doing getting out of bed?" he mumbles, his eyes unable to stay open.

"I have things to do, My Lord," I tut at him. "I cannot be lying in bed all day like my lazy husband."

"You should be resting," he says as he flops over onto his back, his arm blocking the sunlight from his eyes. "You and our baby."

"It is not certain if there is a baby yet," I reply, even though my stomach is clearly beginning to show that there is. I keep that to myself for the moment, for he will be all over me if I point it out to him. He needs rest and I need answers. He can fuss over our growing baby later.

"I shall need to write to my mother and father; perhaps you should do the same," he says as he begins dozing again. I laugh at him before kissing him goodbye.

I choose to walk to Ruth's house, it being such a lovely day, and the fresh air will quell my nausea. Stanley trots by my side, snapping at the odd butterfly that flies too close. Luckily for them, he doesn't have the same ability to jump as he once did. Though, I cannot deny that our new home has definitely put more of a spring in his step. He loves it here, as do I.

Ruth's cottage is a little further out than the rest of the houses, and its garden is more extravagant. The lavender hits me first, just before the honeysuckle. I breathe it all in with vigour, enjoying scents that remind me of childhood, my mother, and a time when I was beginning to take more notice of the world around me. A short window before I was schooled in the ways of being a lady, when notions of being the favourite child was still blissfully unknown to me.

Movement from inside tells me Ruth has already spotted my arrival, which is confirmed when she opens the door with a nervous smile on her face.

"Good morning, Lady Barton," she says, dipping her head.

"I thought we had gotten past all of this, Ruth," I tut as I walk inside of her quaint cottage. "How is he today?"

"In a good mood," she says with a sigh of relief. "And…er…how is Edmund today? I am afraid I upset him yesterday."

"Oh, he is well now," I reply, "I told him he was soon going to be a father."

"Oh, Elsie, do you mean to say…?" she gasps, glancing at my stomach with expectation.

"I believe so," I tell her as she leads me over to a small table with an old tea-set that looks as though it could be a family heirloom.

"And how are you feeling?" she asks, pouring the hot water into one of the cups for me.

"Nauseated most of the time, though I cannot tell if that is through pregnancy or fear," I admit. "I have always wanted a big family, but I am also worried about so many things."

"You will need to see Nancy; she deals with all the babes in town. I am sure Edmund will want you to see a physician, and you should, but Nancy has so many years of experience working with expectant mothers. You will be well taken care of with her."

"Yes, of course," I reply, feeling a little overwhelmed by all this talk of doctors and babies. It only makes it all the more real.

"Elsie, there is something else I must tell you, though, I feel it only fair to speak with your husband first," she says, snapping me out of my troubled thoughts, only to wander into new curious ones.

"Does it have something to do with William and Annie?" I whisper her name for fear of Edmund being able to hear us all the way from his bed. It feels as though I am betraying him in some unspeakable way.

"I am afraid it does," she says guiltily.

"So...so it is true? Edmund is the son of William and Annie?"

"I have already said too much," she says, rising to her feet. "However, your...*condition*, it makes it necessary to reveal all that I know. I did not think this would happen so soon, but it was inevitable, I suppose."

"Why? What does my condition have to do with Edmund's past?" I ask with panic in my voice. If I was scared before, I am absolutely terrified now.

"Please, Elsie, I must talk to Edmund first," she says with her own anxiety coming to the fore.

"Then, we go now," I declare, making it clear there is no room for argument. I will not be kept in this state of fear for longer than is necessary.

"Yes, of course, the sooner the better," she says, placing down her teacup and pacing past me to grab her things. Her agreement should bring me some form of release, but it only has me feeling all the more anxious over what she is about to reveal.

Edmund

At first, we all sit in silence, all frowning over what is about to be revealed about my family history and where I came from. It is becoming worryingly clear that who I believed to be my mother is not the same woman who gave birth to me. My whole life has been a lie.

"I want you to understand that I have kept quiet under William's wishes," Ruth eventually says. "Though, from what I have heard, it was his desire to have you know before he died. Your parents fell out with him because of this, which is why you have not come to visit him in over a decade. As for Annie, she loved you more than you will ever know."

She becomes tearful at this point, putting her teacup back onto the table so she may use her handkerchief to dab at her eyes. She and Annie were obviously very close, and I almost feel sorry for her. However, the need to hear all outweighs any empathy; that and Elsie's peace of mind over our growing child.

"Please, tell me everything," I half-beg, half-order, to which she drops her hands onto her lap and nods.

Chapter 19

Annie

"5, 6, 7, 8, 9, 10, I'm coming!"

I run for the trees first, knowing this is the kind of predictable place Ruth will have hidden. She is so timid; she will never attempt to be more adventurous than the obvious. Where she is clever with facts, figures, and knowledge, I am brave. I go after what I want, always, regardless of my social status or gender. Father taught me to be fearless, just like him. I see her within moments of entering the small forest behind us, her skirt swaying because she cannot even manage to stay still when she is trying to be inconspicuous. I begin to walk towards her, but then I think of my best friend and how she is always found first, so decide to leave her till last. Why should she not win every now and then?

I make a show of pretending to look behind some other trees before about turning and heading to the herb garden where I suspect William will be hiding up in one of the old oak trees. The smell of basil will always remind me of our playing together. I see his foot hanging down almost straight away, it being housed in the finest shoes out of us all. We are but sons and daughters to servants, even Ruth, who is the daughter of a clergyman, compared to William who is the heir to the Colten estate and title. He will be an Earl when his father dies, as will his son, and his son after that. However, William never ever lets on that he is considered better than us. To him, he is just one of the group.

I sneak around the back of the tree so I can creep up on him, holding my breath so he won't suspect I am anywhere nearby. When I see his back leaning over the branch, trying to look out for me coming, I smile to myself, then cover my mouth to stop the laughter from escaping. In my head, I count to three before reaching out and shouting, "Found you!"

"Ahh!" he screams with his face turning ashen and his eyes bulging from the shock of it. Within moments, he is laughing with me and nudging my arm with his elbow. We both sit upon the branch with our legs dangling down, facing the fields of the Colten estate, taking in these last few moments of it being just the two of us. I will never admit it to the others, but William is my favourite, he always has been.

"I don't want to go," he says sadly, making the smile drop from my face. He is to travel to London tomorrow to begin his schooling. We all knew it was coming, but now that it is here, I cannot seem to make my peace with it. Part of me is jealous of his opportunities, but most of me just knows how much I am going to miss him. "I want to stay here with you."

"And Samuel and Ruth?" I correct him, with a small laugh that lacks any true mirth.

"I meant what I said," he simply says, taking hold of my hand.

"You will have so many adventures, William, you'll soon forget all about us," I reply in barely more than a whisper, for I can already feel the ache of a large lump lodging inside of my throat.

"Never you, Annie," he says with a strange look on his face that causes me to blush. "Can I…may I kiss you, Annie?"

"What? No!" I gasp, even though I want to say yes. "Mama has told me not to kiss anyone until I have a ring on my finger. She says kisses must be saved for your husband, and your husband only."

"Oh," he says, sounding somewhat disappointed. I am disappointed too; I would dearly love to kiss him. A kiss to get me through all the days without him. A kiss to savour for the rest of my life. The only kiss I can have with my one true love. William is not meant for a girl like me; he will marry the daughter of a viscount or some other such lady. I do not think I will marry at all, for there is only one boy in the world I would consider marrying. But I cannot have that boy.

"But I will tell you something, William, future earl," I utter, looking deep into his eyes so I can try to memorise them.

"What is that, Annie?" he says with a charming smile. Only thirteen years old and already armed with the talent to render a girl silly.

"If I had to kiss any boy, it would only be you," I admit, ignoring the heat on my cheeks. He smiles with dimples, and it is simply breathtaking.

"Then, one day, I will marry you," he says with a quirk of his lips. "I want to be that husband for whom you save all your kisses."

"We both know you will never be allowed to marry me," I sigh at the same time as I nudge him again. "I am far too lowly for the likes of you, William Colten."

"You are lower than no one, and you will be my wife one

day. But until then," he says, lifting my hand to his mouth and kissing it with a touch that makes me shiver, "promise you will wait for me."

"Always," I reply with my eyes closed for fear they will release tears I do not wish him to see.

William

My bags are packed, my final dinner with my parents eaten, and my goodbyes already given to everyone I hold dear. I shall miss everyone but no one more so than Annie. I meant what I said to her in that tree yesterday; I will return to make her my wife. I might be young, but I already know she is the love of my life. I do not care what anyone else says, my parents or society, I will marry the girl my heart has decided to gift itself to.

The carriage is being loaded up with my bags as we speak, and I am just about to step inside when someone catches my eye. I laugh to myself before asking my father for just a few moments to say my very last goodbye. He side-eyes what has caught my attention and smiles. He then nods his head and steps back to let me run over to Samuel, who is now peeking from around the corner of a nearby tree.

"I cannot believe you are running off to London and leaving me to the mercy of a couple of girls to play with," he pouts.

"Oh, please, Sam, you are secretly loving the notion of having two pretty girls all to yourself. Besides, have you not seen the way Ruth looks at you?"

"Ruth?!" he practically spits, looking utterly affronted by the suggestion. "Me with a clergyman's daughter? Unlikely. I think I am more fit for someone like Annie, don't you think?"

The mere suggestion has me clenching my jaw and balling my fists, but I say nothing; my parents are watching, and I know for a fact my mother has excellent hearing. Besides, I trust Annie more than anyone else in the world. She would never go back on her word.

"Annie is far too much for you, Sam," I reply with a fake smile.

"Hmm, I don't know," he says, teasing me with what he has obviously come to realise about Annie and me. "She's extremely pretty. I would be a good husband to her one day, especially when you desert her to go and court debutantes."

"Annie is not for you, Sam," I whisper through my teeth, "leave her alone!"

"Alright, alright, I'm just teasing," he laughs, and I finally begin to release some of the tension from my muscles. "Though, you know she will never be for you either. Your parents will never allow it. Seriously, I would hate for you to set her up just to have to watch her fall; that wouldn't be fair, William."

"Let me worry about my parents," I tell him as I hold out my hand to shake with his. He stares at it and quirks his lips to the side before wrapping his arms around my shoulders. I laugh as I hug him back. "Look after them both will you?"

"Of course," he says before we let go of one another. "Enjoy London."

"Goodbye, Sam."

As the carriage moves away and down the long gravel driveway, past the grand gates to our estate, I notice a flurry of white cotton and curly dark hair. There, my Annie stands, waving at me. I wave back and notice her weeping, just before she kisses her hand and blows it to me. She kissed me after all.

Annie

Five years later

"Annie? Are you even listening to me?" Ruth nudges my arm from beside me and I cannot help but laugh at her. The sun is warming our faces as we lie in front of a willow tree on the banks of the river running through the Colten estate. Our days of playing hide and seek are long gone, along with any promises William had made before he left for school. His visits have become more and more fleeting over the years, meaning time for his old riff raff friends has been practically non-existent. I shouldn't have been surprised that he moved on from his childhood love for me, but I was, nonetheless. In fact, it was heart crushing; it still is.

"I cannot relax, we shouldn't even be here," she says with anxiety in her voice.

"Oh, please, Ruth, we used to be here all the time," I sigh contentedly under the afternoon sun.

"Years ago, when William still wanted to consort with us peasants," she huffs, being angry on my behalf. We keep nothing from one another. "What a cad to have made such promises, only to break them as soon as you were out of his vision."

"Ruth, we were children," I reply, even though I feel

devastated every time his name is brought up. "I should have known he would find better things."

"You should marry Samuel; he's asked you enough times, the man is practically obsessed!"

"Urgh, don't remind me, he came to ask my father for my hand last week," I grumble. "My father said it was up to me. He's now trying the heavy-handed approach."

"I don't follow," she says with concern in her voice.

"He tried to kiss me against my will," I admit, to which Ruth's mouth gapes open in dismay.

"Well, then, he's a cad too!" she huffs at the same time as crossing her arms in outrage. "Cads, all of them!"

I cannot help but laugh over her outburst; she is usually so prim and proper. William isn't the only one who has changed since that game of hide and seek. When Samuel turned fifteen, he became quite an angry young man. He would rage about William and how he had left us all behind; he missed his friend and the sting of what he saw as betrayal grew bigger with each passing year. At sixteen, he decided I was meant for him, that William had practically gifted me to him. It hurt to hear this, for how could I argue with it?

William or not, my heart did not pine for Samuel in any way. I politely declined and decided to have Ruth tutor me in the hopes that one day, I might become a governess or a nanny. I do not want to spend my entire life in the fields, and I know that without William, I am never going to marry. Alas, Samuel hasn't taken my rebuttal quite so well.

"Seriously, Annie, are you safe? He wouldn't try to hurt you, would he?" Ruth asks with deep concern in her voice.

"I am not afraid of Sam," I tell her with a long sigh, "he is all mouth and no action."

"Hmm," she simply murmurs, relaxing back onto her elbows. "As long as you are sure. What a shame it is that boys have to grow up into such foolish creatures."

"Indeed," I agree before we both fall into laughter, though mine is not as joyful as hers. William may well be foolish, but what does that say about me when I am still so hopelessly in love with him?

A few hours later, when the day is turning into dusk, and I am sitting in the tree William had promised to marry me in, I allow myself to think about him and what our life could have been like if he had kept his promise. How many children would we have had? Would he have given up his title and riches? Or would his parents have come to accept our love? A childhood fantasy, but it is mine, all mine. I might not have William in the flesh, but in my mind, which was once full of fairies and magical whimsy, he is my husband, and I am his wife.

When the light finally disappears behind the horizon, and not even an orange glow is left behind, I concede to leaving this tree and heading off home. Mama and Father will already be in bed by the time I get home, but it is late, and I have an early morning, followed by a session of studying at Ruth's house. She has taught me how to read and write and now she is teaching me basic arithmetic. I must admit, I'm rather enjoying it. Numbers have an order, a logic that appeals to me. Had I been a boy, perhaps I could have become a bookkeeper.

As I wonder back through the woods, following a well-worn path and listening to the hoots of owls as they pass messages to one another, I hear another sound. A sound that shouldn't be here in the middle of the night. Galloping hooves thudding upon the dry, compact earth are growing louder and louder from behind me. I have always considered myself a sensible girl, though in this moment, I lose all sense and freeze in a kind of rigor mortis. Only my lungs are working at double their usual rate, as well as my heart that is beating so vigorously, it is almost as loud as those hooves.

When I finally manage to turn around to see what monster is virtually upon me, I have but fleeting moments before a gloved arm is reaching out and lifting me clear off the ground and onto the galloping horse. Its master is hard to make out, for he holds me in such a way, I cannot see his face, only the trees ahead of us. I think I should scream, but who for? No one is out in the woods at this time at night.

We ride for what feels like miles, to the point whereby I feel my heart is sure to give out. It isn't until we finally reach a clearing, where a large pond lies still, that my captor finally steadies his horse and comes to a stop. I only feel all the more terrified, for now the journey is over, what is to become of me?

I am carefully placed onto the ground where I back away a few steps, just as whoever it is dismounts on the other side of the horse. The tension builds as I wait for him to round the beautiful beast and reveal himself. The intensity of the situation becomes so much that I find myself shouting.

"Show yourself, whoever you are," I cry out. "At least let me look upon the face of the man who intends to do me harm."

A low chuckle hits my ears, which only has me gasping for breath.

"Shh, Annie, I mean you no harm," he says, finally

stepping into the moonlight to reveal his identity. "I did not wait all this time only to hurt my future wife."

"William?" I ask the obvious now that he has shown his face, but I can admit, I am deep in shock to see him here before me in the flesh. How many times have I dreamt of a moment like this?

"I am glad I have not changed so much you do not recognise me," he says as he walks up to cup my face. "But I must say, you have changed considerably, Annie; you have grown more beautiful."

I am lost for words, mesmerised by the boy who turned into one of the most handsome men I have ever looked upon. Tall, broad, chiselled features, and raven black hair; a true Prince Charming.

"You…you…you utter cur!" I yell at the same time as shoving his chest with all the anger and resentment I have been holding onto since he left me.

"Annie, I don't under—" he flusters all the while I begin stomping away from him.

"No, of course you don't understand, you arrogant swine," I continue shouting as I round on him. "You thought you could just show up after years of barely anything, capture me, utter a few charming words, and I would melt into your arms? You…you…you beast!"

"Annie, if you would just give me a moment to explain –"

"What? That you needed time to have your fun? To live your life while I waited patiently for a boy who would never come?"

"No, it wasn't like that at all –"

"As if I could believe a single thing you say, William Colten, you broke your promise when –"

His lips seal over mine, drowning out my words with a kiss that is so immensely breathtaking, I am ashamed to say I am unable to stop it. In fact, my hands find his head and run through his deliciously soft hair, all the while his fingers cling to my back with desperation. He tries to part my lips with his tongue, as is the way some men do with their wives, or so I have been told, but that's when I see sense and pull back with a scowl upon my face.

"You stole that!" I cry with accusation and with my finger pointing at him, looking venomously in his direction.

"I did not," he says with an arrogant smile on his face. "You said all your kisses are saved for your husband; I am to be that husband, just as I had promised. I hope you have kept your promise too, Annie Houghton?"

"What on earth are you talking about?"

"Are you still a maid?" he asks, quirking his eyebrow at me, as if in chastisement.

"How dare you! Of course I am still a maid," I snap with a horrified expression.

"Good," he says as he bends down upon one knee. "Then, Annie Houghton, will you do me the honour of becoming my wife?"

"What! Are you crazy?" I try to shout, but the words come out pitched and weakened through shock alone. "You abandoned me, Samuel, Ruth, all of us. You do not even know me; I am not a twelve-year-old girl who you can make empty promises to anymore."

"I couldn't see you without consequence, Annie, my mother knew I had feelings for you. You were the first name upon my lips whenever I returned home. I was told that if I ever came to visit you, your father would lose his job, and your family would be evicted from our land. I refused to risk that and lose you for good. At least this way, I knew exactly where you were."

"Then why now?" I ask with suspicion still in my voice.

"Two reasons; one, I have been planning this for quite some time, Annie, everything is finally in place. Secondly, do you not think I haven't been watching you, making sure you are safe and happy? I know Samuel is desperate for your hand, and he is beginning to lose patience. I can no longer sit by and let him man handle you as he has been."

"Wh-what plan?" I ask, now sounding more curious than suspicious.

"My plan to marry you, Annie," he says softly, stepping cautiously towards me, as if I am a wild animal that needs reassuring before he attempts to rescue it. "I have two friends who are setting off to Europe for a whole year; my parents think I am going with them. They have agreed to write once a month, pretending to be me. I have secured a small cottage, miles north from here, Annie. Nobody will know who we are; Annie, we can live freely. I can obtain work, as can you…well, up until we have a family. By then, of course, my trust fund will have kicked in—"

"A family?!" I gasp. "William, do you know what you are suggesting? You'd be giving up your birthright…for *me*! A girl you haven't spoken to in years."

"You are still the girl I always knew I was going to marry," he says, reaching out for my arms. "You and Ruth get together every day, straight after you have worked in the fields, to improve upon your reading and writing. You cook, but always burn the bread. You told your father you couldn't marry Samuel because you had promised your heart to somebody else. You still cross the boundary into my family's private grounds because you like to lie beneath the willow tree when it is warm. You climb the old oak tree most nights, just to remember that last time we had spoken properly to one another. You look beautiful with your hair tied up, or down, or wet, or even when you have just gotten out of bed."

"William...?" I whisper, unsure as to what to say; he never forgot about me.

"And as for my birthright," he utters as he wraps his arms around my back to pull me in close, "none of it matters without you. You are everything I want and more. All of this," he says, gesturing around him, "is nothing but bricks, mortar, dirt, and air. You are my heart, Annie Houghton."

"We have spent many years apart, William," I say with a smile I cannot help but let come to the surface. "We were but children when we made those promises."

"And yet, we both kept them," he says before kissing the end of my nose. "But if it would please you, let us spend some time getting to know one another again. Right here, at sundown, each night. By the end of the week, you can decide. Accept my proposal or say our goodbyes for good."

"And if we are discovered?"

"Only my mother has the wherewithal to know what I am up to, and she is in London for the next two weeks. Do not worry, Annie," he says while brushing my cheek with a gentle touch that has me wanting to melt into him, "I have spent years planning how to keep my promise to you."

"Then, yes," I finally agree with his reassuring eyes smiling down at me. "Let us get to know one another all over again."

"I will bring…strawberries," he whispers with a smile. "You always loved strawberries."

"I still do."

"I know."

William

Truthfully, I had expected that to go less smoothly. Annie must be softening with age, for she never would have let me off so lightly when we were children. She would have put me in a head lock until I sang out my apologies for the entire village to hear. But after that kiss, I know she feels just as strongly as I do.

I have been watching Annie over the years, keeping my eye on her ever since my mother forbade me from seeing her again. I have seen her transition from child to woman, right alongside my own transformation. Truthfully, I did not form my plan until I saw Samuel badgering her to marry him. It was the wake up call I needed to make sure I could keep my promise to the woman who was always destined to be my wife.

That being said, Annie is right, the girl always has been, I do need to court her as a man, not rely solely on our memories of being thirteen-year-olds. She deserves nothing less; I am only sorry I cannot treat her as the lady she clearly is, if not by birth, by every other way. She is more than any debutante my mother has tried her hardest to match me with. As if I would ever agree to such a relationship with anyone other than Annie. Annie Colten - it has a nice ring to it. Speaking of rings, I have a date with a jeweller who I hope is as reliable as our family's usual man. My grandmother's ring needs to look as stunning as the girl to whom I'm going to give it to. My grandmother loved me more than my father tenfold; she would have approved of the fact I am going to marry for love rather than status.

"Your Lordship," a familiar voice rings out with clear contempt. "Buying yet more jewels to adorn your holy body with? Should have known you'd turn out to be just another foolish rich dandy who would rather be with other similarly rich fools. How disappointing."

"Samuel," I reply sadly, ignoring his cruel words that would normally have a man of my position castigating him for speaking so out of turn. But I am not like most other men of wealth and title, I am...*was* his friend, and I abandoned him to make sure Annie's family would not be cast out because of my affections for her. My father is ridiculously arrogant, but he is not as nearly as vindictive as my mother. She would destroy an entire family if it served a purpose.

I turn to face him with a sorrowful expression, contrasting completely with the sneer upon his face. I feel equal parts guilty and angry with the man I now see before me. I wish I could have been the friend he needed all the while his father beat him senseless for not working hard enough. But I am also furious with him for taking advantage of my absence, when I could not be here for Annie, the girl I had asked him to look after. I cannot blame him for falling for her, especially when Ruth made it clear that she was in no way interested in boys, marriage, or romance. Of course, he would fall for Annie. But when I saw him pulling at her, trying to put his lips all over her, even when she had turned down his rather aggressive proposal, it took all my willpower not to intervene. In truth, I would have, had it not been for Annie's ability to fight him away by herself.

"I saw you galloping away with my future wife, Colten," he snarls, like a rabid dog that needs to be put out of its misery. "Stay away from her, Colten!"

"I apologise for not being here for you, Sam, but when it comes to Annie, you know she was always going to be mine," I snap, trying to rein in my temper. "And I'll thank you to keep away from her, especially when she has made it perfectly clear that she does not return your affections."

I turn around, ready to walk away before things turn ugly. Though, when a hand grabs for my shoulder, I realise things have already turned bleak for mine and Samuel's friendship.

"You'll never marry her; your pompous family would never allow it. To lead her on like this is cruel. I understand rich people like you do not consider the feelings of those of us who you deem to be beneath you, but I genuinely care about her."

"Then learn to accept her answer, Sam, she doesn't want you!"

He lunges for me with so much force, we end up on the ground, scuffling around in the dirt. The man becomes positively unhinged; he has his father's temper, which is nothing short of heartbreaking. However, it is something I refuse to let Annie be a part of. His teeth are clenched, bared like a wolf getting ready to attack, and the whole time, his hands are wrapped around my neck.

"Le…l-l-let…go!" I try to scream; however, it comes out more as a muffled gurgle. As the world turns blurry, and I feel moments away from blacking out, I give in and use a cowardly move to force him to release his grip. I reach out and squeeze an area that is sure to have him howling in agony.

"Y-you will never have Annie," I cough and splutter as he rolls onto his side, clutching at his manhood. "Even if she turns me away, I will make sure you will never have her. She deserves more than the monster you have become. Touch her again and I will make sure you are taken far away and never seen again. Do you hear me, Samuel Riley?"

"Well, if…" he splutters, in between emitting curses that he can only have learnt from his father's evil tongue, "…if I cannot have her, Colten…you won't either. I promise you that!"

With those threatening words, he slowly gets to his feet, spits at the ground before me, and hobbles away. This is just another reason to execute my plans for Annie and me as soon as possible.

Annie

When I find myself walking through the woods, just after dusk, I begin to feel exceedingly excited over the prospect of seeing William. I then feel ashamed of myself for letting him badger me into this strange outing, and for wanting to run away with him like he suggested we do last night. I was going to confide in Ruth during our study session, however, I couldn't seem to find the right words. Whatever came to mind would only make me sound even more ridiculous than I already feel. Ruth is scholarly and has no interest in marriage and family. How could she possibly understand my weakness when it comes to Lord William Colten?

My troubled thoughts are stopped short when I notice dozens of candles lighting up the clearing in front of the pond. They illuminate the nighttime bugs as they become hypnotised by the light. It is breathtakingly beautiful, like a fairy tale. Is this all this is? A make-believe fairy tale that belongs in the pages of fiction? And is the handsome prince of a man before me just a notion of fantastical thought leftover from childhood?

"Lady Houghton," he says with a smile that tells me I have a look of awe clearly written all over my face. "I trust you are well on this fine evening?"

"I am, at least for the moment, Lord Colten," I reply, playing the role of a debutante. "Though, I am a little worried about all of these open flames about the forest floor. It is positively irresponsible of whoever it was that decided to leave all these candles amongst the kindling."

"You do not approve? I thought it was rather romantic," he says as he begins to walk towards me with a boyish twinkle in his eye. "Besides, being with you in the pitch dark of night might have proved much too tempting for me to remain gentlemanly. You wished for me to court you, so this is me courting you as you well deserve."

"Ah, well, in that case, court away, My Lord," I reply with a theatrical curtsey.

"Are you sure? I am happy to be ungentlemanly with you too," he says, now standing right in front of me and looking positively mischievous.

"No, you are right, Lord Colten, I should allow you to court me properly," I say, reluctantly taking a step back with a wide smile on my face. I cannot help it; he brings out the silliness in me. He always has.

William

Hours later, and we both seem to have lost track of time. I have not laughed this much since leaving this place as a thirteen-year-old boy. But now the birds are starting to sing their dawn chorus and I realise, we must have fallen asleep. It is the most perfect sight; Annie lying across my chest with a contented smile on her face. I kiss her chocolate-coloured locks before rearranging her on the blanket beneath us. I then walk over to my bag and retrieve my drawing tools so I can capture this moment in all its glory.

I have tried to draw Annie many times over the years, but never with her being so still, providing the perfect model pose for me to replicate on paper. When we are finally married and living with the freedom to be together in the light of day, I will paint her. For now, however, I shall use charcoal.

She does not even stir once while I draw, racing against the light of the sun, knowing we need to get going before we risk being discovered. I even finish before she finally opens her eyes that sparkle with disorientation and momentary confusion when she sees me sitting before her, charcoal still in hand, my fingers moving across the page to make some final adjustments. It could never compete with the real beauty before me, but I have to admit, it is one of my better creations.

"William?" she says as she moves into sitting up, rubbing her eyes and looking inexplicably adorable. "It is morning; what are you doing?"

"Well," I begin as I move to sit beside her, where I encourage her to lean against me, cradling her within my arms and kissing her soft hair again. "I was taking advantage of being able to capture my muse without her fidgeting. What do you think?"

"Wait…that's me!" she gasps with shock, moving bolt upright and studying the image I have drawn. "William, when did you become so talented?"

"I could take offence to that question," I tease, to which she nudges me with her delicate hand. "At school, when I was missing you desperately, I decided to channel my frustration into something tangible. My first attempts were not so appeasing to the eye, so I had to take a few steps back and draw simpler objects, develop my craft as it were. I had wanted to give in a few times, but then I would picture you, folding your arms and telling me off for giving up, so I kept at it. This is the result of five years of practice."

"It is incredible, William," she says as she places one of her fingers on the edge of the paper. "The way you have captured the light and shadow is just…" She looks up at me and it takes all my breath away. This, here, with her, is all I want. "It is just beautiful, William."

I lean down and place my lips against hers, dropping my drawing so I can wrap my arms around her. Our kiss turns more passionate, more like the kisses I have been dreaming about. My will power dwindles to nothing as she allows me to move over her, sliding her slender body underneath mine. I feel my body ready itself to take her how it so desperately wants to. Her hands move into my hair, massaging my scalp so I lose all sense of reason, logic, and the potential consequences of what could happen if I took her now. She deserves a ring on her finger before she allows me to have her like I want her.

"Marry me?" I whisper, mere inches away from her silky lips.

"You know I will," she replies with her fingers still moving over my head. "I promised, remember?"

"Then, we leave tonight." I smile before kissing her again because she is too perfect not to. "I have everything planned, even where we shall be wed. All you need are your things. Spend time with your loved ones, but do not mention a word of this to anyone."

"But Ruth?" she pleads.

"Once we are settled, you can write to her, I promise," I reassure her, even though I would rather we left and never spoke to anyone from here ever again. It is too risky. However, Ruth is like a sister to her, and I already made my peace with the fact that she would have to tell her. Ruth deserves to know; she's been there for my love when I could not be, and she is extremely trustworthy.

"You promise?" she says with her eyes melting my heart just that little bit more.

"I promise, and you know I always keep my promises," I tell her, just to make her smile.

Annie

The day is long when we finally make our leave for a new life, away from all that I have known. My family had not seen the tears that lined my eyes when I had wished them good night the evening before. Neither did they stir in the morning when I had whispered my final words over their sleeping bodies. They have been a good family, my parents more than fair, especially considering how most other girls are treated. Both my mother and father have a relaxed view on life, placing importance on happiness instead of social standing and appearances. I can only hope William and I are as content as they are after so many years of marriage.

I had cried once again when we passed by Ruth's cottage,

uttering silent goodbyes and thanks for being the best of friends. William cuddled me in tight, kissing my temple; he understood he wasn't the only one giving up important things to be together. But for him, I would give the world.

A short marriage ceremony had been arranged when we arrived in Edale, with a few witnesses that William paid handsomely. We wore the clothes we had travelled in and feasted on a simple meal from a local tavern, just the two of us. The ring he gifted me fit perfectly and I still cannot stop staring at it with a huge smile on my face.

The small cottage which William has purchased sits near the woods, on the outskirts of the village. It reminds me of home, which helps me stop worrying about what my parents must be thinking right now. I had left a note explaining the reason for my sudden departure, leaving out William's name, and hope they are not too saddened by my decision to leave them.

"Mrs Colten," William says from behind me as I release my hair down my back. His hands reach around my waist, pulling me against his front. A thrilling sensation shoots through me, one that both excites and scares me. "I have waited years to call you that."

"Mr Colten?" I smile, placing my hands over his. "Does that sound strange? To no longer be Lord Colten?"

"Nothing about today feels strange," he whispers before turning me in his arms to face him. He towers over me now, his height having taken over mine from the age of twelve. His physique is broad, strong, and suddenly so masculine. Our childhood is far behind us. "Do you know what usually happens now?"

My mouth turns dry all of a sudden, and the look of

wanting in his eyes has me feeling heady. He must see my anxiety because when I nod, he places a forefinger beneath my chin and offers me a reassuring smile.

"Perhaps we should wait," he says softly, "you must be exhausted, my love, my wife."

"No," I all but whisper, "no, I want to."

He searches my face for a hint of doubt, one I hope he doesn't find, because I am more than ready for the sliver of space between us to finally close.

"You are nervous?" he asks, still unsure as to whether he should seal our marriage by us coming together.

"Every girl must be nervous before their first time," I admit, "but with you, I am also desperate for it."

We both laugh over my admission, and he kisses my forehead with affection, reminding me that it is William, a man who is my friend as well as my husband and lover.

"I trust you with all of me," I whisper, and it turns the air serious, or dare I say it, momentous.

"And I with you, Annie," he whispers back before cupping my face and kissing my lips with every intention to take me like I want him too. "It is my first time too."

"It is?!" I gasp, sounding shocked, to which he laughs. "You never indulged in…I mean, in London…with all of its…*distractions*?"

"Why are you so surprised, my love?" he grins with his teeth, touching my lips with his thumbs, looking more handsome than he ever has before. "I told you I had kept my promise to you."

His voice then drops to a whisper as he leans in close. "How could I possibly have given any other woman my affections when I knew I was destined for the greatest woman in the world, Annie Colten?"

I search his eyes for any signs of falsehood in his declaration, but there are none. No more words are needed to pass between us to convince either of us that the time is right; the time is now.

As we kiss with equal parts passion and love, he begins to untie my dress, but shows his inexperience by not being able to complete the task without getting into a muddle. I smile as I step away and slowly undress myself in front of him, indulging in the hungry look in his eyes as he watches with fascination. With every piece of cloth I drop to the floor, his eyes grow darker, and when I am finally standing before him naked, his breathing has become more audible. He reaches his hands out, only to withdraw them a few times before finally touching me.

"Beautiful," he murmurs to himself as his hands run over my waist, up to my breasts where my nipples are hard, peaked, and my skin is covered in tiny bumps that do not speak of cold, but of nervous anticipation.

"Annie, you have taken my breath away," he utters as he continues to study my body like a beast waiting for a juicy bone. "May I?"

"May you what?" I laugh with nervous breath.

"May I kiss you here?" he asks as he places his fingers over my nipples.

"William, I am your wife, you may kiss me anywhere you so desire," I tell him, to which he smiles.

He leans in and places his lips on my hot skin, kissing me

chastely, exploring timidly. When I sigh over the sensation, he begins to move more confidently, opening his mouth to place his tongue on my skin, sucking on my nipple to the point of my gasping for breath. He trails his fingers down, down, to a place that is the most intimate part of all.

"Oh my!" I gasp as his fingers run through me and I grip hold of his shoulders.

"Am I hurting you?" he quickly asks, looking up at me with concern.

"No," I reply at the same time as shaking my head and he smiles.

"I want to…I mean…Annie…"

Before he can explain himself, he places his mouth over where he had just had his fingers and begins running his tongue through me. I emit a strange sound of desire at the same time as he groans against me. It feels…inexplicable!

He keeps moving his tongue over and over, kissing me like he kisses my mouth, and something begins to build, something I know I want to reach the top of. As he grips hold of my hips and presses even harder with his tongue, I finally reach my pinnacle, and a sensation of releasing overtakes me. I feel as if I might scream with the overwhelming feelings now running inside of me.

"William, stop, you need to stop, it is too much!" I pant as his movements feel much too sensitive. I try to pull him up and he lets me. His fingers reach for my cheeks, his mouth smiling when he sees what he has managed to do to me with just his kisses.

"Good?" he asks with a boyish expression on his face.

"Ridiculously good, William, so good," I fluster as I lean in to kiss him. "But now I wish to see you, all of you."

He steps back, maintaining eye contact all the while he begins his more hurried undressing. His clothes drop to the floor in little heaps, revealing more and more of the beauty that lies under them. A body of muscles that flex beneath his smooth skin, a scattering of dark hair covering his chest, and arms that look as though they could save me from anything.

"My husband is handsome beyond words," I tell him, and he blushes. "Please, continue."

He laughs as he removes his boots and pushes down his trousers, leaving him to be just as naked as I am. I see all of him, including the very thing that is to join us together as husband and wife. I cannot hide the nervous inhale I take when I stare at it. It is strange but also appealing at the same time. The very thought of which has me clearing my throat to try and breathe more easily.

"Annie," William whispers, sensing my inner turmoil. "Annie, I will be slow and gentle, and we can stop if—"

I cut him off by lifting my hand to his lips, stopping him from trying to talk us both out of this. I am afraid, yes, but I still want this more than anything. He keeps his eyes on mine as I reach down to take hold of him, my hand searching to become familiar and comfortable with it. His eyelids droop and his breathing quickens as I explore what is obviously so sensitive for him. He kisses me chastely as I continue moving up and down and all around him.

"Like this?" I ask, and he nods with heavy breaths. "Take me to the bed, William."

William bends to lift me up in the same way he had when he carried me over the threshold of our new home. This time, I do not giggle, I keep my eyes right on his as he lays me down and braces himself on top of me; his muscular, tall body caging me in as he slides between my legs. We kiss, we touch, we relax our fears and make promises to always love one another.

"Now, William," I whisper, and he nods, positioning himself before pushing inside. It stretches, it stings, it burns. "Oh..."

"Annie," he says as he pauses to let me get used to him, even swirling his hips in an attempt to open me up. "Relax, my darling, we have all the time in the world."

I breathe in deeply, looking into his eyes for comfort and reassurance. When I nod, he moves in further and further until, at last, he is all the way inside; we are connected as one. I even emit a giggle, proud of what we now are. I never believed this would happen; it feels like a miracle.

"I love you, Annie," he whispers as he moves his fingertips across my smile. "To think we might have lived our lives without one another, without this."

"I love you, William, I always have."

After these declarations, he moves, thrusts, and caresses, his hips massaging against mine as we pant, sigh, and moan with the pleasure we are taking from one another. We give, we take, we fall that little bit more in love. I hope it will always feel like this.

William

Eighteen months after we were married, Annie and I are living the life I had always wanted with her. I thank my lucky stars every day, for we have had relatively few problems. I work as a bookkeeper at a small firm, while my wife, Annie, stays at home to take care of our beautiful baby boy. It had not taken long for her to fall pregnant, probably due to how much we had remained confined to the bedroom in those early days of marriage. She enjoyed consummating our union just as much as I did. We still do. In fact, I shouldn't be surprised if she were to fall again in the very near future.

Edmund, our son, is only six months old and thriving. He smiles all the time and adores his mother. I cannot blame him; I feel exactly the same way about her. She is truly amazing to have come out of what was an extremely hard birth, for all of us. I know she still suffers from melancholy now and then, particularly when she thinks no one is looking, but she never shows this in front of our boy.

She writes to Ruth once a month, and Ruth always replies. Her father suffers from an affliction of the mind, making him forgetful and childlike at times, but also with sudden outbursts that can frighten his daughter. If things were different, I would offer to help, but I am no longer Lord William Colten. I am just William - husband, father, bookkeeper. And though I cannot help our dear friend, I am otherwise exceptionally happy with that.

"Edmund Colten, look at you, sitting up so strong," Annie coos while we picnic in the beautiful outdoors. It is the end of summer and the perfect conditions for a late afternoon tea. "You are so handsome, just like your father."

"That he is," I tease while playing with one of his toys with him. Annie has become very adept at sewing; she's even taken to mending clothes to earn some extra money. We are by no means wealthy, but we are comfortable. I have a trust fund, but I cannot take much without causing suspicion back home. Mother and Father still think I am travelling around Europe. I take out small amounts to save away whilst my wage pays for our living expenses.

"I wonder if he will have anything of me in him," she says contemplatively. I have to admit, my son is the spitting image of me.

"Perhaps he will have your romantic sensibilities, as well as your nurturing and loving heart," I reply before kissing the side of her head. She smells of herbs; she's been out in the garden, growing more food to supplement what we are able to buy.

"Do you have any regrets, William?" Her words instantly render me as still as a statue, worrying that she doubts my undying love for her.

"Annie, my darling wife, look at me. How could you possibly think I would want anything more than what I already have? You and Edmund are my life. I love you, Annie Colten."

"And I you," she says before kissing me so intensely, I know we will be trying for a sibling as soon as Edmund is put to bed.

William

As soon as we are home, Edmund is put to bed; he had fallen asleep on my shoulder on the way home, leaving a nice patch of baby drool. Annie and I then fall into trying to rip one another's clothes off, kissing and touching, trying to get as close as we possibly can before I can be inside of her. I am shirtless when someone throws open the front door, bearing a rifle and an unhinged look in his eye.

"Samuel?" I shout when I finally make sense of what I am

seeing. Annie immediately runs to Edmund's bassinette to soothe his cries. She then hurries over to me, places him on the bed behind us and stands beside me, the both of us shielding our son.

"Finally!" he shouts through gritted teeth. "I have been searching for a long time, but now I have you, Colten!"

"Samuel, please…" Annie whimpers when Samuel unlocks the barrel of the gun with a loud click.

"Silence, harlot," he growls, "you were supposed to be with me, not living in sin with this swine!"

"Annie and I are married; do not talk to my wife with so much disrespect!" I snap, not even thinking about the gun and what he could do with it.

"You are not the lord of the manor here, Colten, you are just as lowly as I am, as is your wife and bastard child!"

My heart beats with ferocity as a raw red rage blurs my vision. He smiles with menace, knowing he has ignited my fury. I move to run towards him, to release my anger and attack him, but I am immediately blocked by my wife's body, just as Samuel pulls the trigger.

"Annie?" I whisper as she lurches towards me. The heat of my emotions instantly turns cold and grey. She opens her mouth to speak, but instead of words, comes blood. She falls against me, and we sink to the floor in a clumsy heap. Blood seeps out of her chest, staining her dress crimson red, all the while her face turns the colour of fresh snow.

"Annie…no…I…" Samuel whimpers with shock in his voice. He falters for a moment before he turns and runs off into the night. Edmund remains crying but I cannot take any notice of it; the love of my life is dying right before my eyes.

"Annie, no, please!" I cry with such ferocity, I am shaking her dying body within my arms. "I love you!"

Those last three words seem to comfort her, and a sort of peace falls over her face as she reaches up to stroke my cheek.

"I...can't believe...I won't be...living this life...with you...both," she says, completely undoing me, and my cries rival even those of my infant son.

"Annie, don't go, please don't go!" I howl, shaking her to try and make her come back to me, even though it is hopeless; she is already passing on.

"I love...you," she gasps before falling limp.

I've lost her.

Our promises kept, but our lives forever broken.

Chapter 20

Elsie

When I finally look at my husband, I do not know what to offer or how best to respond. Comfort, first and foremost, or space? His expression is indescribable; I have never seen a man looking so lost before. His complexion has lost any colour he had left over from his travels, and his eyes are nothing short of haunted. His mouth is hidden behind his statue still hands, and if I look close enough, there is a slight trembling in his shoulders. *Oh, Edmund!*

"H-how do you know the child is Edmund?" I venture to ask when the silence becomes almost deafening.

"Besides the stark resemblance to both William and Annie? I know the child was given to William's cousin, Jane Barton," Ruth replies with what sounds like shame in her voice. "You see, when William returned home with the infant in his arms, it was clear he was not the same person as when he left; he was a shell of a man. Lost, broken, and completely overwhelmed by everything that had come to pass. He was in no fit state to take care of a child. Though, in my opinion, neither was he in any state to agree to what his parents decided for him."

"I do not understand," I say, still with my worried eyes staring into Edmund's lost ones.

"They arranged for the child to be brought up by Edmund's cousin and her husband," she says, still looking immensely apologetic. "William took years to come to terms with everything, and by the time he was even close to living again, his parents had passed on. Edmund was living in London with his new parents."

"Oh…oh, I –"

"W-Where is he?" Edmund cuts me off with his shaky words, his face now looking more furious than sad.

"Who?" Ruth asks with a frown of confusion upon her face.

"The man who killed her. Samuel. Where is he?"

His voice is quiet, but no less fearsome than if he had shouted at the top of his voice. I have never seen Edmund looking like this before; it is scaring me.

"At first, he ran," she says quietly with what sounds like even more guilt in her voice, something Edmund picks up on almost immediately.

"He ran here. He ran to you, didn't he?" he says accusingly. She looks down to her fidgeting fingers, but it only makes him look all the more furious with her. "DIDN'T HE?"

His temper causes the both of us to jump in our seats. Once I have come to terms with his outburst, I rush over to Ruth who is now trembling with tears.

"Edmund, please?" I beg him, feeling my own eyes becoming glazy for him, for me, and for her.

"He did," she whimpers. "He told me everything and begged me for sanctuary."

"And did you give it to him?" he asks as he paces towards her, and I fear what he might do if she does not give him the right answer. However, after what feels like much too long for my nerves to withstand, she slowly shakes her head.

"I could not," she cries, sounding just as guilty as if she had said the opposite. "Not after killing my best friend, not after leaving her little boy without his mother. I let him rest in the spare bed, then crept out into the night to report him to the constable. I will never forget the look on his face when he realised I had betrayed him."

Edmund merely scoffs with a look of disgust on his face. He cannot understand her pain, but I can, so I wrap my arms around her and let her hold onto me for strength. I try to soothe her with my voice, but I cannot take away her hurt, cannot undo this for her…or him.

"Where is she buried?" Edmund asks sadly. "My mother, where can I find her?"

"William had her buried in the family cemetery, on the grounds of the estate," Ruth replies. "A day never went by without him—"

Before Ruth can finish her sentence, Edmund storms from the room and begins marching along the gravel path that leads to the main road. His strides are much too long for me to keep up. He ignores Phillip calling out for him, asking if he wants to ride back in the carriage. He even ignores me. I wonder if he can hear anything other than the thudding of his own heart beating.

"I am so sorry, Elsie," Ruth whimpers as she runs out to catch up with me.

"It is not your fault," I try to reassure her, but my head feels dizzy, and before I know it, I am slumping to my knees with the world around me turning hazy.

"Lady Barton!" Phillip gasps as he comes running to my aid alongside Ruth. However, all I can see is the back of Edmund becoming smaller and smaller as he marches away without a single look back.

"This is why I needed to tell you," Ruth flusters, pulling back my attention, "Elsie, you are going to have to take great care with your pregnancy."

"What? Why?" I ask as I am practically carried to the carriage so I can sit down.

"Edmund wasn't an only child," she says cryptically, "Annie had twins."

"Twins?! A-as in two babies?" I gasp with shock. I have never heard of anyone I know being a twin before, though I realise it only makes my condition that more precarious. "Where is this twin?"

"Sh-she never made it, Elsie," she replies sadly. "She was born sleeping."

As I clutch hold of my stomach, fearing everything one can when they find themselves expecting a baby for the first time, I think of Edmund and how much more this is going to destroy him.

Edmund

What does one do when everything he thought he knew turns out to have been a complete lie? I could never have expected for this to occur, and yet, here I stand, before a grave of a complete stranger who happened to have given birth to me. Loved me, cared for me, expected to have shared a whole life with me. And now she is nought but bones, as is my cousin, or should I say, my father. Truthfully, I do not know where to begin.

Edmund, you are about to become a father yourself; how can you embark on such a thing when you do not even know who you are?

Father. Yes, a father. Elsie, I should go to Elsie and be the man she needs me to be. I should let go of all this bad feeling and focus on my family. *Who is my family?* I do not know who is who any more. How can I expect Elsie to feel at ease with a man who has lost his very own identity. She is already nervous enough to be carrying my child, and now this has come to plague her. No, I cannot share this burden with her; I must protect her at all costs.

"Edmund?" my darling Elsie calls for me, as if she knew I needed her. "Thank goodness, I have been looking all over for you."

"I apologise, Elsie, I have had much to think about," I utter without emotion, but when I turn to look at her properly, I can see she has already been worrying too much. I immediately reach out for her, and she wraps her arms around me, gifting me with her embrace before I even get to take her hands within mine.

"Edmund, I am so sorry for all of this," she cries sadly, "know that I am here for you in any way possible, you only need ask."

"I am fine, Elsie, truly. I am more worried about you," I tell her at the same time as placing my hand upon the small mound of her stomach. She is already beginning to show, a fact that scares me all of a sudden.

"Edmund, there is something else you need to know—"

"Please, Elsie, no more surprises, I cannot...please...no more..." I try my hardest to be the man I should be for my wife, but it is too much to not give into her soft arms, her soothing breath, and her familiar scent. She is the only constant thing left, all else has been obliterated.

"Ok, Edmund, it is ok," she whispers, stroking my hair as she does and thinking of no one else but me. "Come to bed, Edmund, let me hold you."

"I cannot," I tell her truthfully, "sleep is the very last thing I feel like doing."

"Edmund, I can soothe you in other ways," she says with a small smile that tells me how uncomfortable it was for her to offer this out loud. After all, Elsie is new to intimacy.

"My beautiful wife," I whisper as I run my thumb along her plump, tantalising lips, "I would love nothing more. Alas, I would be lying if I did not tell you my mind would be elsewhere."

"I understand," she says softly, and I know she is being truthful. "What do you want to do, Edmund?"

"I think I need to write to my mother," I reply with a long sigh.

"Then that is what you should do," she says before kissing me on my cheek. "I am here whenever you need me."

"I know, and that is why I love you so much."

Elsie

I should have known a letter from Edmund would have sent his mother and father into a tailspin; of course it would. Between Edmund's procrastination and travelling, a whole month has passed by since we found out everything. Over that month, Edmund has withdrawn from everyone, including me. It has given me much time alone to contemplate everything, and yet, I am still no clearer as to how best to help my husband.

I have tried to remain a little detached from my own feelings; to simply be here for Edmund when I know he is hurting so much. I have not dared searched the waters of my own emotions towards his parents, all I do know is that I would be feeling just as betrayed if I was in Edmund's position. My father may not be the best of parents with me, and I know he has an obvious favourite when it comes to his daughters, but, as far as I am aware, he has never lied to me. And I have always trusted Mama completely.

His parents arrived only moments ago, unexpected and looking deathly pale. I have never known them to look so grave, they have always been overly jovial at every event they attend. I have always felt comforted and welcomed in their company. But now, I can tell they are deeply uncomfortable in front of me; I can sense they already think I am judging them harshly. Perhaps I am, I am still unsure.

"Edmund," I call out softly from the doorway of his cousin's study where he has been spending more and more of his time, even in the dead of night. I cannot tell if being here soothes his nerves or ails him. He is lost in his staring at the painting of Annie, to the point whereby he cannot even hear me. In fact, he has not even realised anyone is here with him.

"Edmund!" I repeat myself, sounding more urgent.

"Elsie," he says with a tired smile, "how long have you been standing there?"

"But a few moments," I tell him truthfully. "Edmund, I am worried about you, if you are not physically in here, then your mind is. Please, will you not talk—"

"I CANNOT!" he shouts using a voice I have never heard from him before, one that silences me instantly. It shocks me so much, I take a step back, dipping my head as I do so. "Elsie, I am sorry, I –"

"Your parents are here, Edmund, I thought you should know."

"My parents?!" he snaps, and I take another step back, which he sees. "Elsie, please, I did not mean to—"

"I shall keep them busy until you are ready to join us for tea on the terrace," I tell him without emotion, only so I might keep the tears at bay. I turn to leave, though before I do, I look at him one more time. He has returned to staring at William's many drawings. "Please do not keep me waiting, Edmund, I am not sure how long I will be able to keep the news of our expecting from them, and I do not wish to tell them without you."

"Of course not, Elsie, I shall be there as soon as I have cleaned myself up," he says.

He stands, ready to step towards me, but I am not yet able to endure his affection after him snapping so angrily at me. He can see it too, so I merely nod, and take my leave.

As I sit with my in-laws, who appear as though they are shrouded in misery, I automatically cling to my stomach, not even thinking about it. Thankfully, they are both feeling so sorry for themselves, they do not notice me. Much like Edmund these days. As I begin to dwell on the fact, Edmund appears beside me, prompting his mother and father to stand and face their son. When I make a move to stand with them, Edmund rests his hand upon my shoulder as if to tell me to stay where I am.

"Please, Elsie, in your condition, do not go out of your way to stand for me," he says, causing a flutter of butterflies about in my chest.

His mother gasps and his father attempts a smile, but when he sees the stern expression on his son's face, it is soon wiped clean. It was not quite the announcement I was hoping for.

"You are expecting, Elsie?" his mother finally asks with a very peculiar expression. It is as if she is trying to appear both guilty and overjoyed at the same time. I notice my hand reaching for my stomach once again; *you were supposed to bring happiness, not sadness.*

I am," I reply coyly, smiling momentarily before seeing the stern expression still marring Edmund's face. I immediately drop it and look down to my lap, feeling as though showing any kind of joy is inappropriate and dismissive of Edmund's sadness.

"This is wonderful new—" his father tries to say to us both but is cut off before he can even finish.

"I cannot indulge in this chit-chat any longer, Father, I need answers and I demand them now," he says with a venomous tone of voice. Hatred is taking over the man I had fallen in love with, and I have no idea how to get him back.

"Edmund, I hardly think the subject of your first child should be referred to as 'chit-chat'," his mother says, but her words only seem to inflame his wrath. "Think of Elsie and how she must feel to hear you dismissing this happy occasion in such a way."

"Do not talk of my wife, Mother, nor my child, not when you have been keeping such huge secrets from me," he growls like a guard dog with his teeth bared in warning. "My happiness has been overshadowed by your deceit."

"My *deceit*," she snaps with anger to rival his own, "was to protect you, Edmund. I loved you from the very moment I saw you. I might not have carried you as I did Stephen, but you are my son, and nothing and no one will tell me otherwise."

With those heart-felt words, she gets to her feet and marches towards the house, leaving me to wonder if I should go after her, or remain here with my husband. Fortunately, the decision is taken out of my hands.

"Edmund, sit down," his father says gravely, and after a moment's pause for thought, he does. "Edmund, and Elsie, this must remain between as few as people as possible. Unless you would like to be the subject of gossip and malicious rumour, I am afraid this has to be kept discreet."

Edmund opens his mouth to argue, however, when I place my hand on top of his, he stops himself. Answers are needed and arguing over details will only delay them.

"Your grandmother, William's mother, was a rather cruel woman, so when she found out what William and Annie had done, she stopped at nothing to find them. Your uncle, your mother's brother, tried his best to talk her out of finding William, but she refused to be bested by someone whom she considered a commoner. She saw Annie as nothing more than a blight upon their good name, a gold digger who was taking advantage of her only son. She had heard William talk many times about the man who eventually found them. After a short conversation with Samuel, she realised he was obsessed with Annie, something she knew she could work to her advantage. She also knew Annie's best friend would still be in contact and could therefore get to her son through her. As you are aware, Ruth's father suffers from an affliction of the mind, a simple fellow who saw innocence in everything and everyone. Samuel had been watching the both of them, and when he saw Ruth's father with a letter in hand, ready to be sent to Annie and William, he intercepted it. He pretended to be doing him a service, taking the burden so he could return home and rest. The gun Samuel took with him wasn't his father's, it belonged to the Colten estate."

"She knew he would kill her," Edmund says through clenched teeth and a glazy expression. I squeeze his hand tighter, but I know he cannot feel it anymore, so I nod at his father to continue.

"When William returned, he was in no fit state to take care of you, Edmund," he sighs. "Your mother and I had been trying so long to give Stephen a sibling, but without success. It was William's father who approached us with the idea to bring you up as our own. At first, we refused; we couldn't do that to William. But when we saw how vacant his mind had become, how he did not even realise when you were in the room, we conceded that it might be for the best."

"It does not explain why I was never told!" Edmund snaps.

"By the time William came back to some semblance of living, you were a little boy, immersed in our family with a mother, a father, and a big brother who adored you. William agreed that it wouldn't be fair to take this away from you. He wanted to be your cousin too, a man who could still show you love but without taking you away from all that you knew."

"But that changed, didn't it? When you fell out with him?" Edmund asks with a voice that sounds close to breaking.

"Just before Stephen died, he said we should tell you who you really were," his father admits sadly. "He knew he wasn't going to survive his accident, and he did not feel right about having lied to you your entire life. William agreed that the time was right, that you deserved to know who Annie was, that she existed."

"But?"

"Your mother and I were scared, Edmund, terrified we would lose you. Stephen passed away and you were all we had left. You were our little miracle we had prayed for when we couldn't have any more children. It is why your mother was so protective of you. The thought of losing you was too much to even consider telling you. William threatened to tell you anyway, so we ceased all contact with him. He…he wrote to you. But I guess he had an attack of conscience, because he gave it to your mother instead. He told her to give it to you when she would one day realise that you deserved to know."

"So, this is why the estate was left to me?" Edmund says sadly.

"Yes," his father simply replies. "As well as William's title. You are an earl, Edmund."

"You think I care about such things?" he cries out at the same time as jumping to his feet in anger.

"Edmund, I don't think your father meant—"

"He is not my father!" Edmund shouts at me before stomping away from the both of us. I do not even recognise him anymore, and when I burst into tears, his father is wrapping his arms around my shoulders, crying with me. I am not sure who is comforting who more, but right now, I am not going to push him away.

Chapter 21

Edmund

I cannot get away from this anger that is surging all through my veins, cannot see anything beyond betrayal and hurt. The only thing that is driving me forwards is a desperation to act upon my anger in a destructive way. I head straight to where the woman who destroyed my family is lying in the small cemetery that sits in the large garden at the rear of the property. It has but a few graves, including that of William's. Annie, my birth mother, lies somewhere hidden, somewhere my villainous grandmother could not find her.

As I approach the gate, I pick up a shovel that the gardener leaves for clearing away weeds and leaves. With a firm hand, I take it towards my grandmother's grave where I proceed to attack her gravestone, chipping the stone and scratching the words so they are no longer legible. I swing and hit until I am covered in sweat and my voice is hoarse from growling with every swing. It is not until I hear a small gasp from behind me that I stop and turn, still brandishing the shovel in my hands.

"Edmund, stop!" Elsie whimpers, putting her hands out in front to protect herself. The fear in her eyes, the look of terror that washes over her entire face, as well as the tremble in her hands has me dropping the shovel to the ground so I can cover my face in shame.

"Elsie…" I whisper in a tortured voice, reaching out for her, but she steps back. She is afraid of me.

"I cannot do this anymore, Edmund," she whimpers, "I do not know who you are at the moment."

"Neither do I," I reply with my anger beginning to build once again.

"You are Edmund Barton, my husband…my *friend*," she says, as though begging me to believe that this is still true. I want to soothe her, to be those things for her, but another part of me is too angry to give up on my rage.

"I am not any of the things you once knew, Elsie," I snarl, only giving into the fury inside of me. "I am bitter, angry, and alone."

"You have me, Edmund!" she cries. "I told you I would go anywhere with you, and I meant it, Edmund. I am who I have always been to you; please do not push me away!"

Moments pass with her staring into my eyes, trying to reach the man she once knew. But he is gone. I have no idea who I am anymore. All I can see is anger.

"Please, Edmund, please…" she whispers, her voice straining against her tears.

"You should go," I tell her, "I am in no mood for company."

She remains silent, the shock on her face undeniable. The

Edmund she has always known is still here, still pleading with me to listen and comfort the woman who is not only my wife, but also carrying my child. He knows how she deserves to be treated, but his voice is not as strong as the one that is telling me to give into my rage. And so, I say nothing, just return to desecrating my grandmother's grave.

"Your parents are leaving, Edmund," she tells me sadly, sounding formal again.

She is disappointed in me, and I cannot blame her for it. I pause but otherwise continue in my endeavour to make this stone look unrecognisable.

"Edmund, I am going to go and see Nancy. She has birthed most of the babies in the town, and is very experienced in these matters," she says with a hopeless sigh. "Will you come?"

"I cannot, Elsie," I answer almost straight away, swinging the shovel and hitting the stone with steady hands. This has now become a distracting chore rather than an act of passion, something to avoid seeing the sadness in her eyes. "Go without me, take Lucy with you."

More moments of silence pass, and I know she is waiting for something, something that will show I still care. I do care, I just suddenly do not know how to show it, how to get passed this fury that is consuming everything that used to be me. I listen as she sniffs back a sob and sighs once again.

"I think…I think I shall go and see Emily," she says. "In fact, perhaps I should stay with her whilst I am in confinement."

"A good idea," I reply, even though I do not want her to leave me. But I also do not want her to be here to see me behaving so abysmally. I fear I will only push her further away if she remains with me.

"You want me to go?" she asks with disbelief in her voice.

It is enough to finally stop me from acting so indifferent towards her feelings. With shame running through me, I slowly turn to face her. I cannot help but take in a sharp breath of air when I see her looking so utterly devastated. I know I am behaving even worse than her father has done in the past.

"Elsie," I whisper as I take hold of her hands, prompting her to finally give into her tears. "I love you."

"I am not sure you do, Edmund," she whimpers, and I cry with her. "Not since everything has come to light. I understand your pain, I do, but why have you stopped caring about me? I am right in front of you; I am your family now, and yet, you would rather I was not here."

"Don't you see, Elsie? I cannot have you here whilst I am so lost in who I am," I try to explain; badly, I'll admit. "I am so angry, I do not want to risk losing you by having you here to witness my falling into this darkness that has consumed me so."

"But is this not what we should be working through together? As man and wife? In sickness and in health?" she pleads with me.

"Not this time," I reply ashamedly.

"But if I am not here, how can I help you?" she begs, clawing at me to see sense, but I turn away. She needs to go before I give into her. I am not ready to let go of everything that pains me, not yet.

"Please, Else, just go!" I cry, pushing away from her so I can hide from her tear-stained face. "Please!"

"As you wish," she finally whispers. "Whatever you want, Edmund."

Long moments pass before I turn around to wish her a safe journey, but by the time I do, she is already walking away from me, looking huddled and sad.

Elsie

I arrive late. Very late. A rider had gone ahead of my carriage to warn my sister of our impending arrival, so when I come in the dead of night, she is already waiting for me, looking deeply concerned. Even Tobias has come to see me inside, but his worry only has me feeling all the more wretched. I never ever thought my brother-in-law would be having to offer comfort over Edmund's treatment of me. Edmund has always been an angel to Tobias' sometimes devilish demeanor. And yet, here I am, seeking solace in my sister's house.

When I first step outside of the carriage, Emily doesn't say a word, she simply runs to embrace me. It is enough to have me crying yet again. Nancy had warned me of how emotional one becomes when carrying a baby, but I fear I will never be rid of these feelings after having had the love I had always craved, only to have lost it again in such a short space of time.

"Let us get inside, then we can talk," Emily says, looking right into my eyes to try and soothe away my melancholy. "You can tell me as much or as little as you like. You know I am always here for you, Elsie, you and your baby."

When I look at her again, her eyes are cast down to my growing stomach, which is appearing more pronounced with my cloak billowing around it. She smiles at me, and for the first time in weeks, I smile back at her.

"Come along," she says, offering her arm as we walk inside. "Molly in already on the job of getting you some warm milk."

After explaining the whole thing to Emily and Tobias, who remained silent throughout, they are both staring at me with perplexed expressions. Speechless. Though Monty, who always knows when someone is in need of comfort, comes trotting up to my knees where he rests his head and slowly wags his tail. I scratch his head, prompting Stanley to look up from his bed beside the fire. He grumbles a little but otherwise turns around and goes back to sleep again.

"He is just hurting, and justly so," I try to argue for him. After all, he is not only my husband, but he is also my best friend. "I am not quite sure how to help him anymore."

"You cannot help him," Tobias says so suddenly, all eyes immediately turn to him. "Trust me, you cannot help someone when they are not in a rational state of mind to be helped. Alas, I can tell you from personal experience."

"Then I just stay away forever more?" I ask with the feeling of a painful lump in my throat.

"Hopefully not," he says, stepping towards the light so he looks less sinister and more human. "But for now, yes."

"Tobias, what about his child?" Emily cries, gesturing to my growing abdomen. "He has a duty to take care of his wife and the mother of his unborn child, does he not? I feel for Edmund, I really do, but he cannot shirk all his responsibilities forever more; it simply isn't right."

"Emily, my darling, you are so very black and white at times, but you cannot force someone based on rational argument when their rationality has temporarily taken leave," he says, his eyes still holding their warmth whenever he looks upon her. "Time will heal."

"Tobias, time is limited in Elsie's case."

"That is true," he says contemplatively. "How long do you think you have until your baby will be born?"

"I was told I must be about three or four months," I tell them after having seen Nancy earlier today.

"It gives Edmund at least a few months to try and clear his head a little," he says, though I am not sure he is convinced of that fact.

"She told me something else," I murmur, "something that makes things a little more difficult, and worrying. When she felt around my stomach, she told me that I might be carrying more than one baby. And when I told her that Edmund had been a twin, she said she would place money on it. I am likely to be expecting twins, Emily."

Saying the words out loud only has me bursting into floods of tears. If I was scared before, I am absolutely terrified now. Twice the babies, twice the risk, twice the heartache if something goes wrong, and all without my husband by my side. Emily is immediately holding onto me as I let out all my anxiety. Tobias paces towards the fire to try and soothe Monty, who is now all of a fluster over my distress.

"That changes things a little," he says, almost to himself, "twins are more risky and likely to come early. Edmund will need to step up sooner rather than later."

"What am I going to do?" I whimper over Emily's shoulder.

"You are going to spend this time with your sister and nephew, get lots of rest, and leave your husband to me," Tobias says whilst looking at his pocket watch. "Beginning now. Emily, best show your sister to bed."

"He is right, Elsie, you need your sleep now more than ever," Emily says as she helps me to my feet.

Edmund

It has been months since I let Elsie go. It was for her sake; hers, and the baby. At least, this is what I like to tell myself, to fool myself into believing. The truth of the matter is I sent her away to save myself from pretending to be alright. To have to be a husband when I am so lost and angry has been entirely draining, to the point where I cannot think properly. Emily and Tobias can take care of her while I cannot. Tobias has kept me informed of Elsie's condition, and though it breaks my heart every time I see her name written by another man's hand, I tell myself it is for the best.

"Excuse me, My Lord, but a letter has arrived for you," Phillip announces as soon as he enters William's study. It still houses everything in the exact same way it had when we moved here. All his pictures of my mother keep me hypnotised for hours, so many hours. "I believe it is urgent."

"Right, thank you, Phillip," I sigh as I hold out my hand for the letter. Once placed inside my hand, I drop it on top of the desk and continue studying all that I can inside of William's study, greedy for whatever knowledge I can find about my true mother and father.

"Is there something else?" I ask my butler when he remains standing by the door, looking quite out of sorts.

"Forgive me, My Lord, I wondered if you were going to read the er...the...letter?" he asks, looking most confused by my refusal to open it straight away.

"I will, Phillip," I snap with annoyance, turning back to the papers in front of me, "when I have time."

"Yes, of course, My Lord," he replies, still sounding awkward, "though—"

"That will be all," a familiar voice says as he pushes his way in, "I can take it from here."

"Lord Hardy," I sigh, leaning back in my chair as I ready myself for the reason of this unexpected visit. "To what do I owe the pleasure?"

Tobias does not attempt to look at me until Phillip has safely departed the room and we are in complete privacy. I merely release a small breath of pent-up anxiety over his being here, then wait for his speech to begin. One that will no doubt aim to shame me into submission.

"Firstly, I am most put out by having taken the time to write a letter to you, only for you to discard it without even giving it a moment's attention," he says, picking it up and handing it to me.

I stare at the envelope before finally taking hold of it and ripping at the seal. He then walks over to the window and begins to study the garden whilst I read.

Barton,

It is with sadness that I am writing to inform you that Lady Victoria Brown, wife of Lord Fredrick Brown, has succumbed to her long illness. Her funeral is to be held at their local church in Whitstable. You and I shall be attending. Pack up your things immediately and be ready to leave at precisely midday on Tuesday 8th September, in the year of our Lord, 1812.

Tobias Hardy

Duke of Kent

"Oh," I murmur sadly, covering my mouth with my hand. The news isn't entirely unexpected but is no less sad to hear. "This is terrible news."

"Quite," Tobias replies whilst staring out the window with his hands neatly positioned behind his back.

"This is today," I say with my brow furrowed, pointing to the letter.

"It is," he says, now looking at his pocket watch and tutting at me. "And you have precisely thirty-four minutes. Which brings me to my second grievance; I cannot abide tardiness; it puts me in a worse mood than usual. I suggest you get a move on, Lord Barton."

"Do I have any choice in whether I attend with you or by myself?"

"Thirdly, I cannot be bothered with ridiculous questions; life is much too short," he says, now making his way to the door through which he exits without another word.

With one last look at my mother, something Tobias chose not to comment on, I get to my feet and fall into line with him. It would not serve me well to fall out with a duke, especially one who happens to my wife's brother-in-law.

By the time I reach the carriages outside, Tobias is already waiting inside the largest of the three, theatrically checking his pocket watch with a long sigh. I move to the carriage behind, which is my own, but a loud cough from the duke tells me I am to travel with him. I would laugh if I could remember how to, but I cannot even begin to smile, let alone show any mirth beyond that.

I climb inside and adjust my cloak so it doesn't bunch beneath my legs, then give the footman a nod of my head, signaling that we are ready to depart. Tobias remains silent, brooding, until we are at least a mile away from the driveway of Maybrook House. We pass by the Langford's cottage where I see Ruth's father sitting in the garden, staring into nothing. Ruth is walking outside to see to him, showing patience and kindness to someone who must have lost his mind decades ago. For a moment or two, I consider her own heartache, her own sad history, and I feel guilty for having lost my temper with her.

I know Tobias is watching me, watching them, but try not to let him see my face. It is sure to give away how utterly wretched I feel.

"Are you not going to ask after your wife?" he eventually says with contempt in his voice.

"I assume she is well," I reply ashamedly. "I will not...I mean, I cannot..."

"As far as I can tell, she and your unborn children are

well," he says.

"*Children*?!" I snap, frowning at his strait-laced expression.

"Yes, children," he replies while removing his gloves, "there are two."

"I…I had no idea," I gasp with barely enough breath to make much of a noise beyond a whisper. "Your letters…they've never said."

I am gifted with a pointed look, one that says he has purposefully left out this vital piece of information, most likely as punishment. It also tells me to not be so pathetic as to get angry with him when we all know my wife's current predicament is not any fault of his. It is mine, all mine.

"She found out the day you sent her to Emily," he says with obvious judgement. "I believe she had asked you to accompany her, but you declined. And before you send yourself into a fluster and begin casting aspersions my way, I am not trying to goad you in any way. I too, once banished the one I love most."

"Thank you, I appreciate your understanding."

"I may understand, but that does not mean I condone your actions," he says sternly, "just as you did not condone mine. I have to ask, Edmund, how long do you intend on turning your back on your family?"

"I have not turned my back! I am simply taking time to try and come to terms with all that has transpired. Now, please, let us talk of something else."

"Very well," he says gruffly, "let us talk of unimportant things and pretend all is well with the world. After all, I am sure Elsie is currently doing the very same thing. Though, she has had very little choice in the matter, has she not?"

"ENOUGH!" I shout, though he does not flinch in the slightest. "Good God, Tobias, please!"

"Careful, Edmund, you do not want to raise your blood pressure," he says after a few moments. "Your wife has enough to contend with. In fact, perhaps it is best we do not speak at all until we arrive."

"Agreed," I murmur, but loud enough for him to have heard me.

Chapter 22

Elsie

My stomach swells with each passing day, carrying the children of a man I have not seen in months. Does he miss me? I cannot even sink into my melancholy with free abandonment, for my sister refuses to leave my side. Any signs of my falling into sadness and she is on me as much as her ridiculous hound. Do not misunderstand me, I adore her for it, the dog too, but ultimately, she cannot bring back the joy I had once felt for so fleeting a moment. Only my husband can do that, but he is choosing not to. So, until he decides otherwise, in sadness I shall remain.

Today is Victoria Greyson's funeral. A wife, a mother, a daughter, all gone. I cannot help but think of Annie, how she had loved so fiercely, only to have such a short period of happiness before tragedy struck in the most brutal way. I wonder what could possibly be going through Fredrick's mind right now – fear, despair, anger – is he feeling as lost as Edmund?

"You are thinking about him again," Emily says with a disapproving expression.

I smile momentarily when Monty comes by to join her in staring me down. Stanley grumbles from his basket but makes no attempts to move. He has been moving less and less since we got here; he is my very own empath, mirroring my despondency. However, unlike me, he refuses to try and hide it.

"I am always thinking about him," I admit with a shameful smile, "how can I not?"

"Edmund is my best friend but even I am mad at him right now," she says with her arms folded in silent outrage. My dear little sister, how I once believed she would take Edmund's side over anyone.

"I love you, Emily, have I ever told you that?" I declare, looking at her with genuine affection. "We argue as sisters do, but when all the nonsensical bickering is swept aside, I truly love you."

"Oh, Elsie, I love you too, but do not talk like this," she says with a haughty look, making me laugh over such a strange response to my declaration of sibling love.

"You act as though I have offended you," I gasp through laughter. "I thought we would share a moment, and yet, here you are folding your arms and pouting at me."

"Because this is just another sign that you are sinking into a kind of depression from which I won't be able to pull you out," she says. "It will not happen whilst I am here with you. Now, then!"

"I suppose this is your way of telling me you care for me too?" I grin as I walk over to embrace her, though my growing abdomen is making the task somewhat impossible. "For your sake, I shall try not to think of him today."

"Good," she says with her nose still pointing high in the air. She lasts another few short moments before she falls into laughter with me. "Come, I am going to make you play stick races with me."

"Oh, no, must we?" I grumble as she takes me by the hand to pull me towards the door. "I never liked that game, and you made us play it continuously when we were children."

"Yes, we must, because today especially reminds us that we are all mortal, and life is precious," she says with a dramatic far-off look in her eye. "We must play childish games for Victoria's sake, for Fredrick's sake, and for little Thomas' sake. When everyone else is mourning, let us behave as children, and remind ourselves of a time when life was so blissfully easy."

"I think I can see your logic," I sigh softly, smiling when I see her grinning over her winning. But perhaps she is right; when today is so sad for so many people, let us celebrate the fact that we are alive and well. "And I suppose I must get outside whilst I am still able to."

Confinement in my sister's house is proving to be more than a little dull and I am sure the fresh air will do me good.

Edmund

Fredrick Brown is a broken man. I suspect he is only functioning for the sake of his son who is a mere two years old. He barely communicates with anyone, but for his boy, he tries to be the man he once was. I cannot help but feel sad, and perhaps angry; why could William not have looked upon me like this when my mother was killed? Instead, he sunk into his own misery and left me to be brought up by strangers. He abandoned me.

"Fredrick," I finally utter as I approach the small wooden bench on which he is sitting with his infant child. The boy has finally succumbed to sleep and is currently drooling over his father's shoulder. "My sincerest condolences."

At first, he offers a semblance of a smile whilst looking towards the floor, as if he knows something I don't.

"Have a seat with me, Barton," he says, gesturing to the empty space beside him.

"I did not want to offer you such a cliché sentiment, but quite honestly, I cannot think of a single thing to say that would sound any less ineffectual. So, it was a last-minute decision to stick with tradition."

"That is fair," he says, staring into the distance as he rubs his baby's back. "You are expecting a child too, no?"

"I am, two in fact," I reply with a genuine smile. But then I remember the state of my life at the moment, and quickly drop it again.

"That will be an interesting time for you," he laughs sadly. "I remember when Thomas was first born, Victoria and I were so happy. Back then, we had no idea how ill my beautiful wife was."

"Fredrick, I really do wish this had not happened to you," I tell him with my most sincere sympathy, "or your son."

"Barton, promise me something," he says, still unable to look at me, "you go home, and you kiss your wife; you never know when it will be the last. And when your children are born, you pledge your life to making them feel as loved as they possibly can. Nothing else matters, trust me."

I cannot answer him with words, for a lump has lodged itself within my throat. If I even attempted to open my mouth, I am sure I would end up breaking into a thousand pieces. I do not deserve to do such a thing in front of this man who has lost everything.

The child begins to stir, prompting Fredrick to get to his feet and walk him inside. I am sure he is grateful for the reprieve from all the mourners. Once he is out of sight, I return to my seat so I can hide from everyone. I cannot face another exchange of meaningless words just to be polite; I want to converse as much as Fredrick does.

"Edmund Barton," a familiar but unwanted voice says from behind me. When I look up to confirm my suspicions, he moves around and gestures towards the empty seat where Fredrick had just been sitting.

"Lord Boreham," I reply, "I was not aware you knew Lord Brown."

"I was Victoria's godfather," he explains, "Thomas' too."

"Thomas never mentioned you," I tell him truthfully. "Though, he never mentioned a lot of things. I cannot imagine how the Greysons must be feeling right now. We have had our differences, Boreham, but I am truly sorry for your loss."

"Thank you. Though you should know, I will always harbour a grudge against you for Elsie," he says, sounding mildly jovial about it. "I sincerely hope you are making her happy at least. I know you thought I could not possibly have treated her as well as you, but I would have done everything in my power to make her feel as loved as she deserves. Everyone knows how much Rothschild favours his youngest, and I would have made it my mission to let her know she was my one and only."

"She *is* my one and only," I snap, "always."

"Really?" he questions, turning to face me with a haughty expression. "Because I could have sworn, I heard the duke telling

Fredrick about her staying with him and his wife. Did I hear wrong?"

"Whether you heard what you heard or not, it is none of your concern, and neither is my wife!"

Before he can respond in any way, I get to my feet and march back towards the house. Fredrick is nowhere to be seen so I am sure he will not mind if I leave without any other exchange of words. I refuse to remain in the same space as that odious, pompous man. I am so furious; I begin to hyperventilate. The last time I felt this vexed was when I first discovered where I had come from, and the only person that was able to bring me back down to some semblance of normal, was Elsie. It is of no surprise, I have been in desperate need of her comfort, her love, and softness, every day since I sent her away from me. For her own good.

"It would be extremely rude to go ahead and die at somebody else' funeral, Barton," Tobias says without emotion as he paces up towards where I am still struggling for breath. "Not to mention inconvenient."

"Did you know Boreham would be here?" I gasp whilst trying to get a hold of my breathing.

"Of course," he replies with a half-hearted shrug.

"You could have mentioned such a thing," I snap, "forewarned me before he appeared without notice."

"Oh? Did he say something to offend you?"

"Yes, the man offended me; he was asking after my marriage, implying I wasn't being the husband Elsie deserves!"

I watch him as his brow furrows into a pensive expression. It has me remembering how much I used to loathe him, for I know he is purposefully acting the fool at this point.

"I fail to see why you are feeling so angered by the insinuation; is he wrong in his assumption?"

"How dare you?!" I positively growl, stomping up to his haughty expression and stature, my finger raised to his face in warning.

"Careful, Barton," he replies, not even flinching over my threatening behaviour. "You are only so angry because you know he is right. I know it, he knows it, but what is really upsetting for you, is the fact that you know it too. Whatever your reasons, however supposedly noble they are, you sent your pregnant wife away from her home and husband. And though I have never agreed with the man, for he is a contemptable cad with an onerous reputation, on this one occasion, I do."

"At least my intentions were somewhat honourable," I try to argue, pathetic as it is. "You banished your wife without even telling her the reason for your deplorable behaviour!"

"Whilst I am somewhat flattered over you basing your moral code on mine, your argument is at best, weak, at worst, ridiculous. I believed Emily had betrayed me, whereas Elsie has only ever been there to support you. That is until you decided your wallowing in self-pity was more important than her."

"What would you know about—"

"Family heartache? Please, Barton, let us not get into whose past is more tragic than the other," he sighs. "Eventually, one has to remember the present and the future. Are you not doing exactly as the man who killed your mother did? Letting your temper destroy the lives of people who are not to blame for your hurt. And are you not doing exactly as William did when he lost your mother? Pushing aside your children to focus solely on your own melancholy?"

"That is not what I am doing at all! I just need time away from everyone to figure out who I am," I try to explain, but even I can hear the doubt in my voice.

"Do you envy Fredrick right now? Because I can guarantee he would most likely give anything to swap places with you. And yet, here you are, purposefully putting yourself, as well as Elsie, in the exact same position as he is. Why don't you let that sink in, Barton, because I know Elsie will eventually get through this. After all, she has lived her whole life with a fool like you, being overlooked and undervalued. But when you realise what you have thrown away, I very much doubt you will pull through as well as her."

For once, I have no words with which to argue; Tobias Hardy is irritatingly correct. Even worse is the fact that this means Lord Boreham was right too. Right now, I have to concede that Elsie might well have been better off with him. How on earth did I let it come to this?

"One more thing, Barton," he says, turning back to look at me with a condescending smile that I more than deserve, "what happened to Annie and William was tragic. Your life could easily have been just as tragic had it not been for your mother and father who took you in and treated you as their own. And though your recent behaviour may contradict what I am about to say, you are, in fact, a respected and successful man. I would go as far as to say your parents did an excellent job in providing you with a life that could have been so sadly different."

Elsie

"Be honest with me, Emily, how much is it going to hurt?" I ask as we sit side by side beneath her special tree. Admittedly, memories of catching her with Tobias in this very spot, has me shuffling uncomfortably every few moments. That and my protruding abdomen. "I am becoming more and more impatient to have my body back to normal, but I am also incredibly frightened."

"You know I would never lie to you, Elsie," she says contemplatively whilst she scratches Monty's head, "which is why I have to tell you that pushing your child out of your delicate area is as painful as that sentence sounded."

"Oh," I reply, not hiding my disappointment at all. "You were supposed to say it was merely a pinch and I have nothing to worry about."

She laughs in such a way, I cannot help but laugh along with her. I did ask for honesty after all. And besides, the notion of childbirth being no more painful than a pinch is a fairly ridiculous one.

"I will say this, however, once you hold your baby, or *babies* in your case, you will no longer care about the pain. When I held James for the first time, I was so in love with him. Not to mention the look on Tobias's face when he first cradled his son; it was everything."

"I can only imagine," I sigh sadly, with a lump so large in my throat, I am not sure I will be able to keep it from coming to the fore.

"Elsie, he will come back to you, I promise," she tries to convince me with her hand resting on top of mine. "He is hurting after a fresh wound, but he will come back."

"I wish I had your confidence," I whimper, bursting into

tears the moment she takes me inside of her arms. "I don't want to face this alone, I really don't. I feel as though I have been alone ever since you left home."

"You will never be alone, Elsie, I will always be here for you," she whispers, "you and your babies."

"I keep worrying that history will repeat itself," I admit, "that I will not survive the birth, that I will be taken from them. Edmund is already just as lost as William was."

"Don't talk like this, Elsie, please, you will be fine," she says, sounding tearful herself.

"Promise me you will do as Edmund's parents did. Promise me that if I do not make it, you will look after them for me."

"Elsie, you are becoming hysterical, please calm down," she says, and maybe she is right, maybe I am losing a hold of my senses, but I still need that promise from her.

"Please, you have to promise me!"

"Of course, Elsie, I would treat them as my own, just as I know you would do with James," she says, the words instantly soothing me, if only enough to stop my tears from falling.

"It's been months, Emily. I have to come to terms with the fact that Edmund has abandoned me. I was never enough to have him choose me over all else. Just as I was never enough for Papa."

"I do not agree with you, but I can see why you think so," she says with a long sigh.

"I need to think of the future, to think of my children," I tell her resolutely, "and that means returning home. He can live in that study or move elsewhere, but my babies deserve to have their own home with love and security, even if it only comes from their mother."

"Actually, sister, I think that is the first thing you have said with which I can agree this afternoon. Edmund has had his time, now it is your turn."

"And you know what else? My children will be loved equally; they will never have to try and prove they are just as worthy as the other."

"Of course they will, Elsie, because you will be their mother, alive and present," she says with a stern look in her eye. "When do you plan to return?"

"Tomorrow," I declare.

"*Tomorrow*?! In your condition? Oh, Elsie, are you sure?"

"Emily, don't go and lose that feisty edge of yours now, I need you to give me the encouragement to go through with this," I tell her before laughing at her furrowed brow.

"Right, yes, of course," she says, nodding as she does so. She looks so serious, I have to laugh even harder. "Elsie Barton, you have my full support."

"Good," I reply with a sigh that knows the future is going to be hard but at least I now have one…of sorts. For the first time since arriving here, I feel a little less hopeless, a little less stuck, and a little more in control of my own path.

Chapter 23

Edmund

I have been standing in front of my childhood home for a time I cannot even quantify anymore. Having thought and thought on everything ever since Tobias had chastised me at Victoria Greyson's funeral, I can no longer make sense of it all. I am still angry, sad, and confused, but I also feel a strong sense of shame. Up until now, I have not taken a single moment to consider how those closest to me are feeling. I have only seen my own heartache, and in doing so, I have inflicted pain on the people who care about me the most.

Elsie.

She is the most important thing in my life, and yet, I pushed her away. I am no better than her father. I can only hope she will forgive me, and not because she is good and compassionate, but because she can see that I am truly sorry, and because she knows I love her more than anything else in the world.

However, I know it is going to take some time and will need to be my sole focus. With that in mind, I have decided to face the other important people in my life – my parents. The people who took me in and brought me up. Yes, they lied to me, but only because they were afraid to lose me. I owe them so much; I do not even know where to begin.

Taking in a deep breath for courage, I knock on the door and wait anxiously for Harold, my father's butler, to open it. I hear movement long before he actually gets around to opening the door, leaving me time to work myself up into even more of a frenzy. By the time I look upon his tired old face, I am about ready to pass out.

"Lord Barton, we were not expecting visitors today," he says with concern on his wrinkled features. "I am afraid your father has already left for town, and your mother is still resting in bed."

"Apologies, Harold, I only came to the decision to visit earlier this morning, but now that I am here, I must speak to my mother," I tell him as I begin stepping inside, flustering with my hands to show how desperate I am.

"I shall let her know at once, though, I must warn you, she is very unwell," he says as he closes the heavy door behind us. "She has barely been out of bed since returning from your estate, months ago."

"I…I had no idea," I reply contritely and with the sensation of blood rushing from my head whilst my heart begins beating with rapid force. "Is it serious?"

"Forgive me, My Lord, but you will have to ask your mother and father," he says as he leads me up the staircase with the same steps that still creak under my heavy feet.

I have lived through everything here, and yet, I have never felt so afraid of what I might find when I finally see the woman who cared for me like no other. If Annie could see what her son has become, I am sure she would be so ashamed of me. Perhaps as much as I am ashamed of myself.

"And my father? Is he well?" I ask, swallowing back the lump in my throat, though it only returns as soon as I have completed the action.

"I believe so, but I must say, he very rarely smiles these days," he replies.

"I see," I utter just as we reach my mother's door, on which he delivers one swift knock. Moments later, the housekeeper opens it, appearing flustered and angry over the intrusion.

"What on earth, Harold--" Marie begins to whisper shout at the poor man, so I intervene on his behalf. She has always scared the gentlemen of this house, my father included, but I can no longer allow someone to suffer because of my actions.

"Forgive me, Marie, but I must speak with my mother," I interrupt as I take a step forward. "Is she able to see her son?"

"Oh, My Lord, I did not see you there, my apologies," she says, standing up straight and nodding her head in my direction. "I am afraid your mother is much too unwell to accept visitors."

"Edmund, is that you?" A frail voice from inside calls out from behind the housekeeper who does not do a very good job of hiding the roll of her eyes. "Marie, let him in please."

"She is not to be upset," Marie whispers, talking to me like I am a child again. I suppose, on this occasion, I deserve her disdain.

"Of course," I reply, trying to convince her with the sincerity of my words through eye contact alone. With a sigh that tells me she would love to send me packing, Marie finally moves aside to let me in. As soon as I see my mother lying inside of her bed, looking frail and half the size of her usual self, I instantly want to punish myself in the most brutal way possible. What a truly ungrateful son I have been.

"Oh, Edmund, I never thought I would see you again," she says with a smile on her face. It only has me feeling all the more ashamed of myself.

"Mama," I end up whimpering as I run to her, grabbing her hand like I did so often as a little boy. She grips hold back and begins to run her fingers through my hair with her other hand, my head resting upon the side of her bed. "I cannot even begin to apologise for my inexcusable behaviour; I deserve to be pushed away, to be cast out of the house, yet you still embrace me."

"It is every mother's job to forgive their child when they have made mistakes. And besides, I don't think any of us are innocent in all of this."

"You are! You are my mother, and I am so sorry," I cry, looking into her glazy eyes while wishing I had handled things so differently. "I was just so angry with the world."

"I know, dear, I have always known that," she says sadly. "I just feared you would never stop being angry."

"When I heard their story, of what happened to Annie, I did not know how to *not* be angry. She had wanted her family so desperately, and yet, she only got to have it for such a short time before it was stolen from her. And William? I feel both heartbroken and furious with him. Why did he not fight for me? His son, the product of his love for her."

"Why do you think I was so fearful, Edmund? It was not for my sake, nor your fathers. It was because I know how damaging holding onto your anger can be. William was so angry for so long; he lost the only thing he had left of her. You, Edmund, *you*!"

"Did you really think I would abandon you if you had told me the truth?"

"You did for a while, my son," a voice from behind me says with sadness. I turn around to find my father looking aged, tired, and forlorn. For a few moments, I simply look at him, not knowing what to say, but when he holds out his arms for me, I run to him. And this is why I love them so much; they do not place social expectations above love. He embraces me with so much warmth, I end up shuddering against him.

"I know, and I am so deeply sorry," I cry against his shoulder.

"We know, Edmund," he says with a little more joviality to his voice.

"And we forgive you, Edmund," my mother says from her bed. "I did not tell you because you were such a happy, rounded, caring little boy; I knew I risked your wrath later on, but I could not bring myself to put an end to your innocence and your love of life with such sadness."

"I know, and I understand," I reply with a sigh that tries to clear away my tears. "I just wish I could have had one conversation with one of them knowing the truth. I feel like that was something we were all owed. After everything."

"Well, I cannot give you a conversation, my darling, but I can give you this," Mama says as she reaches over to her bedside table and retrieves something that looks like a letter. She turns it over and over inside of her hands, as if still doubting whether to give it to me.

"Here," she finally says with unshed tears in her eyes.

"What is this?" I ask as I look over the letters of my name.

"It is from William," my father explains, "he asked us to give it to you when he would no longer be around to tell you the words himself. But then you went away on your travels, married Elsie, and we shamefully put it off for another day. Today is that day, Edmund."

"Elsie," I utter with a pain in my chest so strong, I have to clutch my hand to it.

"How is she?" Mama asks, unaware of our separation.

"Well. I think," I admit shamefully. "She has been staying with Emily, ever since…I told her to leave me."

"Edmund!" she gasps with horror on her face, and I end up tearing up again.

"Please, do not say what I have already said to myself a hundred times," I whimper. "I messed everything up."

"No," she coos, "there is nothing you cannot do to try and fix things. I always knew Elsie was the Rothschild for you. She is patient, forgiving, and so in love with you, I wonder how you never saw it before you did."

"And I am so in love with her, which is why I sent her away from me; she deserves so much more," I confess.

"Well, my boy, it is time to go and put things right," she says, patting my hand from her bed, "by any means possible. In fact, do so before you read William's letter. It is time you made her your priority, not sad memories."

"Mama, how serious is your malady?" I ask the question I have been putting off for fear of what her answer will be.

"I am physically well…as well as a lady can be at my age," she says. "But after I thought I had lost you forever, my mind has refused to let me get up. It has been punishing me for the part I played in lying to you for all these years. I shall be fine, Edmund. Your marriage, however, needs your attention, and fast. So, go now. We have time for all this later."

"I love you, Mother," I tell her as I lean down to kiss her on her pale cheek, praying that she is being truthful with me. "I will write as soon as I am able."

When I reach my father at the door, I hold out my hand to shake his, but he merely smiles before pulling me in for an embrace that reminds me of childhood.

"Go and get her, my son," he whispers before releasing me to go and do just that.

Edmund

Once I left my parents' house, I arranged to head straight to Kent so I could begin trying to make amends for all I had done to the woman I love most in the world. I do not expect Elsie to forgive me straight away, in fact, I know she might never forgive me. However, I also know I must try, and keep on trying, even if I die doing so. What I do not expect to find is that she has left the Hardy estate and taken herself back to Witney. I also did not expect such a frosty greeting from my best friend and sister-in-law, Emily, which was folly on my part. I should have known Emily wouldn't hold back from telling me exactly what she thought about me.

"Emily," I say her name ashamedly, looking down to my feet because that is how low I feel. She merely cocks her head to one side, folds her arms and audibly sighs. She is going to be an accomplished mother when she finally has to chastise James for acting just as ridiculous as I have. She has made me feel so much worse without even having to utter a single word.

"Edmund," she finally says back to me, "I suppose you had better come inside."

"I take it Tobias has returned?" I ask, if only to try and ease the tension.

"He has, though you need not fear him when I am the one who is so furious with you," she says as we walk through the long corridors to the courtyard outside. "I do not believe I have ever felt this way about you, Edmund Barton. To say I am disappointed is an understatement."

"Believe me, Emily, I understand," I reply, just as Tobias and James come into view.

"Sit," she says, gesturing to a chair in front of the table where an array of cakes and teacups are teasing the poor hound, Monty, who is now drooling from both sides of his panting mouth. He momentarily wags his tail but soon returns to his role of guarding the delicious offerings on top of the table. Meanwhile, Tobias is looking the epitome of the proud father with young James squirming around inside of his lap.

"To what do we owe the pleasure?" Emily asks with short, curt words.

"Brave, Barton, very brave," Tobias says without looking away from his son.

"Tobias, now is not the time for your sense of humour,"

Emily snaps, to which I have to duck my head to hide my smile.

"Dearest, please, you must let me enjoy this moment," he argues. "It is very rare to see you losing your temper with someone who isn't me."

"You can enjoy the moment without talking, can you not?" she says with a haughty expression.

"Duly noted," he replies, nodding his head and leaning back to continue playing with his son.

"As you can see, your wife isn't here," she says, focusing those angry eyes back onto mine. "Against my physician's advice, she returned to Witney a day or so ago. I am afraid she has moved passed the heartache of her husband abandoning his responsibilities, and has now transitioned into anger, defiance, and fierce independence."

"Take it from me, Barton, that is not a place in which you want your wife to reside," Tobias adds, his eyes still on James. "You will have quite the battle on your hands, as did I not too long ago."

"Tobias!" Emily snaps.

"Apologies, darling," he says before leaning over to kiss her flushed cheek.

"I deserve all that I am about to face," I admit. "In my defense, I have not been myself. You know more than anyone, Emily, I would never have planned to hurt someone I care about in my normal state of mind. I lost sense of who I was, but I promise you, I have found him now."

"I appreciate what you've been through, Edmund, I really do, but the way you handled it... Well, in truth, you have not handled it, have you? You simply lost your temper and let it take over everything you hold dear."

"I know," I murmur, sounding as pathetic as poor Monty is looking over those cakes.

"So, what does *he*, or rather *you*, plan on doing to fix all of this?"

"Whatever it takes," I declare with determination. "I will not abandon my children as William did to me, and I will not let Elsie doubt my feelings for her a second longer. She is my priority, as are our children."

"You know, Edmund, I am thinking," Emily says with her finger resting on her lips, looking pensive, like she used to as a child when she had some ridiculous scheme in mind. This is a good sign; she wants to help me, which means I am beginning to move back into her good graces. "I am thinking you cannot simply grovel, like you deserve to. Elsie will no doubt accept it straight away, all the while believing you do not really love her as you say you do. The way to make it right, and to make it up to her, is to convince her she is everything you need to make it better. You have to convince her of your love all over again. Honestly, Edmund, you really have messed about with her confidence, and after all the effort you put in to convincing her of your affections the first time around. I ought to set Monty on you."

"I agree, I do deserve that, but it will not help Elsie, will it?" And besides, Monty looks about as ferocious as the teddy bear I had once had as a small infant.

"No, but it would give me great satisfaction," she says before sipping on her tea. I turn to look at Monty who is still keeping a watchful eye on the food. I think, when it comes to Monty, I am in the clear.

"Court her," Tobias says plainly. "She was robbed of that honour because of Lord Boreham, but now you have all the time in the world. Show her that you have put some thought into her happiness."

"Tobias," Emily gasps with a shocked expression on her face, "that is a good idea!"

"Well, do not sound so surprised," he says with indignity in his voice.

"It is a good idea, a great idea," I gasp, feeling positive for the first time since everything came to light all those months ago. "And I know exactly what to do; I only hope she is still able to indulge in my plan."

"Actually, Barton, your first hope should be that she agrees to it," Tobias points out.

"I believe you *forced* me into your idea to win me back around," Emily teases as she rests her hand on his shoulder. "Which only ended up with me having to assist with the birth of Ethel and Marley's brother."

"Well, that too, might be a possibility in Elsie's condition, so I must make haste," I tell them, getting to my feet and readying myself to leave.

"Good luck, Edmund," Emily says, "do not disappoint me again."

"I don't plan to," I tell her resolutely, "*ever* again."

Chapter 24

Elsie

Every time I feel one of the babies kick, it gives me hope. Hope that I can be happy, even without a husband. Plenty of ladies in my position live a separate life to the man to whom they are married; indeed, it is unusual to live as closely as we once did. It is only that it feels all the more unfair that I had but a moment of what I have been dreaming of for so long, only for it to be ripped away from me. But love comes in many forms, and I can think of nothing more warming than knowing I shall be meeting my babes in the very near future.

As I walk about the nursery that has been adorned with fresh linen, all ready for the upcoming arrivals, a pang of fear hits me. What if something happens and I never get to see them grow up? What if I meet the same fate as Annie? Or worse, one of the babies is born sleeping, just as Edmund's twin sister had. I cannot fathom how Edmund's mother ever coped with such a loss. As for William, I can understand his falling apart. Perhaps he did Edmund a service by letting him go, or was it pure selfishness? It is all so complicated.

"Lady Barton," my maid, Lucy, calls meekly from the doorway, curtseying as she does so. I smile and stand with my hands clutching hold of my stomach; I do most of the time now. It has become so big, it seems natural to rest my hands upon it. "Ruth

Langford is here to see you. Shall I tell her you are well enough for visitors?"

"Yes, of course, thank you, Lucy," I reply with a hint of excitement over having a visitor. Confinement is such a tedious affair. "I need a nice distraction."

She curtseys one more time before making her way downstairs. I take a moment to breathe in the smell of fresh linen, then make my own way down to meet my friend.

"Elsie, how are you?" she practically beams when she sees me wobbling down the staircase. "I cannot believe how big you have gotten. You must be very close."

"I must confess, I am more than ready to meet them in the open," I tell her, even if I am scared of how that is going to happen.

"Do you have any names in mind?"

"No," I reply quietly, as if ashamed of the fact. "Every time I try to think of one, I can only think of Edmund and how I want him to be making such a decision with me. It is simply easier not to."

"I see," she says sadly. "Let us go for a walk, take in the sun; it will make you feel so much better."

"In my condition? I have been told to rest, rest, and then rest some more," I reply, laughing at her suggestion.

"And how are you finding that?"

"Awful! But I do not want to risk having my babies out in the open."

"Trust me, we will not venture far, and if you feel any kind of niggling, we will head straight back. Please, Elsie, do say yes. It is a beautiful evening, and the woods are breathtaking at this time of day. Why, Annie and I used to… Never mind."

"Oh, alright," I sigh, sounding as if I am conceding when in fact, I am desperate to get out. "Let me grab my shawl and I will be with you."

"Perfect," she smiles. "I will take great care of you, I promise."

As Ruth and I slowly walk down one of the garden paths, we remain lost in our own thoughts, content to be in each other's company. Though, I suppose I am more like three instead of one; what a puzzling thought. The rhododendrons are in full bloom and even in the dusky light, they look magnificent. The air seems alive with insects whilst birds noisily come into roost. I love this time of day; it is perhaps the only time of day when I do not feel like I miss Edmund so much, I want to break down and cry. Maybe he will come back to me one day, when his melancholy finally releases him, and he realizes he isn't alone; he has me. He will always have me.

"Annie and I used to play hide and seek over there," Ruth says, pointing in the direction of a small collection of birch trees. "She always found me first. That is until she discovered her true feelings for William. Then she would pretend not to see me and go and meet him at the oak tree in the herb garden. They'd sit up in that tree and tease one another, pretending not to like each other, when in fact, I believe they knew back then that they were destined to be together."

"It is heartbreaking to know they only had such a short time together," I add sadly.

"Well, that depends on how you look at it," she says contemplatively. "They had a whole childhood together before they became husband and wife. They had the best of relationships, full of innocence, laughter, and never having to see the other one get old and slip away. And they also had new life, Edmund, which in turn, has also led to new life."

She gestures to my pronounced abdomen and smiles. I automatically move my hands to rub over the children growing inside of me, hoping they know how much I love them already.

"I only wish he could see it that way," I murmur.

"Perhaps he does," she says with a smile that tells me she knows something I don't. When I look at her quizzically, she merely lifts her chin, gesturing to something behind me.

"Hello, Elsie Barton," a familiar, though now strange voice says from behind me. I do not turn straight away, for my feet refuse to move. Instead, I clasp a hand over my mouth, gasping over the shock of hearing his voice for the first time in months. "Please, Elsie, please turn around."

Ruth looks at me with a mixture of concern and encouragement, but I still cannot move; I'm too afraid this is all a dream. Eventually, I hear the crush of twigs underfoot as he walks around to face me. He looks so much leaner than when I last saw him, and his hair and eyes have lost their usual shine.

"Elsie," he whispers, drawing my name out like a prayer. "My God, look at you; you are so big, so...*amazing*!" he says as he reaches out to touch where our children are growing.

"Are...are you really here?" I ask so quietly, I am not entirely convinced the words actually left my lips.

"Oh, Elsie, what have I done to you?" he asks with tears

filling his eyes and with so much pain written across his face, I want to reach out for him. But I can't. "I am here, Elsie, I am here for always. I will never leave you again."

After those words, I cannot help but release the ball of emotion from the back of my throat. A stifled breath leaves my lips and I begin to fall. I would be a mess on the floor had Edmund not swiftly moved forward to catch me, wrapping me up in his arms at the same time as he begins crying with me.

"You sent me away!" I whimper. "You did not want me anymore. I have spent my whole life not being wanted."

"I did want you, Elsie, I wanted you so damn much," he cries, "but I was so afraid of myself, of losing myself to my anger and grief. I could never subject you to what I was going through, could never risk hurting you."

"But you did hurt me, Edmund, you rejected me just as much as you had felt rejected and lied to," I argue. He releases his grip but then grabs hold of my hands to keep me steady, and I notice Ruth is now gone. We are left alone to work this out as man and wife. *Can we work this out?*

"I know that now, I know you must be so mad with me, Elsie, and you have every right to hate me, but I—"

"I am not angry, Edmund, and I could never hate you."

"Then tell me, tell me how you are feeling."

"I am feeling...I am feeling sad, Edmund, so incredibly sad."

My admission has him looking confused, as though he cannot understand. In fact, he stares at me for a while, trying to work out what to say. I have shocked him, and I have no idea why.

"I expected you to be furious with me, Elsie, to want to punish me," he says, "just as Emily did with Tobias when he had acted as foolish as I have."

"How could you think that? This is completely different, Edmund. And I am not Emily, I never have been. She craved adventure in a way I never have. I was brought up to be the debutante, the perfect role model for my wayward sister. I hated it. I thought I envied her spirit, her freedom, but when I saw the love she felt for Tobias, I realised that what I envied was the love she had from everyone. It is all I have ever wanted, Edmund, love and family. I might have hated the frills and frocks of trying to find a husband, but a husband and family is all I have ever craved."

"Elsie…"

"I started to believe I would never obtain it, that it would have been all for nothing," I sigh sadly, thinking of how very real that belief was when Emily had left for her happily ever after. "But when you returned home from your travels, and I saw you at the Bartlett's ball, a small spark ignited inside of me. A hope I once had but lost, began to let itself be known all over again."

"I felt it too, Elsie," he says ever so quietly. "I remember wanting to challenge Boreham right there and then. I returned home only when I saw your mother escorting you back to your carriage. You were so sad, Elsie, and all I wanted to do was hold you."

"When you made love to me for the very first time, I finally believed, Edmund, I finally felt from you what I had always wanted."

"I love you," he whispers as he presses his forehead to mine, his eyes closing as if in reverence.

"But when you gave into grief, which I fully expected you to do after finding out about what happened to Annie, and William, and how you were seemingly abandoned, you pushed me away. I never needed a Shakespeare sonnet, Edmund, but I do need a love that will never break. It might become complacent, it might argue, it might need reminding of how to show itself now and then, but it never breaks. Do you understand, Edmund?"

"I do," he says before momentarily pressing his lips against my forehead. "But know my love for you never broke, it was I who broke for a while."

"Then always let me stay by your side to help mend you," I tell him as I look deep into his sad eyes before leaning in to kiss his pale lips.

"I promise, my love," he says, kissing me as he had before all of the suffering; a kiss of new beginnings.

"Then," I tell him as I stroke his face, "even though Emily would curse me for forgiving you so quickly, I do. Our children are nearly here, and I do not want to waste a single second of it being just you and me."

"Oh, God, I love you so much, Elsie," he says, practically beaming as he wraps me up in his arms. "And speaking of not wasting a single second, I decided to take a leaf out of William's book and have arranged to court you as I should have. Beginning with a candlelit picnic by the lake."

"Can we dance?"

"Yes, we can dance…well, as much as one can in your position," he laughs, and I laugh with him. "But yes, we can do whatever you want, for the rest of our lives."

Chapter 25

Edmund

"This is beautiful, Edmund," Elsie gasps when we finally reach the lake where I have arranged countless candles to create just the right atmosphere. "Did you do all this yourself?"

"I did," I reply proudly, now feeling thankful for carrying out the onerous task without help. "It felt only right to do all of this with my own hands, to show you how much you mean to me."

"Well, your efforts are appreciated," she laughs, "even your babies are kicking around inside."

"Really? Can I feel?" I ask, desperate to experience this amazing miracle.

"Of course, they are part of you after all," she says as she takes hold of my hand and places it over her stomach. I feel the softest of movements before one big kick, which makes her laugh. "They know who their father is."

"Hello, my darlings," I whisper to where my hand is, "your mother and I cannot wait to meet you both."

"You do not know how good it feels to have you here with me, saying those words," she tells me and it kills me that she even needed to. "Edmund?"

"Yes?"

"If you want forgiveness, it has to include your own," she says with a beautiful smile. She is going to make the greatest of mothers; so patient, so understanding, so selfless. "No more dwelling on the past when the future is very nearly here."

"I sincerely hope they take after you, Elsie," I tell her as I turn her back to me so I can wrap my arms around her waist and begin swaying, dancing just like she wanted to.

"As long as they are brave like their father," she says, leaning back against me, making me feel so good for the first time in months.

"I think *you* are incredibly brave, my darling."

"You would not say so if you knew how scared I am of these little ones coming out of me," she admits, sounding extremely anxious. "What if something happens? What if I—"

"Shh, Elsie, I will be with you every step of the way," I try to reassure her, "and we will live happily ever after, like we deserve to. We will live the life Annie and William should have had."

"You promise?"

"I swear," I tell her before kissing her temple. "And I am going to spoil you every day and night leading up to when these little dears are ready to come out."

"Well," she says with nervous laughter, "I do not think you

are going to have to wait too long for that, Edmund. My stomach has been tightening and releasing for a few hours now. According to Emily and Nancy, I believe my body is preparing itself."

"They're coming?!" I gasp with shock as I turn her around to face me. I cannot imagine what I must look like because the moment she sees me, she laughs. "Now?"

"Well, I think so, but Emily said—"

"I have to get you home, I have to get Nancy, I have to call for the doctor, I have to—"

"Edmund, breathe!" she cries out and I do, because she is my wife and I forgot how to listen to her, until now. "One step at a time, they are not going to fall out of me. First, we blow out the candles, if only to try and keep me calm."

"Right, I see…of course," I tell her with a confidence I am not sure I have. "Then let us do it together."

I take hold of her hand and begin to lead her around the flickering lights, trying not to show any signs of fear when her hand squeezes mine every so often. She is a master of hiding her true emotions, so continues to smile and act as if she is not experiencing any kind of fear or anxiety when she feels pain. When we reach the last candle, I take hold of it and begin to lead her back towards the house, finally taking charge like I should have done instead of flustering in panic.

"I shall call for the doctor as soon as we are inside," I tell her, "and then I will send someone to fetch Nancy."

"Will the doctor approve of her being there? I do not know the protocol, but from what she has told me, I would say they do not like each other very much."

"I do not care, Elsie, I will have whoever I can to make sure you are well looked after," I reply. "You and the babies are the most important people here and no pompous physician is going to tell me otherwise."

"If you say so," she says as she winces in pain.

"Elsie, it is alright, you can let out the pain, I'm here for—"

"Ahh," she groans, clutching at her stomach and doubling over. "Edmund…Edmund…they're coming, and oh, God…"

"Harold!" I shout at the top of my voice from where we are standing, not too far from the front door. He comes rushing out to help just at the right moment. I am not sure I will be able to keep her from falling at this rate.

As we each take one of Elsie's arms, pausing every now and then to let her get over her pain, I begin barking orders to each and every one of my staff. The doctor is sent for, and once Elsie is settled inside of her room, I shall be getting on my horse and heading to Nancy's house in town. No one can ride as fast as me and I think I have finally run out of staff to ask.

By the time the doctor arrives, Elsie is well and truly red in the face and sweating. She groans with pain every few minutes, panting in between, and clutching hold of whatever she can to release her agony. I would be lying if I said I wasn't scared. She looks so unlike herself, so full of fear, exhaustion, and pain. If I could take her place, I would in a heartbeat. Alas, a man's position is to watch on whilst feeling entirely helpless.

"Elsie, let the doctor examine you whilst I fetch Nancy, you are in good hands. Lucy is here, she will offer you comfort until I am back."

"No, Edmund, you promised you'd be here!" she cries,

reaching for my arm with an expression that breaks my heart.

"Fathers are not permitted in the room whilst---"

I cut the doctor off when I turn to glare at him with an expression that tells him to hold his tongue or risk the consequences. No one is going to tell me what I can and cannot do inside of my own house. Neither will they stop me from being there for my wife and children. Fortunately, the man makes a show of clearing his throat, then returns to unpacking his bag so I can comfort Elsie, the matter seemingly being dropped from his end.

"Elsie, look at me," I tell her as I take hold of her hand and push back her hair from her sweaty brow. "I will come back; nothing will keep me from you longer than is necessary."

"I am scared, Edmund, it feels as if I am going to tear in two," she says with tears running over her crimson cheeks. "What if I never see you again?"

"You will absolutely see me again, as soon as possible," I reassure her.

"I would be quick, Lord Barton, if you do insist on being here, baby number one looks as though it will be born in the next hour or less," the doctor says without emotion.

"Elsie?"

"Go!" she says, nodding in acceptance before releasing a loud moan.

Elsie

The doctor peers between my legs and nods his head, otherwise showing no emotion; at least, nothing I can read.

Anything could be happening down there, good or bad. He merely removes his glasses, cleans them with his handkerchief, then puts them back on his long, bony nose. He then walks over to the bowl of water to wash his hands. I look at Lucy in question, but she merely smiles with a wince across her face. I wish Edmund was here, he would be asking him everything I want to know the answers to. I tried speaking only moments ago but was met with the palm of his hand and a heavy sigh.

A knock on the door has me whipping my head around in the hope that Edmund has returned. Though, I doubt he would have knocked.

"Elsie?" a familiar voice sails across the room. "When Edmund stopped by, he explained what was happening and asked if I could sit with you. I hope my being here is alright?"

"Oh, Ruth, thank God you're here," I groan as another bout of pain hits me full force. She rushes over with concern written all over her face. As the intense sensation begins to subside, I breathe as deeply as I am able to, to try and get over the pain.

"I remember Annie telling me how much it hurts," she says, making herself comfortable while gripping my hand in support. "But she also said it was more than worth it when you held your baby."

"What if history repeats itself? What if I lose one of them?" I ask with panic taking over.

"You cannot change the what-ifs, Elsie, you can only do what you can do to help get those babies out. That is what you need to focus on, Elsie. Worrying will only take up precious energy you do not have to spare right now."

"Easier said than done," I huff as a new sensation takes

over, a strong desire to push.

"I am sorry, Elsie," she whispers as I try to battle through the pain, gritting my teeth whilst trying to breathe through it. "I cannot talk from experience so I can only use what I have read. I sometimes sound like a book, but I do stand by my words. You can do this, and you can get those babies out."

"Where is Edmund?" I whimper.

"Baby is crowning," the doctor says, still without any emotion.

"Oh, my goodness! I need Edmund here!"

"I know, but in his stead, I am here," Ruth declares resolutely.

The pushing sensation soon becomes unbearable, and I cannot stop myself from bearing down, all whilst groaning from the back of my throat. After a few more pushes, the doctor throws up his hand, presumably telling me to stop. I wonder if he even talks to his wife, or does he simply communicate only with gestures?

"Excuse me," Ruth says with a tone of voice that I have never heard from her before. She sounds forceful and thoroughly frustrated by this man. He peers up from between my legs and looks at her without any fluster. "This is Lady Elsie Barton, and she is about to give birth to the Earl's baby, the least you can do is use words to tell her what is going on."

"The head is delivered; I am now turning the baby so she can deliver the rest of it," he says.

I look at Ruth with a confused expression; this man is like a closed book. No emotion whatsoever. The desire to push soon distracts me from this strange man's persona, so I clench my teeth and allow the sensation to follow through. I couldn't stop myself from pushing for all the world. This baby is determined to come out, almost as much as my body is determined to push him or her out of it.

"Come on, Elsie, you are doing so well!" Ruth cries as the feeling of the baby sliding out takes over from the sheer pain of giving birth to it.

"Elsie!" Edmund shouts as he bursts through the door. I want to shout back but I am still clenching my teeth as I push with all my might. "Oh, dear God, I nearly missed it!"

He crosses the room within moments, taking over from Ruth as the baby is born and I can finally let go of my held breath. My whole body trembles from the relief, and the delicious sound of a brand new life filling its lungs with air has everyone smiling and cheering. Apart from the doctor. He simply hands the baby to Nancy, who has shuffled into the room with her bag and is now cooing over the bundle in her arms. The doctor returns to his position between my legs, though I soon forget about him when Nancy brings my crying baby to my arms.

"Elsie, it's a boy!" Edmund cries with sheer pride and happiness on his face. "I cannot believe how amazing you are to have brought him into the world. He is perfect, just like his mother."

"Oh, Edmund," I whimper as tears take over me. "I cannot believe I did it either."

"Second baby is breech," the doctor says, sounding no different from before.

The pain begins again, tenfold, though, instead of a dull

ache like before, it feels as if a knife is cutting through me. I cannot hold back the screams of agony as the building aches come in fast waves and with no relief. Edmund hands our son to Ruth who steps back to try and calm his little cries. Edmund grips my hand, trying to offer soothing sounds in between barking questions at the doctor.

"On her feet!" Nancy shouts.

"That is not the protocol –" the doctor tries to argue but he is merely shoved out of the way by Nancy.

"I have delivered hundreds of babies over three decades, and I have seen this plenty of times before," she says without even sparing him a glance. In fact, I think she is saying it more for my benefit than his. "This is more common with two."

"Are they going to die?" I cry.

"Elsie, you have to concentrate on getting baby out, not the worst-case scenario. Now stand so we can encourage baby to work its way out. Lord Barton, help me to get her up."

Edmund and Nancy take an arm each and pull what must feel like a dead weight. I try to help them, even though I would rather remain on the bed, for the pain cutting through my abdomen feels as though I am going to die if it doesn't stop. I brace myself against Edmund, my hands gripping hold of his shoulders.

"I-I'm scared, Edmund," I cry, feeling exhausted. "And I can't do this anymore."

"I know, darling, just a little more," he says, looking devastated that he has had to ask such a thing. "This is the life we have always dreamed of, and here we are, doing it together. I am so happy with you and when this pain is finally over, I am going to dedicate my life to making you just as happy."

"I am h-happy…ahh," I groan as something feels like it's shifting inside of me.

"It's working, Elsie, trust me, baby is dropping," Nancy shouts from her position on the floor. I have never felt so undignified - if mother could see me now! "Not long now, love, I promise you!"

Her ruddy cheeks and beaming smile reassure me. I wouldn't trade her for the doctor, though he is obviously well skilled, I feel comforted by her straightforwardness. Something else shifts, then a sound of running water, and our second baby finally falls into Nancy's hands. I gasp with joy, right up until the silence hits me. Why isn't my baby crying?

"Edmund?" I whisper with horror in my voice. "Edmund, is it well? Why isn't he or she crying? Edmund!"

"No need to worry, love," Nancy says as she gets to her feet with the silent baby inside of her arms. "Come on, baby, cry for your mother," she says to the bundle as she begins rubbing its back. She isn't gentle either, she rubs at it fast and furiously. I open my mouth to say something but then I remember what she said before; she has done this countless times, she knows what she is doing, far more than me.

With bated breath, we wait for Nancy to work her magic, a time that seems to last forever.

"Look at me, Elsie," Edmund whispers as tears fall in rivers down my cheeks, "keep looking at me."

"Edmund, I can't –"

The sound of a baby gurgling ever so softly from where Nancy is still rubbing its back silences both of us, and it feels as though every part of my body is being held in suspense. The baby begins to cry, and I release every ounce of emotion trapped inside of me.

"There, there, my love, you gave your mama quite a fright, little one," Nancy coos as she rocks the bundle in her arms, now stepping this way with our second child. Both our babies are alive. I am alive. Edmund is here. Surely, one person doesn't deserve this much happiness.

"You have a daughter, Elsie," Nancy says as she hands her over to me, now looking pink and alert. Ruth has handed our son to Edmund, and I suddenly want to yell for joy.

"I do not even know where to start," I laugh and cry at the same time. "Or even who to thank first."

"Thank *you*, Elsie, for your love, your forgiveness and your courage to do all this," Edmund says with such love in his eyes, I end up crying uncontrollably.

"Thank you, Edmund, for loving me, and for giving me everything I have always wanted and more."

Epilogue

Edmund

Annie and Charles are officially crawling and taking over the entire house. Poor Harold is having to take extra pauses in his duties to catch his breath. I doubt he has ever been cut out for small children, but at least he is trying. Their nanny is the perfect mixture of nurture, patience, and discipline. Discipline in the form of not letting them roll down the staircase or pulling at Stanley's tail. And as for Elsie? My darling wife has taken to motherhood like a bird to flying. But what is more beautiful is that she loves it, all of it, even the hard parts. And with twins, there are plenty of hard parts.

I am learning on my feet, enjoying this time when they are small and full of wonder. Charles, named after the man who gave me a father when William could not, is full of mischief, reminding me of Emily when she was a child. However, Annie is Elsie through and through. She is quietly curious and finds contentedness in just being with her mother, father, and anyone else with whom she has a strong bond. She is my princess and always will be. Tobias has already teased me about having to keep her protected when she comes of age, and of having to 'beat back' the countless suitors she is bound to attract. However, he should watch what he says, for Emily is expecting their second child. He could easily have the same problem.

The main thing Elsie and I have agreed on though, is that both children will know they are loved in equal measure. Neither of them will feel second best to the other. The same will be said for any other bundles of joy that may come our way. We never want our children to feel as Elsie once did. Even if her father eventually did make his apologies to his daughter. His weaknesses as a father when it came to his eldest means they will never have the same relationship that I hope to have with all of my children.

"Elsie, I want to ask for your forgiveness for all the mistakes I made with you, especially at your wedding. It was foolish of me to drink so much when I knew I was going to be saying my final goodbyes. The emotions I had felt that day hit me by surprise, many of which I did not want to face. And so, being a weak-willed man, I drank to keep them at bay."

"Emotions?" she asked with a confused look on her face. Annie was curled up inside of her arms sleeping whilst I bobbed our son up and down, trying not to watch as he finally admitted to being such an unfair parent on her.

"Immense pride, happiness, and relief that you had found a good man. But also sadness, Elsie. You were the last of my children to leave, and I knew I had hurt you, knew that I had failed to let you know how much you mean to me."

"Oh," she said in such a way, I knew she thought he was lying. *"I wasn't aware that I did…mean anything to you."*

"Of course you do, Elsie!" he said, shuffling over to the edge of his seat. *"I am not a wise man; I have made my peace with*

that. You made things so easy when it came to parenting you; you were a perfect little girl. Between you and your mother, I did not feel at all needed. I kept my distance for fear of doing it all wrong and risking undoing all that made you so incredibly good. Emily was always the wilder child who needed a stronger presence to rein her in. She also let me pretend that I was educating her. I suppose we bonded because she was the more unruly child. But that was so incredibly unfair on you, Elsie, and if I could go back, I would give just as much of myself to you."

"I see," she said with emotion threatening to spill, for he cannot go back, and neither can she.

"I love you, Elsie, you are perfect," he declared.

"I never wanted to be 'perfect'. It is a hard act to maintain and only has you feeling thoroughly isolated."

"I want to make amends, Elsie, I want to be more present with you and my grandchildren, to give them what I should have given to their mother," he said with hope in his voice. "With your permission, of course, yours and Edmunds."

"I would like that, Father, but on one condition," she said with a confidence I am so proud of, "you do not treat them any differently. You never show either of them if they make you feel uncomfortable or inadequate. You show them that you are their grandfather, the adult, not the other way round."

"I more than agree," he replied with a smile spreading across his face. "And I hope to get to know their mother better, if she agrees?"

"That would be nice too, Father," she said, but with caution in her voice. George will have his work cut out for him, but I cannot help but feel a little prouder of Elsie for making him work

hard for her forgiveness and love.

Elsie and her father had come to an agreement to try and build a relationship that should have been there from the moment she was born. A relationship I will try my hardest to maintain with my own children. However, in order to achieve such a feat, I know I need to do one last thing so I can move past any lingering resentment I still have. If not, I know the past will return to bring me down again. I never want to forget William and Annie, which is why I had her portrait moved into the main house.

As I turn William's letter over and over in my hands, feeling anxious over what I am about to read, I consider what I want it to say. Do I want to hear him telling me how much he cared about me? How much he wished he had done things differently? Or will such declarations only make me feel all the more frustrated? At the end of the day, however, it matters very little what I want it to say; it will be what it will be.

Dear Son,

I wish I could tell you how many times I wanted to call you that, to tell you the truth, but I honestly lost count. You mustn't blame your parents, for though they argued with me over telling you, the only reason for my silence was I truly believed it was best for your wellbeing. Edmund, you had already suffered through so much tragedy in your short life, I could not risk tipping you over the edge; I couldn't risk you turning into me. At least I got to see you during childhood, and your mother always wrote to me, even after we stopped seeing each other. I cherished those letters, my son, read them over and over until the paper was at risk of falling apart. By the time you turned eighteen, becoming a man, I was already too ill to come and find you so I could lay myself bare. Or perhaps I was too cowardly. In truth, I could not face seeing Annie in you, seeing that I had lost her twice over.

*The point of this letter is this: live, Edmund, live! Annie and I made you with so much love. A love that was cut short far too early. Your mother, Annie, would be so proud of who you've become. She would thank your parents for doing such a fine job and for loving you as much as she did. You and I were her world, and in my grief, I forgot that. I am not sure how she would feel about my failings to you, but I like to think she would know I made the right decision. You would have led a very melancholy life with me, for part of me died with Annie in that once, happy home. The first year of your life was the best of mine and not a day goes by that I don't think about how happy I was. You and your mother were **my** world.*

Your grandfather, Annie's father, told her she mustn't dwell on the past, that life still moved whether you decided to live it or not. The past is but memories, the future is your true potential for happiness. It is in part why she forgave me and decided to marry me. So, I say the same to you; do not dwell on what happened to your mother and I, find your own happy ever after and live it for both you, and for us. Especially for Annie.

I shall be with her soon, and Edmund, you have no idea how much I am looking forward to seeing her beautiful smile again. She was…there are honestly no words. I am truly sorry you never got to know her beyond infancy. I know my life was complete because she loved me. And you, Edmund. No mother could have loved her child more. I only hope you one day meet the love of your life, a woman who loves as fiercely as Annie once had.

Live, love and be happy, my son, and one day we shall all see each other again.

Your ever-loving father,

William

As I feel the gentle touch of Elsie's hand over my shoulder, knowing she has read what I have, I lean on her and let my emotions win out. Just this once. One more time to remember the tragedy of what happened to my parents. My wife holds me until I let happiness take over, for I have managed to fulfil William's wish for me. I have the love of my life right here, and so long as she is by my side, happiness will always follow.

Let's connect!

Facebook Taylor K Scott | Facebook

Instagram: Taylor K Scott (@taylorkscott.author) • Instagram photos and videos

Website (including my blog) www.taylorkscottauthor.com

Author Dashboard | Goodreads

Sign up to my monthly newsletter through my author website or through the link below:

Taylor K Scott Author (list-manage.com)

Other works by Taylor K. Scott:

Learning Italian

A romantic comedy, which is available now on Kindle Unlimited

The Darkness Within

An enemies to lovers romantic suspense.

Gabe

A contemporary romance standalone. This is the second book in 'The Darkness Within' series.

Claire's Lobster

An age-gap, romantic comedy novella

My Best Friend

A Friends-to-Lovers contemporary romance

Mayfield Trilogy

A dark, suspense romance.

2023

The Carter Trilogy

A set on contemporary romances, including 'The Gentleman', 'The Knight', 'The Fool' and 'The Devil'

Here is an excerpt from Fredrick's story, 'A Marriage of His Mercy', which is available now for pre-order: https://geni.us/dnFA6ah

A Marriage of His Mercy

Fredrick

Where is Tobias when you need some light relief from the stuffiness and pompous one-up-man-ship of self-important gentlemen, who are currently parading around Lord and Lady Feltham's neatly landscaped garden? I cannot even remember what we are officially here for, only that if I do not bring Thomas to at least one of these 'societal necessities' at least once or twice a year, his grandparents begin mentioning their interference in his parenting, or rather, arguing the need for him to have a mother figure in his life. Alas, this does not only come from my parents, but also Victoria's. Though, I cannot blame the Greysons, he is all they have left of their daughter.

Victoria, has it really been eight years already? Our son is nearly nine, which can only mean it has. Are you laughing at me

now? Having to act responsibly and respectfully in front of a horde of people who can barely tolerate one another behind closed doors. I know I can only tolerate one more hour of this at best. No, do not mock me, Victoria, you are the lady here, we have always known this. I may rule in other areas of our relationship, but when it comes to formalities, you are definitely the one to lead me.

No, you are right, this is for Thomas; to stop tongues wagging about his father being unable to properly look after him and bring him up in the proper manner. Though, I would argue that pretending to be his horse whilst he jousted against a tree with one of the maid's brooms yesterday, proved to be much better parenting than parading him around such a tedious event this afternoon.

Speaking of Thomas, he is now salivating over a line of marzipan fruit that a rather rotund child is counting out along the rim of one of the tables. I desperately want to intervene, to tell the greedy unlicked cub that it is exceedingly rude to empty the entire bowl of such delicacies and order him to put them back this instant. However, something tells me to at least let Thomas try and deal with this situation himself. I am consistently told Thomas should have been schooled by a governess, that I concern myself far too much with him, hinting that I am much too protective of a boy of his age. I whole-heartedly disagree, but I still find myself remaining at a distance during this moment in time, silently willing him to say something to the boy.

"Lord Brown? By God, I cannot remember the last time I saw you," a female voice says from behind me. Rolling my eyes over having to converse with someone from this rigmarole of a social event, I release a quiet sigh and turn around to give this lady my most charming smile. I shall need to massage my cheeks for at least a few minutes afterwards, but at least I will look the part.

"Lady…?" I wince at the poor lady, feeling utterly embarrassed by my faux pas. She will either leave in a dramatic fashion over my forgetting her name, or, if I am extremely lucky, she might take pity on me and simply remind me of her name.

"Well, now let me see, the last time I saw you, I was Miss Benton, but now you may call me Lady Winton," she informs me with a mirthful smile that does not seem the least bit forced. I release a breath of relief and in my state of relaxation by this welcomed reprieve, I suddenly remember her name.

"Francesca?" I clarify whilst she laughs at me.

"Ah, so, I at least made some impression on you," she teases.

"Forgive me, I am rather out of the 'loop' of who is who these days. In fairness, I cannot say I have much been in 'the loop' since Victoria…well, er…"

"I understand, Lord Brown," she says kindly. Her warm smile tells me she is a friend to have, one who will be loyal to you because she genuinely cares, not because of any title you might have.

"Please, call me Fredrick?" I ask, almost as if I am begging her to in the rigidity of this garden party.

"I am afraid to say I never met your late wife, though I have only ever heard good things said about her," she says as we look back over to where Thomas is still looking longingly at the line of marzipans. "Is that your son? He looks just like you."

"Are you referring to his physical features or the way his mouth is watering?" I joke at the expense of my poor boy.

As soon as the last word leaves my mouth, I see a young

lady approaching him, with a look of pure curiosity on her face. I cannot help but begin to edge towards them, wondering what she is about to say to him. Francesca fortunately falls into step with me, so it looks entirely natural and not the least bit as thought I am rushing over in an attempt to rescue him.

"Do not look so concerned, Fredrick, her name is Miss Viola Fox. Her father is Lord Marcus Fox. He remarried a few years ago. The poor girl's mother died when she was only eight years old," she says, then pauses our walking to apologise. "Forgive me if that sounded…ungentle. Sometimes, I forget myself and I end up saying the completely wrong thing. Truthfully, I saw one awkward lone person trying to avoid all of the pomp and pageantry and felt immediately drawn to you. My husband has always been so much better at all of this than me; he does enough socialising for the both of us, which I more than appreciate. Though, it often leaves me circling these sorts of functions all alone."

"I appreciate you coming to offer your awkward company with mine," I reply with sincerity. "So, Miss Viola Fox is not some predator about to gobble up my son?" She merely laughs at me, confirming my suspicions, that I must look as though the ridiculous thought had seriously crossed my mind. "He is very important to me."

"Of course, he is," she says with an understanding smile. We begin walking again but stop short when we are close enough to listen.

"Those marzipans look quite delicious, Bernard," Miss Fox says to the chubby boy still eyeing up his horde as though they are his children and is ready to fight to the death for each and every one of them. "Though, sometimes it is better to share than to keep treats all to yourself; you might even make yourself a friend."

Thomas, who looks as warm and gentle as his dear late mother, smiles and nods his head at the boy, his attempt at offering this friendship of which she speaks so eloquently. The boy pauses in his task of ordering the treats, and I believe he is about to accept Thomas' friendship, but when he eventually smiles, it is more of a sneer than a welcoming gesture.

"No!" he practically spits before gathering them all up in his greedy arms, squashing the majority of them. One or two even drop to the floor, which catches Thomas' eye almost immediately, but as soon as he bends to pick them up, the horrid little boy stamps on them with his foot.

"Bernard! Apologise this instant!"

Miss Fox' raised and outraged voice catches the attention of the repugnant child's mother, who gathers him into her arms.

"Mama, she shouted at me when he tried to steal my marzipans!"

"Oh, Bernard, you must not get upset," she says with a cruel expression on her face before turning back to her friend who looks as equally ugly in her sharp features. "There's a reason some ladies never receive any offers of marriage."

Miss Fox takes the intentional insult like a knife to her heart with an audible gasp that has me beginning to march towards the woman and her beastly child. However, before I can even put my foot back on the ground, Francesca places her hand over my arm to stop me in my haste to offer my own form of chastisement.

"You will not do anyone any favours if you intervene, Miss Fox's especially. Be content in the knowledge that neither little Bernard or his mother are revered or indeed liked, by anyone."

Whilst I consider the full meaning behind her words, Miss

Fox turns and walks away with her shoulders slumped and no doubt, tears in her eyes. Thomas, on the other hand, is staring at the boy and his mother with anger in his wide, blue eyes, which are perhaps the only feature that has nothing to do with my family's genes.

"I should like to say a lot of things to you right now," he says clearly and confidently, "but my father taught me it is not polite or gentlemanly to use such words in public."

With that, he turns around and makes his way back to me, an expression of justice having been delivered on his face. It almost has me laughing, but I am much too proud of him to not give him a stiff nod of approval. The boy and his mother, on the other hand, are looking completely shocked by my eight year-old-son's mature but condescending rebuttal.

"Well, Fredrick, I would imagine Victoria is looking down at her son and husband with immense pride," Francesca says as she turns to leave me and Thomas to talk. "I know I would be."

Our son is amazing, Victoria, I only wish you were here to tell him so yourself.

Precisely one hour later, past due the time I had promised myself we would leave, I begin to make the rounds with Thomas so we can say our polite goodbyes and leave as quickly as possible. Francesca has me promising to take Thomas for tea one afternoon next week. Surprisingly, I do not find myself completely adverse to the idea as I normally do when asked to visit people outside of close family, which includes the Hardy household. Tobias, as miserable as he likes to pretend that he is, is like a brother to me, which makes Emily my sister. And I daresay James and Thomas will be as close. With three daughters, Tobias and I may well end up being related through a union between our children.

"Father, look, there is a maze, can we go through it? Please?" Thomas begs of me, and who am I to deny the boy after having lost out with the marzipan bowl. One will be pleased to hear that Bernad was last seen throwing up in the bushes after scoffing the whole lot in one helping. Serves him and his horrid mother right.

"Oh, alright, but then we will be leaving," I tell him as he begins leading us towards the entrance. The exit has a few couples leaving with smiles and laughter, so it cannot be all that long or difficult to navigate.

We begin in much too much haste, which only causes us both to get horribly lost. In fact, I soon realise we have not come across another soul in quite a while. No matter, Thomas is still smiling with extreme enthusiasm. He tackles the maze with avid curiosity rather than logic, but being only eight years old, this is part of the fun. And so, I simply laugh alongside him, pretending not to be praying to Victoria that we make it out of here alive. It is only when he turns a corner and does not appear for some time that I drop my laughter and rush over to see where he's got to.

"Thomas?" I cry out, kicking myself for not keeping up with the boy. "Thomas, where are you? Answer me now!"

When I turn the corner myself, I see only his back standing still, all the while looking down on something. Perhaps he has found a dead animal, or another lost soul.

"Thomas, whatever is the…"

My words are stopped short when I see what has caught his attention. The poor girl from before is huddled on the floor, sitting virtually inside of the bush, as though hiding. Her face has lost all colour and her eyes appear to be begging for something out of pure fear.

"Miss Fox?" I venture, but this only causes her to slam a finger to her lips, silently telling me to be quiet.

"I just found her like this," Henry says to me, dropping his voice to a whisper for her sake. "What's wrong with her, Father?"

"Miss Fox, I must insist you let us help you," I whisper too, for her eyes only widen more with fear over being caught here in this strange situation. Perhaps the vulgar woman from before was referring to a mental condition when she so rudely said there was a reason for Miss Fox being neither engaged nor married. "Can we go and get someone for you?"

She shakes her head much too quickly, and her eyes bulge out even more, just as tears escape from a rapid fluttering of her eyelashes. An affliction of the mind or not, she is absolutely terrified. I step past Thomas and bend down lower so we are almost eye to eye with one another. Her eyes, a warm chocolate in colour, look at me with desperation, so I take a risk and reach for her hand. She lets me, even slumps a little in relief that I am here to help, not give her away.

"Miss Fox?" I whisper just as an unfamiliar voice calls out 'Viola'. The sound of which only sets her to trembling all the more vigorously. Whoever that voice belongs to, he is the source of her terror.

"D-don't let him find me, please!" she begs, clawing at my arm in such a way, I half suspect a monster to turn the corner when he reveals himself. I simply nod my head, reassuring her that I will keep her safe and hidden. I then beckon Thomas over to stand in front of the poor girl, so she is not only camouflaged by the bush, but she is now covered by my son.

Just as I stand up to my full height, the monster in question turns the corner. He is an older man, older than me. His hair is thinning and the colour of pale slate, his cheeks red and covered in thread veins and he is at least a full head shorter than me. He could easily be this girl's father; perhaps he abuses the poor girl. Perhaps he shouts at her, or even uses his fists against her. Well, not with me in the vicinity, he won't. I cannot abide a man beating a woman, especially when she tried to help my son earlier on.

"Oh," he says with surprise when he finds Thomas and I here. He smiles, bearing yellow teeth and the distinct smell of alcohol upon his breath. "This maze is a bit of a brute, isn't it?"

"Quite," I reply stiffly, unable to hide my instant dislike for the man.

"Well, yes, I was wondering if you had come across my niece, Miss Viola Fox. She was much too enthusiastic and has gotten herself lost."

He laughs nervously, clearly picking up on my hostility. Even Thomas is looking bemused by his presence, his little nose sticking in the air with judgement.

"No," I simply reply without room for question.

"I saw someone turning the corner over there," Thomas adds, "someone in a dress, so maybe that was her."

His face instantly morphs into one of desperation to run after Thomas' fictitious lady, his expression looking nothing sort of lascivious. I shudder over the thought of him harming the poor shivering girl behind me.

"Thank you, both of you," he says hurriedly, "excuse me."

He turns and practically runs to turn the corner, greedy for the prize that awaits him at the end. When sufficient time has passed to appease my cautiousness, I turn around to see the girl sighing with relief. She flutters her eyes closed and releases fresh tears that trickle over her flushed cheeks. Her ebony-coloured curls frame her face like a painting, and the redness of her lips have me thinking of Snow White, caught in a hell from which that she cannot escape.

"Thank you, both of you," she eventually says before rising to her feet with a look of humiliation. She brushes down the back of her dress and attempts to look at us both, but soon ends up staring at the floor with shame.

"Has that man hurt you?" I ask almost straight away, concern lacing my words.

"I…I cannot talk about it," she says with her cheeks blushing even brighter. "But I thank you for your discretion."

"Miss Fox, please, I need to know you are going to be safe," I tell her with urgency in my voice.

"I cannot tell you what I do not know," she utters with a furrowed brow, as if in thought. "Though, perhaps Thomas might be so kind as to escort me out of the maze?"

Thomas struts out his chest, looking proud as punch; she is indeed, a very pretty woman, I can only imagine how enchanted he is by her. She offers me a discreet smile over his head, to which I return the gesture.

"It would be my honour," he says haughtily, only to release his chest and look at her with a curious expression. "How do you know my name?"

"Lady Winton always takes a turn with me at these events, reminding me of who is who. I must confess, my memory does not serve me well when it comes to names. Though, I am sure I won't be forgetting such a handsome face in such a hurry."

"Well, then, Thomas, you must. I hope you do not mind if I join you both?" I play along.

"Of course not, Father," he replies before offering his small arm for her to hold onto. "Come, Miss Viola, Father and I will ensure no harm comes to you whilst we navigate this maze."

"I have no doubt about that," she says before gifting me with a beaming smile over my little gentleman in the making.

Look at him, Victoria, he's already courting beautiful ladies.

I keep a little distance between us, not least of all because I do not want to cause a scandal with my consorting with a young, unmarried lady who looks like she does. I wonder how she got herself inside the maze all by herself in the first place, especially with that seedy fellow following her around. Is he really her uncle?

When we eventually reach the exit, a few pairs of eyes fall on our strange little trio and frown with curiosity. Thomas, of course, plays his part to perfection by turning to release Miss Viola and offering her a formal nod, as if thanking her for letting him escort her out. She nods back with a small curtsey and a shy smile.

"I fear you are going to break many hearts, young Thomas," she says before turning to offer me a curtsey, her cheeks pinking. "Thank you so much, Lord Brown."

"I am still not going to rest easy until I know you are safe from whoever that was that had you shaking so," I tell her, most likely breaking several social protocols. However, I have never been one to adhere to such things over basic human kindness. "Is he really your uncle?"

"Lord Brown, I appreciate your concern, really I do, but I have been taking care of my safety with that man since my father married his sister."

"Forgive me, but I am not convinced you have been managing to do that so well, not after I saw you shivering so violently today. Does your father—"

"I must go, do not concern yourself with me," she says, no doubt having been schooled how to answer such imposing questions. She then turns to escape my interrogation, but still, I cannot leave it like this. I will never forget the look of her terrified eyes.

"Miss Viola," I call out, prompting her to turn and face me one more time, as well as a few nosey ladies of the ton. I walk up to her so I can whisper what I need to, keeping my words between just us. "If you ever need help, please, ask Lady Winton; she knows who I am and that I just want to help."

She says nothing, simply smiles and walks away; the proper answer given we now have an unwanted audience. As I watch her walk away towards an older couple, her father and his wife presumably, I feel Lady Winton sidle up beside me so she can do the same.

"You are right to feel concern for her," she says quietly. "Her step-mother's brother, Archibald, who is at least twenty years her senior, has been sniffing around that poor girl for years. Rumour says he has already made his intentions known to her father, but he has so far resisted. However, with no other suitors in sight, the step-mother is gradually beginning to talk him round."

"How in God's name are there no suitors? She is by far the most beautiful lady here...present company excluded. I would have thought she would have them lining up along her father's extensive property."

"Can you think of no reason?" she asks, turning to look at me with a sorrowful expression. I pause with anger sweeping over me for the poor girl.

"The cad!" I growl under my breath.

"As soon as a gentleman shows any form of interest, he is in their ear, either talking her down or threatening the man himself. He is obsessed with her."

"Can no one talk to her father? Surely, he would want to protect her?"

"Manipulation runs strong in the family; his wife is not to be trifled with and will do anything for her brother. Unless...?"

She smiles with a hint of deviousness behind it.

"What?" I almost demand of her.

"Well, unless there was someone who would not be so easily talked out of marrying her. Someone who has a young son in need of a kind mother figure perhaps?" she hints heavily, and I laugh over her matchmaking. "What do you think, Lord Brown?"

"I think, should you have daughters, you will make an excellent matchmaker."

"That's not a no, Fredrick," she says, to which I release a sigh.

"I already have Thomas to protect from the world, I cannot take on anyone else," I reply. "I am not in the market for a replacement for Victoria. I vowed I would never marry again when she passed."

"Yes, but who says Viola would need to be anything beyond a wife by name? This need not be a romantic transaction; it would be of mutual benefit to you, Fredrick. She is rescued from a miserable life with that odious man, whereas you would have a mother figure for Thomas. A governess, if you will. You not wanting a wife is precisely why this arrangement would work out so well."

"And what of her? Surely, she is going to want a family one day? I cannot give her that."

"Could not? Or would not?" she pokes me, to which I smile at the mischievous woman. "Either way, I am sure, given the alternative, Viola would be more than happy to bring Thomas up as her own. You saw the way she looked at him; she would make an excellent step-mother to the boy."

I turn to see Miss Viola looking at the ground whilst her step-mother fusses over her father, only to physically flinch when the revolting 'uncle' comes creeping up behind her, whispering something inside of her delicate ear. She shivers; I can see her, even from here.

Could I save her, Victoria? Would you understand? Of course you would, you were the warmest woman I know. But could I really do it?

"Think about it, Fredrick," Francesca says close to my ear. "And bring Thomas over for tea."

"Of course, Lady Winton," I reply, "but no more matchmaking."

"I promise nothing," she says with a shrug of her shoulders and an innocent flutter of her eyelashes. I simply laugh before taking Thomas' hand to lead him back to the carriage. As we pass by the Fox family, I look at Viola and notice her tear-stained cheeks.

A marriage of mercy.

Interesting.

Printed in Great Britain
by Amazon

32897709R00188